V.J. Groom was born in England, raised in Australia, and has spent much of her adult life living in south west France and travelling in Europe.

She has degrees in History and Art History and a doctorate in Mediterranean Studies. She now lives in Devonshire with her family and her dogs, chickens and ducks.

LAST RITE IN ROCAMADOUR

V.J. Groom

LAST RITE IN ROCAMADOUR

AUSTIN & MACAULEY

While the author has tried to ensure that the facts in this book are correct, there is no historical evidence that the sacred relic of Cahors cathedral was stolen, or that the miraculous bell of Rocamadour sounded on this particular occasion.

A CIP catalogue record for this title is
available from the British Library.

ISBN 978 1 905609 598

www.austinmacauley.com

First Published (2009)
Austin & Macauley Publishers Ltd.
25 Canada Square
Canary Wharf
London
E14 5LB

Printed & Bound in Great Britain

DEDICATION

To David,
travelling companion, *par excellence.*

ACKNOWLEDGEMENTS

Thanks to all those kind people who
helped me along the way.

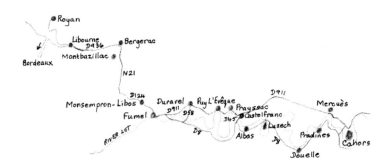

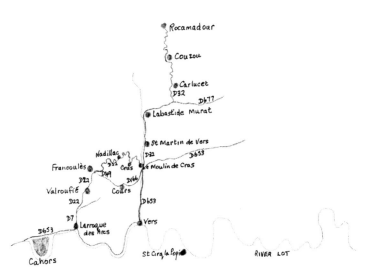

THE BEGINNING

Guilty.

The defendant had been found guilty as indicted. That was a relief. I pushed forward through the crowd, elbowing aside two grey-robed friars who had come to provide him with spiritual guidance. I had something much more helpful to offer.

The tall man standing before the inquisitors' table looked bemused. As well he might do. It's not every day you are found guilty of aiding and abetting heretics and sentenced to wear the yellow cross, not to mention carry it on three routes of penance. But this was south west France, in the great province known as the Quercy. The black-gowned Dominicans were making their tours of the local towns and villages. Called by some the Dogs of God, they were well named. They knew how to dig out local rivalries and quarrels, and to encourage gossip amongst neighbours. They were skilled in rooting out information about the local heretics, those citizens who held beliefs that the church could not allow. Even to give shelter to a heretic was liable for punishment, as my client had just discovered.

Still it could have been worse. All the centres of pilgrimage were fairly local. A journey to Rome, even Jerusalem, had been considered but the man's riches had told in his favour. A spanking big donation to the local seminary and a pledge to aid the restoration work at the cathedral in Cahors had worked wonders.

'Look,' I said. 'Just get it over as quickly as possible. You've got the *sous*, I've got the expertise. It's no big deal. Let my organisation take care of the details and before you know where you are you'll be back in the bosom of your family.'

I reminded him of this when he quibbled at the prices I put forward.

'I'm not guilty you know,' he protested. 'This is a miscarriage of justice.'

'I'm sure you're right,' I consoled. There was no point in telling the poor bastard a guilty verdict was the inevitable outcome of these courts. 'Like I said,' I repeated, 'get it over with as comfortably as possible. Leave the arrangements to me.'

A sudden thought struck me. 'You have got the necessary, I trust?'

'Necessary?'

For a local tycoon he was pretty dense but the shock of the verdict had unnerved him.

'The necessary finance,' I explained, 'to cover the costs.' That was when I outlined the price involved. I'd upped it as much as I could to be commensurate with his state of shock.

'Yes.'

I held out the parchment hoping he wouldn't notice the small print. He didn't.

'Sign here,' I pointed to the space in the bottom corner and he dutifully put his mark. It was all I had time for before the court officials came to strip him of his cloak. He was issued with the tunic of the pilgrim with the great yellow cross on the front and back. Someone stuffed a bag and a staff into his hands and gave him a receipt to show to his family. It would take a few days, however, to get through the rigmarole of the court and present himself for the necessary blessing at church before his departure. I had time to present my own bill first.

'Let's get you out of here,' I said. He didn't demur. 'Anyone here to see you off?'

'My daughter.' He looked round vaguely. She could not be seen in the crowd.

'Don't worry,' I assured him, 'I'll get a message to her. All part of the service.'

This was my first real job with Penance Way, the pilgrims' support service, but it had not taken me long to learn the basics. It was run by a canny old Jew called Bon Macip. I had no time for him or his organisation but in my present circumstances the post of tour manager suited me well. My real boss, or should I say my liege lord, was Edward of England.

Until recently King Edward, or Longshanks, as some dared to call him, for he towered over most everyone at court, also ruled parts of south western France as Duke of Gascony. His lands stretched from the river Charente, south to the Pyrenees and from the great sea eastwards to the frontier at Périgord. In the days of his great grandfather, King Henry, the second of that name, the territory of the kings of England had been much greater. Henry had married the fair lady Eleanor of Aquitaine and together they had ruled all of France from the Loire to the mountains that bordered the lands of the rulers of Aragon and Castile.

It was common knowledge, however, that Edward's grandfather John had carelessly forfeited much of this territory. There were still parts under dispute. Edward claimed the Quercy, where I now found myself, as his possession, but that was hotly disputed by Philip of France. The whole matter was in the hands of their lawyers and it was anybody's guess when they would arrive at a decision.

For his territory in France, Edward had to swear allegiance to the king of France and that was where all the problems had started. Some ten years earlier Philip, called 'Fair' by those who admired his beauty, had succeeded to the throne. At first he had accepted my lord's words of fealty but later he proved to be a troublesome man. He wanted to rule all of France himself and he used any devious means to trick the English ambassadors. There are those who say that this was not difficult to do. Edward's envoys were skilled in court etiquette. They did a good job of charming the queen of France but were complete buffers when facing the skills of the French lawyers.

There are others, however, who recall the king's infatuation for the lady Blanche, and wonder if this lay at the root of the problem. Our fair queen Eleanor was dead these past seven years and Edward's ambassadors had brought him news of the beauty of Philip's half sister, Blanche of Brabant. Our lord yearned for the consolation of the marriage bed and was prepared to give up his Gascon lands for the fair lady. It was almost arranged when news came that Blanche had married Rudolph of Austria. Rumours from court said that Edward was inconsolable. I could not possibly comment on this, of course, being unskilled in the blessed state of marriage but I have heard my father tell of the king's fury when it was discovered that Philip had outsmarted him once again.

I should inform you that my lord did not stay celibate for long. He agreed to marry Marguerite, Blanche's little sister. She was only eleven years old so he had to wait a little longer than he hoped. Still he went on to have three more children so the delay hadn't caused him to lose any of his skills.

Despite all this the two kings had spent most of their time, from then till now, at war. Recently, however, with this new agreement a truce of sorts had been declared. Edward now needed agents to keep him informed of the situation in France, for Philip had shown he was never to be trusted. As you will come to see, I had managed to get myself involved in all this.

I now found myself a tour leader in the city of Cahors, the capital of the lands of the Quercy, not exactly English territory but close enough to the lands under threat from the soldiers of the king of France. My present engagement was to take a group of pilgrims to Rocamadour. Some were locals, citizens of Cahors or the surrounding villages. Others had arrived in Cahors on the Via Podiensis, the great pilgrim route which follows the river Olt down from Figeac. Their journey would end at the shrine of St James of Compostela in Castile.

My present client had been convicted of harbouring heretics and so the pilgrimage was meant as a punishment. For many, however, it was the journey of a lifetime, planned for and anticipated with great enjoyment. A pilgrimage was the chance to visit exciting new places, such as St Michael's Mount in Normandy, the tomb of St Thomas Becket at Canterbury, St Peter's in Rome or St James of Compostela in northern Spain. The most impressive pilgrimage was a journey to the holy places in Jerusalem.

There was also the opportunity to meet people from outside the confines of ordinary life and above all to find favour with God. Not that any of this, you understand, applied to me. Pilgrimages were well known as journeys fraught with danger. The roads were often impassable, wild animals, bears and wolves lurked in forests and robbers awaited the unsuspecting pilgrim. Food was often difficult to get as many villages did not welcome extra mouths to feed. The lucky pilgrims found a bed for the night at wayside inns or in the crypts of monasteries or abbeys, but those not so fortunate had to sleep by the road, huddling in groups for safety.

Most pilgrims went on foot. The rich, however, rode on horses or in carts. Some pilgrims took retainers or servants with them to ease the discomforts of the journey.

Still, despite the dangers, which some said added to the adventure, pilgrimages were very popular and on the roads you could always meet groups of people making their way to the next holy shrine on their itinerary. My new boss, Bon Macip had seen the possibilities and set up his company, Penance Way, some four years earlier. Already he was doing a roaring trade. He had branches in other towns but Cahors was his main office.

This city had proved a useful stopover for travellers from the east, especially for those wanting an excursion to Rocamadour, which was one of the most visited centres in Christendom. Cahors itself was also popular because of the reputation of the sacred relic of its ancient cathedral. This relic, the Sainte Coiffe, or Holy Cloth, was part of the shroud that had covered the head of our Lord while in his tomb. It had been brought back to Cahors, from Jerusalem, by Bishop Gerald III who had ventured on a pilgrimage to the Holy Land. It was this same old boy who had built the great cupolas on Cahors Cathedral to commemorate the sights he had seen on his trip. I had learned this as part of my induction day organised by Bon Macip.

'It's just as well to know one of the city's main benefactors,' my boss had said, adding under his breath, 'if that's what you can call him.'

Once every ten years, at Pentecost, the Holy Cloth was brought from its chapel and paraded through the streets of Cahors. This day was the most holy occasion in the calendar of Cahors Cathedral and many pilgrims came to stay and watch. They crowded into the city finding rooms where they could. The inns filled up immediately as I had found out to my cost. Local visitors from neighbouring villages also flocked in to pay their respects to the relic. They were hoping for a favour or two from on high for themselves and their families.

This year the sacred relic was due for its ten-yearly outing. The great day was to fall on the Sunday of Pentecost and old Bon Macip had grasped the opportunity. He had organised a quick trip to Rocamadour on the Tuesday before the solemn procession through the streets. Taking pilgrims off to Rocamadour for a few days would relieve the accommodation situation in Cahors while at the same time adding substantially to his takings.

I contemplated my instructions. It was the end of May, a good time to travel. The roads such as they were would have dried out after the early spring rains. The sun would be strong enough to keep up the pilgrims' spirits. This pilgrimage lark is no soft option you know. Granted my lot were the luxury end of the scale. They travelled in carts and stopped overnight at the usual bed and breakfast places. Still the going was hard. We had to travel over the high Causse, as the hills round here are called. The water in the streams might be low but the bridges were often washed away during the winter. Bon Macip had warned me not to get the carts stuck in the mud of the fords. He didn't want any claims for a refund from a rich client jettisoned out of his seat as a cart tipped over. Some were unfortunate enough to take a kick or two from the horses or the oxen. As I've said, you wouldn't get me on a pilgrimage, except of course in the present circumstances.

Rocamadour has always had a lot of pulling power in the tourist trade. According to my boss, that is. I had not been there, nor had I ever wanted to. You might think that odd for a tour guide, but then I'm not the usual sort of employee.

Bon Macip had called me to his office. It was situated on the second floor of a smart house in the centre of Cahors. He spoke in a funny mixture of Occitan, the local language, with some Aramaic words thrown in. I had come to understand it. Perhaps I should mention here that, disturbed as my education had been, I had always had a flair for languages. There were many foreign ladies in our fair land. Some had come to England with Queen Eleanor. They spoke the language of Castile. Others had come from Provence with the fair Eleanor, the king's mother. I had picked up the basics from their maids, young girls sent by King Edward on occasion to our castle at Torre. It was his way of returning a favour and my father Lord John had rendered the king many of those. I could master a dialect pretty quickly. Some of the maids sent from France in moments of truce between the two kings spoke the language of Paris. There was many a starry night when I put my knowledge of foreign words to good use. I think it was this skill, more than my prowess at arms, which mainly kept me out of trouble.

'My dear boy,' Bon Macip had said as I entered the room. I didn't let that influence me. He called every one by some endearment and the greater the flattery the more he would do you down. 'Sit down please.'

I preferred to stand until I knew what was coming.

He overlooked the fact and continued, 'I have a quick excursion for you.'

That meant he had a job for me that would pay almost nothing, or worse, a job that involved a problem. 'Excursion?' I asked as if I had never heard the word before.

'Just a pleasant little trip,' he went on, 'to Rocamadour. I have a small group of clients who are here in the city for Pentecost and to see the procession of the Sainte Coiffe. That's about five days away, just time enough to make a quick visit to Rocamadour and be back ready to continue with the main tour to Castile.'

'What's the catch?' I asked.

'My dear boy!' One could almost think he meant it. 'Catch? What is this word? I do not know it.'

I said nothing and after a pause he continued. 'If you mean will there be any problems, let me assure you…'

I butted in then rather rudely. 'There's always a problem,' I said. 'Just tell me what it is.'

'Just a small issue,' he went on. 'You do not need to know all the facts. It will be better if I just give you a resumé.'

'Please do,' I invited him.

'I have a good friend, a merchant,' he stopped and then added for good measure, 'an elected consul of the city.' He paused while I reflected on the extraordinary fact that he had any friends at all. What he really meant was somebody was prepared to pay him well.

'This friend,' he continued, 'does have a small problem.'

'Well nothing unusual there then.'

He ignored my interjection. 'He is devoted to his wife, the mother of his five children.'

I wondered for a crazy moment if I was to be involved in paying off some hussy to avoid divorce proceedings but it was not as simple as that.

Bon Macip tried unsuccessfully to look concerned, 'Unfortunately that good lady is dead.'

I considered if I was supposed to offer some sort of condolences. Bon Macip hurried on however. 'It is fortunate that my friend has the support of his late wife's mother to help him raise his five beautiful daughters.' He fiddled with the quill on his table. He looked up at me under his eyelids with a slight smile. I had early on

21

learned that he thought this expression endeared him to his employees. He was mistaken there. 'I understand you may know the family in question?'

He knew very well that I did. Without doubt he was aware that I had arrived in Cahors but a short time before in the cart of this so-called friend, Jacques Donadieu. I had said as much when he had interviewed me for my present post.

Bon Macip, however, gave me no time to answer 'This dear lady has a brother, himself a good man. Indeed, a man of the church.'

I had no idea where this was going, so I avoided the temptation to say something clever and just listened.

'This brother,' went on Bon Macip, 'is the sacristan of the cathedral.'

I am not a regular worshipper at church, much to my mother's shame, but I knew what a sacristan did. He looked after the fabric of the church including the treasures.

'As sacristan,' hurried on Bon Macip, seeing my brain start to work it out, 'this good canon will prepare the Sainte Coiffe for the glorious Sunday at Pentecost when it will be paraded for all to see. The good citizens of Cahors, not to mention all the visitors, will be able to renew their vows to the dear Lord so he can forgive them for their sins.'

To hear him talk you would have thought him a pious Christian not the old Jew that he was, with but a withering contempt for all the trappings of the Catholic Church, particularly its relics.

I knew, as well as he did, how important relics were. Many had come from the East brought back from the wars of the Cross. I had heard tell of the many holy pieces that our own King Edward kept in his halidom, his sacred treasure chest. Their power had proved helpful in his hour of need, especially when fighting the Welsh and the Scots.

Take this Sainte Coiffe for instance. As I've said, it is a piece of sacred cloth, part of the shroud which covered Christ's head. Later in my journeys I would visit many a shrine and view some wondrous relics. I have seen so many pieces of Holy Cloth that I have marvelled at the size of the head of our Lord which could accommodate them all.

That day, however, in the office of Bon Macip, I had no time to consider further, for the old man was carrying on.

'I come to the little problem,' he said.

I listened more carefully. Finally we were coming to crunch time.

'The problem is, the Sainte Coiffe isn't there.'

I almost laughed but restrained myself and covered the moment by repeating, 'Isn't there?'

'No,' said Bon Macip. 'When the sacristan went to check the relic and prepare it for its great outing, he couldn't find it.'

I swear Bon Macip had a smile on his face, as he said this, which he quickly hid.

I could not help myself. I laughed out loud.

Couldn't find it,' I snorted between giggles.

Bon Macip glared at me. 'It's no laughing matter for the poor man. He is responsible for the great treasure of the church and now it has gone. He is completely devastated and does not know what to do.'

I stopped laughing long enough to ask how I came into this.

'Ah now, there is a way you can help.' Bon Macip had become again the businessman that he was. 'This is a rare opportunity.'

'For me?' I asked facetiously.

'Well for the firm,' admitted Bon Macip. But he hastened to add, 'there will be benefits also for you. Financial ones. Monsieur Dona... Bon Macip checked himself, 'my friend is prepared to pay us well.'

'Pay us well for what?' I asked, beginning to suspect the worst.

'Pay us well to get it back,' said my boss, a note of irritation in his voice.

'So it's not exactly lost then?' I questioned.

Bon Macip hesitated. I assumed correctly that he was pondering how much of the truth to tell me. He made a decision. I was to know most of it. It was only later that I was to discover he had left out the most important bit.

'It's been stolen,' he said, leaning forward and lowering his voice as if the walls had ears, which knowing his outfit might seriously have been the case.

'Right,' I replied. 'Do we know who might have stolen it?' I had thought this rather a foolish question, but in the circumstances it was the best I could do. To my surprise Bon Macip nodded his head.

'Not precisely,' he admitted, 'but we know the set-up.'

This was beginning to sound a bit complicated for me. 'Set-up?' I asked.

Bon Macip hesitated again. It was really costing him hard to divulge the whole story. After a few moments he went on. 'It's a gang.' Before I could comment on this he continued, 'It's a group of rou... he amended the word 'routiers' to 'dealers' to make it sound less problematic. Unfortunately for him I had already heard about routiers, bands of young men who roamed the countryside plundering and murdering and worse. Well worse for young maidens that is.

'Dealers,' he continued, 'the world is now full of them.'

Well he should know. He was a past master at wheeling and dealing. I began to appreciate the difficulties he had narrating the facts. He could almost have been describing himself.

'This group of... dealers,' he said, 'have acquired the Sainte Coiffe.' He hurried on again before I could ask any questions. 'They have contacted my friend the merchant, the son-in-law of the dear lady and demanded a ransom for the treasured relic.'

'So,' I asked rather too casually perhaps, 'Can't he pay?'

'Pay!' Bon Macip almost choked on the word. 'Pay!' he repeated again, clearing his throat of the poisonous word. 'You do not understand the citizens of Cahors, my dear boy, if you think they will be held to ransom like this.' He quickly followed up with the real point of the conversation. 'Pay,' he chuckled to himself this time. 'No certainly not.' Then he added almost as an afterthought. 'No, the only payment will be my fee for I have told my friend you will get it back.'

'Me!' I exclaimed. I know. It was not the cleverest remark in the world but I was stuck for a reply.

Bon Macip rose from the high-backed chair in which he always sat to conduct business. This was seriously worrying, even more so when he clapped me on the back.

'I have put the reputation of the firm in your hands,' he said. 'I have committed the future to you. I have…'

'OK,' I interrupted, 'you needn't go on. Exactly what have you said I will do?'

Bon Macip let out a small sigh of relief. I had obviously replied as he had hoped I would. He knew I could not turn my back on the family who had welcomed me to this city.

He returned to his chair and assumed a more business-like posture. He adjusted his yellow cap. 'This gang,' he said, 'is well known to the authorities.'

I didn't ask which authorities they were. I really didn't want to know.

'We have reports that they are moving on to Rocamadour. They have their sights on the Blessed Virgin in the sanctuary there.'

I don't hold with gangs, believe me, especially ones that put the wind up an old boy of the church but I whistled none the less at the daring of this group. The Sainte Coiffe was a nice enough bit of old cloth but the Madonna of Rocamadour! She was something else, one of the great icons of the pilgrimage world. I saw now why Bon Macip had agreed to help. If she were to be stolen it would upset the whole peace of Christendom, not to mention probably put him out of business.

'But,' I almost stammered out the question, 'how will they get the ransom for the Sainte Coiffe if they are leaving town for Rocamadour?'

Bon Macip leaned forward for the second time at that meeting. He lowered his voice now to barely more than a conspiratorial whisper. I had to lean forward too so that I could take in what he was saying.

'They do not trust the authorities so they wish to be outside the walls of Cahors when they make the exchange. It is arranged that you will take a group of pilgrims to Rocamadour. One of these villains will travel with your party. En route, in secret, you will procure the Sainte Coiffe.'

I noticed, rather too late, that the word 'villains' was now openly used.

'If your negotiations are unsuccessful, of course, you will have to resort to payment.' Bon Macip added, 'But we hope it will not come to that. You will have assistance in this matter,' he went on. 'We would not expect you to do it all on your own.'

'Well thanks for that.'

'So you will undertake the project... the pilgrimage?' he hastily corrected himself.

I thought of my own problems, of the money I needed. 'You said it will pay well?'

'Oh yes,' replied Bon Macip, rubbing his hands together. 'Very well for both of us, dear boy.'

'All right,' I said.

'Dear, dear, boy.' I had never known two 'dears' before. This was going to be some pilgrimage.

As I turned to leave the room, Bon Macip added one extra little detail. 'Of course,' he said. 'The returns would be even better if you can ensure the safety of the Blessed Virgin of Rocamadour and prevent her theft.'

CHAPTER 1

You might well be wondering what brings a simple English boy like me to be acquainted with the upper classes of Cahors, let alone leading a pilgrimage to Rocamadour. Don't worry, I've asked myself the same question more times than I can recall.

Given the choice in my employment, I would now be managing the lands of Lord John de Mohun in the West Country of England. But choice is a rare commodity, and it's not come my way too often.

The estates in question are at present controlled by Lord John's son Reginald, a handsome enough fellow but of feeble constitution. Mind you that's being kind. Most think him a complete fool. I have serious doubts that he can cope with the task. He has my mother's help, of course, which hopefully should mean he does not make a complete mess of his duties.

Isabella, my mother, is all but Reginald's mother. According to her account she was summoned to the great house when Lord John's wife, Beatrice, died in childbirth, leaving a puny runt of a child to the vagaries of the world. I say, according to mother, because she has been known to embroider the truth.

A poor country girl she was, as she likes to tell, but with a good head on her, for all that. Apparently she had found herself at seventeen the mother of twin babies, only one of which survived the travails of birth. My mother having milk for two was called on by Lord John to act as wet nurse to his motherless son. Naturally I went too. So it was, that having been deprived of one brother, I obtained another but a few days younger.

Lord John himself was now languishing in a prison somewhere in France. He had responded to a call to arms from our sovereign liege King Edward, joined the army led by Edmund Crouchback, the king's brother and departed for Gascony. There, our army hoped to curb the skirmishes made by the soldiers of Philip of France who had confiscated King Edward's inheritance.

Lord John was a brave enough knight, but good feasting from the fruits of his estates had lent a pound or two to his girth. Unseated from his horse in the fracas at Bonnegarde, he had been easy pickings from the field of battle. The ransom for his release was more than the estate could stand and we needed a good strategy to find the wherewithal.

Mother had come up with the idea of petitioning the king. She reminded us that Lord John had not only fulfilled his duty to the king, his liege lord, but he had often done undercover favours for the old man. Favours largely connected with getting his son Edward, the Prince of Wales, out of scrapes.

'I'll leave it to you two boys,' said Mother, 'to decide which one organises this.' She said it in the tone of one who means, get it sorted or I'll do it myself. Knowing my mother, that would no doubt be the case.

There had not been much discussion. Reginald had pointed out that his father had given mother and me a good home. I couldn't argue with that. Further he had reminded me that Lord John treated me as if I were a son. That was also true. Next he mentioned that I had picked up a good deal of French from the serving maids lent to Lord John by the king. Finally he declared that, unlike him, nature had provided me with a body more fitted to the exploits of arms than the formalities of court life. I capitulated.

I could have pointed out that Reginald himself was in a real spot of bother. There had been trouble on our lands in the village of Avetone. Some years before, in a gesture of generosity, Lord John had given the rights over the mill there to the abbot of the great monastery at Torre. One of Lord John's tenants, a certain Geoffrey de Bosco, a difficult, overweening fellow, maintained that he had secured a concession from the abbot to have his grinding done first. Needless to say this bit of arrant queue jumping had put Reginald in a fit of temper. He took a group of men down to the parish to sort things out. I cannot say what happened but it ended with the miller's boy receiving a clout on the arm, which broke it in two places.

Normally matters like this would have been settled at the manorial court, but Geoffrey de Bosco claimed that Reginald had deliberately caused the affray. He now had a valid excuse to make trouble for my brother, for whom he had nothing but contempt. He accused Reginald's men of grievous wounding and threatened to bring the matter before the king's justice at Exeter. If he were to be found guilty, Reginald would be a felon and liable for conscription to Edward's army. A campaign to Gascony might well have even more serious consequences for him than those which had befallen our father.

Naturally I had hot-footed it to the abbey at Torre to speak to the abbot. I intended to point out that with Lord John away, concessions had to be made and to remind him that, as controller of the mill, he could bring the matter to a speedy conclusion.

The great red sandstone monastery at Torre rose high above the meadows that rolled down to the sea and the wide beach of sand and pebbles. It commanded a sheltered bay and now there was a quay in the little harbour built by the monks to serve the boats which took their produce to France. The abbey was old, built in the reign of King Richard. It was Lord John's forbear, Lord William Brewer who had first given the land to the monks. They were followers of Saint Norbert and had brought the rules of his great abbey to our town of Torre. My father had added to their territory.

Lord John's generosity had provided Abbot Richard with many hides of land and all the holdings, churches and mills that lay within the boundaries. As abbot he was said now to govern the greatest Premonstratensian house in England, and I have never found anyone who disputed that claim.

It was indeed an impressive pile with its towers and crenellated walls. There was a small gate that led to the almoner's house and the guest rooms where weary travellers could find a welcome. I hurried past that towards the main entrance, barred as usual, with a huge iron portcullis.

Luckily I knew the fellow on gatehouse duty. It didn't take much of a bribe to negotiate access to the main tower and the cloisters from where a fine circular stairway connected with Abbot Richard's hall. The old monk had received me with his customary courtesy.

I had put my case. The news that King Edward was desperate for fighting men was common knowledge. Things it seemed were going from bad to worse in Gascony. More troops were urgently needed. The sheriff of Devon had announced that the sentencing of felons could be deferred or abandoned if they were prepared to fight in the great enterprise overseas. I suggested that I would serve in the king's army to wipe out the wrong done to the miller's boy, clear the de Mohun name and, moreover, find Lord John and secure his release.

I knew the abbot had the ear of the king and I counted on the fact he could arrange these matters. He was wise enough to ask few questions. 'You have thought of this action long and hard?' was his only question to me.

'I have, my lord,' I replied.

'It is true that the king has problems with our neighbours in France.' Abbot Richard looked genuinely sad. As well he might for the mother house of the abbey at Torre was in Prémontré in France. From time to time he welcomed brothers from across the waters to stay at the abbey.

'He has need of good fighting men to secure the peace. It is surely your brother who should go, but the manor has need of a manager in these hard times.' He looked through the huge window that gave upon the rolling fields and the sea beyond. I said nothing. I feared that the abbot had heard of my own frequent scrapes. They were the despair of my mother.

'Your services would be welcome,' he said finally. 'I shall inform the king.'

And so the agreement was made. For the moment Reginald would manage the estates. Meanwhile I awaited the answer from the king's court at Winchester. It was not long before I learned the price of the king's assistance.

The conditions were simple. I was to take the place of my adoptive father. Not on the field of battle in the open challenge of arms but in King Edward's secret service in France. The old king had a mission for me. In the telling it seemed to offer two services; the first, for my country, was the honour of safe guarding the realm from the intrigues of the French, and secondly, for my family, there was to be the chance to raise the funds to secure my father's release and to clear the name of his true son. Furthermore wily old Edward promised to pay me well and to turn a blind eye to the means I used to secure the information.

Naturally I did not discover then what secret plans Edward had for me, though truth to say I think I would still have been willing to undertake the adventure.

I had crossed to Gascony by way of Dartmouth on St Augustine's day. Normally I would have sailed in a nef from our little quay at Torre. I had learned, however, that a cog was anchored in the deep harbour at Dartmouth, bringing wine and sherry from the ports of Portugal and Spain. It was said that these large ships, which had recently arrived at our shores, were better able to withstand the stormy seas we had to cross. I abandoned the idea of anything smaller and hastened to Dartmouth.

The ship was lying low in the waters, laden with the wool from our estates. Our main income came from the sale of fleeces of wool from the blackface sheep we raised on our pasture land high on Dartmoor. We dyed the fleeces ourselves and sold them to the monks at Torre, who arranged their export to Flanders. It was also carrying barrels of dried fish, herrings and congers as well as quarters of grain and beans. All of these could get a good price in the markets across the Channel.

I mingled with the crowds at Bayard's Cove. This was always busy with market stalls and vendors. The houses of the town crowded above my head. From Lower Street, where the quay stretched out over the mud, I studied the vessel which would be my home for the next seven days. It was a clinker-built ship with overlapping strakes of wood nailed on to provide strength in the stormy waters by our coast. I could see the caulking of rope teasings and pitch between the strakes. There were others like me eyeing this newfangled ship hardly knowing whether to be pleased or alarmed at the sight of it riding high and proudly in the waters of the bay. Rising up from either end of the ship were wooden towers, the fore and aft castles with ladders hanging down the sides.

I was informed by one of the passengers waiting on the quay that these structures gave clear viewing over the sea and were useful in giving early warning of pirates or enemy vessels. I thanked him for the information. It did nothing to ease the turmoil in my stomach.

The cog had been constructed in the northern port of Bremen. My new companion, who seemed to have appointed himself my tutor in matters of sea travel, pointed out to me the vertical timbers at the end of the keel and the steer hung rudder which could pivot on its stout pintles from a tiller. I was reliably instructed that these ships were good merchant vessels, able to dock on either side in the harbours where they plied their trade.

I saw for myself the great spar of wood stayed by shrouds of stout cordage running from the sides and front of the vessel. These had rungs on them to assist the sailors to ascend the mast. The great sail was bent onto the long yard with the rig resting on the deck and the yard ends hanging over the stern of the ship. The centre of the yard was held close to the mast by parrels. I knew from experience that these wooden bobbins were really heavy and I wondered at the small number of crew until I noticed the capstans on the deck.

At mid morning our ship left the shelter of the harbour, the comforting sight of St Petrock's chapel soon fading from view. As we made our way down the Range and passed the Black Stone on our starboard side, the ship's men slackened the reef-points tied below the yard. The running rigging was made up of sheets of canvas at the corners of the sail with braces to set the angle of the yards. The sail was hoisted as they tested the strength of the wind. It was a fair breeze blowing from the south as we rounded the Mew Stone and entered the open sea. I was heartened to see the sturdy-looking sprit jutting from the bow and the sharp fluked anchor hanging well clear of the side of the ship.

Despite the strength of our vessel and the skill of the sailors, my initial enthusiasm was sorely tried by the retches of seasickness. It was a fine May morning, the sun having risen to a clear sky, but the swell of the tide was strong. The ship pitched and rolled as it cut its way through the green water. I sought the fresh sea air on the deck, hoping for solitude as I emptied my belly over the side, but I was not alone.

I had taken some note of my fellow travellers. Several had stayed the night at Torre. The abbey offered bed and breakfast for those guests who had travelled a distance. There were a good few of these, for to leave from our fair Devon coast was considered the safest route to the king's possessions in Gascony. The sailors of the Cinque ports, as usual, were in fighting mood. They were fresh from their success in defeating a fleet of Norman ships off Saint Matthieu in Brittany and sacking La Rochelle. Given also the dog fights between the men of Yarmouth and a number of French vessels harassing our southern shores, it was a very brave ship that put to sea from the eastern ports.

One passenger in particular had caught my attention. He seemed a taciturn fellow. Amongst the excited jabber on the quayside, he had kept a close counsel. He was about my height but probably twice my age. He wore the embroidered surcoat of the seasoned traveller. It was made of fine brocade lined with miniver and betokened a man of means. He carried a great leather bag, which I was to learn later contained the transactions of his business with the king and the special pass which gave him free passage through the lands of both Edward and Philip of France. For now he said nothing. I gave him a nod as we encountered each other but he made no response save for looking hard at my face.

For the first few hours I had little time or care to consider his or any other's passage on the ship. My face must have been as green as the sea. Taken up as I was with my own problems, I had no thoughts of the crossing save to get across the water. The next days passed in a haze of sickness. I ate very little and drank only the ale that was offered to me. I slept and woke and emptied the last bile of my starving belly over the side. When I had not the strength even for that, I lay on the pile of bales on the deck of the ship. Once, when I dragged myself into consciousness, I found that a roughly woven blanket had been thrown over me. Despite its rank smell I thanked the unknown hand that had kept the worst of the cold night mists from my body.

At last, as we entered the calmer waters of the outer reaches of the great river called the Gironde, I had the stomach to consider our good fortune. Despite the malaise of many of the passengers, for I was not alone in my sickness, the sailors considered it a good crossing. True to its reputation the cog had weathered the storms which rise with fury in the waters off the coast of Aquitaine. We had provisioned at St Mathieu without incident and had encountered no threat to our passage as we approached the coast of Gascony.

I sat against the wheelhouse and considered the scene before me. As we entered the river we passed great water plains of marsh riddled with canals. Further into the wide estuary, we sailed between high cliffs of greyish ochre with huge trees right down to the water's edge. Although, until now, we had encountered no threat to our passage, we were constantly on the lookout for French ships. King Philip's men had control of Bordeaux, where we would normally have harboured. Our ship was making for the town of Libourne, which was still loyal to King Edward.

Soon the great Benedictine church of Sainte Radegonde rose on its promontory of white cliffs. It was an awesome sight with its great north gate and its huge square tower. I had learned of its reputation from the monks at Torre, but nothing prepared me for its magnificent presence seeming to stand as it did almost in the waters of the river. In stormy conditions it offered succour to those beleaguered by the treachery of the waves. But Lady Fortune was smiling on our ship and we had no need of the comfort of the monks. Our captain saluted their watch guards from the forecastle, but kept to our path in the middle of the river. He knew these waters well, for the Gironde had long served the kings of England as part of their Gascon territory and he was aware of the vast mudflats which ran along the shore. Any ship venturing into one of the pretty inlets would surely have been beached.

We passed many small harbours where we saw the locals with their nets and pots. Muddled with these were the farmlands that reached down to the shore with chickens, sheep and the odd cow or two living at the water's edge. It contrasted strongly with our steep red cliffs at home, and the thrill of adventure was strangely mixed with a longing for my old life.

The sun was setting as we approached our port. It lay at the end of the great fork in the river where the Gironde was divided by two islands. To the right lay Bordeaux along the waters of the Garonne. As I have said, in less dangerous times we would have made for the king's harbour there, but earlier news had warned us of skirmishes taking place with the soldiers of the French king so we tacked to the left and entered the river they called the Dordogne. We arrived shortly at Libourne, one of Edward's fortified towns, known as bastides, built to counteract the influence of the king of France. As I have said it was still loyal to the English. Or so we hoped.

Despite its size our ship manoeuvred neatly into one of the bays allocated for foreign vessels. Dusk was almost upon us and the lights of the quayside flared in the evening breeze. With legs that trembled I joined the other passengers and made my uncertain way on to the land of France.

CHAPTER 2

You may well be waiting for details of my first morning in France. Well truth to say, it's not anything to write home about, for I had awoken in a ditch. It wasn't my usual homely ditch with moss at the sides, good comforting red soil and a cover of herb Robert, lady's smock, fat hen and meadowsweet. You know, the sort of place which after a night's carousing offered a soft bed for the hours left till dawn.

No, this was something else, a great deep scar in the earth with sharp stalks of yellowed barberry and lumps of greyish boulders protruding from the sides. I opened one eye fully although the effort made my head throb. I surveyed the small area of world that was available to me. I recognised nothing. Lifting my eye which now had the other to assist it, I viewed the lower part of my body which was lying in some inches of water. I thanked St Blaise for my succour, for had I fallen, face first, into this wretched hole I surely would have not survived the fight.

Despite the dull throb in my head and the sharp pain in my shoulder I had a clear memory of the events which had brought me to this situation. There had been three of them. I had first noticed them when I left the tavern in Libourne.

For that I must go back to my arrival in this wretched country. As I have said we had arrived at the port of Libourne in the late part of the day. By this time my sickness had left me and I surveyed the scene as we approached the quayside with interest. It was so different from our port at Dartmouth. This was a much bigger place with a long quayside where countless boats were tied up. I was told that they were the barques which had come down the great river, the Dordogne, bringing the goods from the interior to be shipped to England and Holland. They carried river fish, coal, flax, goats cheeses, goose feathers and above all wine. There were passenger ferries too to move the people about in this busy town. The seaman called 'huep, huep, huep' and this signified a boat was about to leave. People would pour out of the taverns that lined the quay carrying huge baskets of produce to sell at the markets further along the river.

I had arrived on the quayside with a confidence I didn't yet feel but there was no point in looking the tourist. My taciturn friend from the ship had bumped shoulders with me as we jumped the last few steps on to the wharf side and caused me to stumble. He didn't bother to excuse himself. I expect he thought I should do that.

Instead I turned away looking for some way to decide what I should do next. It was late in the day. I was almost faint with hunger. I had no idea where to go other than to avoid the road to Bordeaux where the king of France's men were in command.

I made the decision to use some of the money my mother had given me to pay for a meal and a room for the night. There would be plenty of time to rough it later on.

With that someone touched my shoulder, but this time in a more friendly fashion. It was once again the taciturn man from the ship. He gestured to me to follow him and made a sign to indicate eating. I did as I was bidden. As I have said I needed food, and he looked as if he could afford a supper. I decided that I had misjudged him and he wanted to make amends for his former lack of manners.

I looked around me. I had not seen the like of this before. All along the quay were places to get food. Hot or cold. I went a little closer and studied the selection. It was enough to make any traveller hungry. Great trenchers of meat were laid out on stalls. Alongside these were piles of stuffed mussels, huge cheeses with black coatings, bowls of walnuts and almonds and pine nuts, not to mention a vast array of herbs. Looking quickly I could recognise water cress, leeks, fennel, rosemary, parsley, violet petals and primrose all appearing as fresh as the moment they were picked.

I'm a fish man myself and when my new friend gestured to me to enter an inn to sit and eat, I could not resist the stuffed sardines and the fennel soup. There were chunks of delicious white bread freshly cooked, enormous salads of marjoram, sage, rosemary and mint mixed with ginger and nutmeg and ladles of olive oil. I hadn't eaten like this before and despite the chance of appearing greedy, I finished with apple dipped in honey and a delicious fruit mixture of raisins, currants and saffron in a mulled sauce. A bowl of red wine appeared at my elbow and it was not long before the thought of retiring to a feather bed was all that filled my thoughts.

Doubtless you are concerned at my lack of manners. I have no excuses save the light-headedness brought on by the vagaries of my journey, not to mention the wine I had consumed. When it was clear that my meal had been paid for, I barely had the wit to realise I had not thanked my companion. He had stayed only to see me served. The last I saw of him he was talking to the innkeeper before disappearing through a side door.

I stood up to look for the possibility of somewhere to sleep. The inn was full. The first passengers had had the sense to take the few rooms still free. This was a busy port and lodging was rarely available once dusk had fallen.

I staggered through the door of the inn and swayed along the wharf, narrowly avoiding the crates that lined the water's edge. I had seen three men close beside me as I left the inn but had not the sense to think much of it. In truth I had little idea where I was going and soon the cobbled street ran out and I found myself by the edge of the river. And that is almost the last I remember.

I was not conversant with the look and smell of the locals. They could have been mercenaries of the king of France. More likely they were routiers spoiling for a fight. I had been warned of these casual thugs by the abbot at Torre. They roamed the towns and countryside of France causing problems wherever they went. Not that these hooligans were confined to France. I had heard talk of similar hooded villains on the roads of my fair land.

They must have thought me easy pickings. Well they were right there. I like to think that I gave as good as I got. But that might be stretching the truth beyond fair measure. I certainly landed a few good punches before a cudgel blow caught me on the side of the head and I knew no more.

I suppose I was fortunate that they had not killed me outright and the ditch they pushed me into had little water for the season. But my bag had gone and the knife I carried. Also I saw with annoyance they had helped themselves to my cloak and shoes. I pulled myself out of the ditch as best I could with my good arm, the other being of little assistance. It was no easy task but I had great clumps of tough grass to help me. Eventually I lay along a hard ridge of earth and I surveyed the heavens above.

The sun was climbing high in the sky. The warmth of it eased my sore bones and started to dry my hose. I could hear the sounds of the harbour and the cries of the boatmen but I was lying beside a path which obscured my view of the water below. As I lay pondering my next move, painful as that might prove to be, I heard the rumble of cartwheels and the steady beat of horses' hooves. I was obviously on a path that was well used. I thought of rolling back into the ditch for cover but decided that whatever lay ahead it could not be worse that the confines of that dark, dank prison.

I lay quiet hoping that the cart would pass me by, but to my dismay the creaking of the wheels ceased and instead of the comforting sound of hooves clattering past I heard instead the snorting of horses at rest. Suddenly two figures appeared above me. I wondered which pieces of clothing left to me would now be taken. Or perhaps my life. I closed my eyes for a moment. Then I felt myself being lifted. I groaned a few times I have to admit because doubtless you want the full truth. My shoulder was an agony of pain. The two fellows carried me the short distance to the cart and I was placed on some sacks. The smell was malodorous but the bed I was given was soft enough. I stayed still wondering what would happen next.

With that another face appeared and to my surprise I recognised once again the taciturn fellow from the ship who had provided my meal. He said nothing to me nor did he even show that our paths had crossed or that I had supped well thanks to his generosity. He spoke briefly in the local dialect to the two men who had lifted me. It was as well that I had no idea what he said, for with that they held me fast down to my makeshift bed while he took hold of my injured arm and wrenched it upwards. A great explosion of pain filled my body and I screamed aloud. I cannot repeat what curses I used but I surely blasphemed as well as any infidel.

As quickly as it had come, the pain passed and I soon realised with relief that it had largely left my shoulder. Furthermore my arm which I had been unable to move now hung down neatly by my body. The throb in my head took longer to pass. Indeed the blow must have been stronger than I thought for when I tried to utter my thanks for having my arm restored to its shoulder socket, I found the words difficult to form.

Not that my feeble attempt would have been heard, for my fellow passenger had already mounted his horse. One of the sturdy fellows who had lifted me took the reins of the large grey percheron, and the cart and I rolled forward.

I had no idea where we were heading but at first I was content just to lie there and recover my wits. I cannot tell you how many hours passed. Night fell but we continued onwards, the flare of torches guiding our path. We changed horses regularly but still moved on. Much later when I sat up and tried to speak to my rescuer, I learned little except that his name was Jacques Donadieu, he was a merchant and that we were heading for the city of Cahors.

As I have said he was not a man given to unnecessary speech, and what was more it transpired that he was not in good health. I learned in time that he had the stone, a very painful condition. He did not complain, however, for the duration of that long and arduous journey, and my estimation of him went up when I thought of the agonies he endured in that rolling cart.

When I learned the name of the city which was his home, I understood his fine clothing and general air of prosperity. I had heard tell of the great city of Cahors and the famous businessmen of that city, merchants who travelled widely in the realms of King Edward bringing their wine and other merchandise which they exchanged for our fleeces. They were some of the richest men in Europe and many had become successful bankers. It was said that they financed the wars of our own kings. Doubtless that had been my rescuer's reason for his visit to England. It certainly explained the permits he had from both Philip of France and Edward to travel freely through their lands.

As my head cleared and my sense returned, I discovered that we travelled a path that hugged the banks of the Dordogne river. Finally we reached the town of Bergerac. There the two men who had travelled with us made their farewells. There also, Jacques left his horse and took up the reins of the cart. We turned away from the river and travelled a road that headed south-east to Cahors in the lands of Quercy.

I went along with it. There was little else I could do. I summed up my options. I had no idea yet how I would best serve the king in this strange place but one thing I knew. With no shoes and only my tunic and hose it was going to prove more difficult than I first thought.

Jacques kept up a steady pace. His mood lightened with each hour that we travelled. The terrain became more rugged and the crops growing in the fields changed. We left behind the trees of fruit and nuts and we entered wine country.

We passed many a vineyard. The rows of neat vines were carefully tied with lengths of dyed twine to stakes set along the sides of the ditches. At the end of each row was a strong growing rose bush. Though the season was early some were already in flower adding great splashes of red and white to the scene. It was still hilly but as we journeyed, the countryside became less rolling and soon we were in the plain of another great river called the Olt.

By evening we had reached a border town called Fumel. We passed through its narrow streets which wound their way along the river under a high cliff. At the top stood an imposing castle. This guarded the route along the valley of the Olt. My rescuer broke his usual silence to inform me that this small town had given its allegiance to the kings of England. Not that this had brought the town much benefit. King Richard had built his fortress some short distance along the river at Penne and from there the English controlled the Olt on its journey west to the join the waters of the Garonne. To the east of Fumel stretched the lands of the Quercy. There, authority lay with the person who could take it. The lords of Fumel suited their friendship to the strength of the nearest forces and took the opportunity to do a little pillaging of their own. It was my first taste of the politics of this strange land. Not that it mattered a fig to my companion. With his writs of travel, we proceeded eastwards with no challenge to our passing.

From Fumel, we kept at first to the banks of the Olt, passing through flat river meadows where plump geese scratched and goats wandered. There was no terracing here. The soil was rich, too fertile for the black wine which was shipped down river to Bordeaux to liven up the city's gentle clarets. Any vineyards here climbed the stony hills which enclosed the pasture land like comforting arms.

At first our route was shaded by branches of walnut and sweet chestnut. As we approached the villages that straddled the river, I noticed that the orchards were filled with golden plums, apricots and figs. It was too early to collect the fruit but I marvelled at the power of the sun which would ripen this great harvest.

We passed through many places, for our road often left the water's edge. This was the most tortuous of rivers with its great loops and cingles. Sometimes our path rose above the river through forests of chestnut, lime and willow, but then the Olt would curve away from sight of our cart and the road would descend to take us through a town with its yellow walled houses, shops and taverns. Every other while we came across fortified towers which kept a watchful eye on the crossing places of the Olt. There, small flat ferries were chained to solid posts rising from the riverbank.

About noon we came to Duravel where we stopped to feed and water the horses. I'm glad to say we found some nourishment for ourselves for my returning strength made me heed the pangs in my belly. We found some seats in a tavern and ate well on eggs and cheese. Rather it was I who ate with vigour, Jacques toyed with his food and I noticed that each mouthful was an effort.

The town was busy with noisy crowds and soon the tavern was full. Most were visitors who had come to visit the priory and its marvellous relic of holy bones. Three hermits were buried there according to Jacques Donadieu, in another moment of rare conversation. Their bodies had been brought from the east by some crusading knight. It was as well I had no idea then what trouble relics can cause.

We stayed at Duravel only long enough for my hunger to be satisfied and then we took the road to Puy L'Evêque. Now our path became more rugged rising all the time under the shadow of steep ochre cliffs. We entered the town on a high plateau from where I could see the river far below us winding its way eastwards through fertile plains and prosperous-looking farms.

We arrived in a square by a huge donjon. This, I learned, was part of the Bishops of Cahor's country palace. It was well fortified. Apparently the Bishop was taking no chances. I didn't blame him. What with the English claiming jurisdiction at Fumel, the king of France with an eye on control of his diocese and the trouble caused by the difficult citizens of Cahors but a morning's journey upriver, the bishop surely needed a safe retreat. It was a fine town with its tall, round stone towers set high above the river and its sloping cobbled ramps which led down to the Olt. Jacques Donadieu was known here, judging by the signs made to our passing cart. I discovered later that he owned many of the storage sheds which lined the banks. This town had a safe harbour. That day I saw many gabares being laden with barrels and heard the cries of sailors taking a rest before they sailed the dangerous waters of the river. They were heading for the sea at Bordeaux. I could but hope they had less trouble there than that which had awaited me.

Leaving Puy L'Eveque, we kept to the north bank of the river and soon we reached a place where a fast flowing stream added its waters to those of the Olt. Here the new bastide town of Castelfranc was being built. On our journey south we had passed through many of these strange towns with their straight streets and fortified walls. Some owed allegiance to the English and others to the king of France. I'd made a note of this for my journey back.

Here, not to be outdone, the bishop of Cahors was building his own town. At least he could pass down the river with a safe stop on the way to his country house. Our path was barred by an officious clerk controlling the road from his wooden hut. He demanded evidence of our right to travel. Jacques produced his passes in English and French. These shut him up and he stamped the papers with no further word.

Doubtless you will think me idle for I passed the journey sitting on the cart with nothing to occupy me save memorising, as best I could, the road we followed. I had given up any thoughts of leaving our transport for I knew that my best hope of returning to Bordeaux was to reach a large city with all its opportunities. As for taking the reins, that was out of the question. Jacques sat hunched over them and I didn't fancy his reply if I suggested I took a turn.

The hours since noon had almost gone. Evening was approaching. We avoided the difficult passage across the Olt at Luzech and took a smaller track which passed through cultivated river meadows. The fields here were well tended with crops of vegetables and herbs. In the fading light I saw the strange round bories looming like watch towers on the sides of the hills which hugged the pastures below. They offered shelter to the men who guarded the sheep and goats.

My rescuer said nothing, but I noticed his back straightened and his hand grew firmer on the reins when we reached Mercuès and passed a magnificent castle perched on the hills above us. This Jacques told me was the seat of the Lord Bishop, the ruler of Cahors. I soon gathered that the bishop retreated to this palace when things got a bit tough for him in the city. The rich merchants had their own ruling council there and didn't appreciate interference from the church. Not that Jacques actually expressed such sentiments, but he made it plain you couldn't push anyone around in Cahors.

It was dusk as we approached the walls and the fortified ramparts. A bell suddenly sounded, its great tolling voice echoing beyond the city to the vineyards which lay outside. As we travelled, we had passed men and women with their baskets of produce and their chickens and goats trudging back from the markets in Cahors to their villages beside the Olt. Now, hurrying beside us were men and women carrying hoes and baskets of twine. These workers tended the vines growing on terraces built along the craggy hills which sheltered Cahors to the north. They had the right to live within the city and hastened back to the security of its walls each evening before the great gates clanged shut for the night.

Of course I had not the slightest idea of this then, not being acquainted, you understand, with the agricultural practices of growing vines. Rearing sheep was more to my understanding and the shearing thereof and the sorting of fleeces. I was to learn about wine much later as I did many other things.

No, at that moment my thoughts were more taken with my first view of the city of Cahors, where the citizens were so proficient at making money.

I saw at once that this was a big place by any standards. The approach was pretty impressive. The city lay in another great loop of the Olt. It was defended on all sides by the waters of the river. The only roads in and out were guarded by watchtowers and heavily fortified gates. We approached the entrance of St Michel just as curfew was about to begin. Jaques was obviously a familiar face for we were waived through without any difficulty. We then found ourselves just to the south of a huge open tower.

'Impressive building,' I volunteered pointing to the tower. I offered this comment to my companion in the hope that a bit of civic pride would unloosen his tongue.

'It's the tower of St James, the pillory for the city,' was his reply.

Oh well, it was nice to think that they hanged the citizens caught doing wrong in a decent-looking place.

As we descended the main thoroughfare of the city I saw the huge ditch which protected the most densely populated streets. Cahors had over-spilled its original site and now the houses stretched beyond the ancient walls to the plains of the river. I also caught many glimpses of the towering remains left by the Romans. In the final conquest of Gaul they had made Cahors the capital of this region and given it a great arena and stately forum. This was something else I didn't know at the time, but like any other visitor, I marvelled at the beauty of the place and its formidable position.

We travelled some distance down the main street and then turned left and entered a narrow alley. These tiny thoroughfares served the citizens well, for the heat of the midday sun failed to penetrate far below the roofs of the dwellings. Now in the deepening gloom it was difficult to make out where we were.

A few paces to the right we stopped in front of a large town house set behind a fine carved gate. Jacques' demeanour changed as we entered a beautiful courtyard lit with many torches and set with flowers and a fountain. Our presence was noted by several barking dogs. We brought the cart to a halt and the horses whinnied in anticipation of a feed and rest.

With that an inner door flew open and a young girl with streaming black hair launched herself forward. She would have reached the cart in but a few strides, if a hand had not grasped the ribbons around her kirtle and pulled her back. A young female body then appeared attached to the hand accompanied by three more girls of various heights and ages. They formed a line in front of the door to the house and peered anxiously at the cart. Jacques eased his frame forward and descended without a flinch of pain. He said nothing but in an expansive movement he held his arms open and the five maidens surged forward and embraced him. The youngest, she who had been restrained, hugged his legs while two young girls clung to his arms. The fourth threw her arms around his neck. The fifth and oldest planted a kiss on his cheek and then drew back.

Jacques caressed them all in turn. Then he turned to the cart just as I got down and stood by the horses feeling, I am bound to say, not a little sheepish. For the first time, to my observation, joy seemed to have entered the heart of this canny old merchant. He smiled as he beckoned me forward.

'May I present my daughters,' he said with pride. Somehow the occasion seemed to demand something special so I touched my forelock and bent low to the ground. On raising my head I smiled at all five and said in my best French, 'Enchanté.'

This produced much laughter and giggles all round. Later I learned that I had spoken in the accent of the north, the langue d'oïl. The citizens of Cahors spoke the langue d'oc of the south. There was little time for embarrassment, however. The girls were so delighted to see their father, and he them, that there was much hugging all round. They withdrew inside the house as an excited crowd. I followed at a respectful distance.

When the merchant had a moment to break free from the embraces of his daughters, I noticed that an older woman had entered the room. She was of small stature but of regal bearing. She did not approach the group but waited by a great chest that ran along the wall of the room. Jacques shook himself free from the last attentions of his daughters and approached the lady. Then he took her hands in his and kissed them both at the same time inclining his head in a slight half bow. Turning to me with affection and pride in his voice, he presented his mother-in-law.

Later I was to learn that she was Sébélie Beral, a woman of great renown in Cahors. Her ancestry, her marriage and her personal abilities as a matriarch and a merchant in her own right made her a force to be reckoned with in the city.

But at this moment she was a mother and a grand mother and as she caressed the head of her son-in-law. I could see that he was held in esteem by her. What she made of me I cannot say. In fact I mean I would rather not know for I must have looked the unkempt wayfarer that I was, hardly better than the beggars who thronged the streets of this prosperous city. Anyway I did not want to intrude on a family reunion so I begged to take leave of them.

In truth I was now beginning to wonder what I was doing here. The blow I had received on the head had not deprived me of all my senses. Naturally I was grateful to Jacques for rescuing me, but I was far from the place where my own father had last been seen. I was sure that he would have preferred me to get on with the task of raising his ransom after I had discovered exactly where he was imprisoned. To do my task and honour my commitment to Edward, I must seek out the places where the troops of the king of France were stationed. Clearly it was not here. I was soon to learn that the citizens of Cahors cared for no authority, not the king of France, not the king of England nor even their own lord bishop.

But I had no money and only the clothes that I wore. Jacques had provided me with some shoes and a jerkin. It was now up to me to find employment. With a little money to my name, I could consider my options a bit better. But darkness lay over the city now and it seemed sensible to stay the night in Cahors and to resolve what to do in the morning.

For all his own tiredness and discomfort, Jacques saw me well provisioned for the night. He took me to an inn a short distance from his house and there paid the landlord to find me a bed and a good meal into the bargain. His daughters asked to accompany us but he shooed them back into the courtyard and the last I saw of them they were peering excitedly through the bars of the entrance gate.

CHAPTER 3

I was to discover in the morning that my benefactor had in fact set me up well for a week, with a bed and meals already paid for. Given my sorry state, the offer of free board and lodging was very tempting. I donned my underclothes which I had aired by the open window and gave thought to my mission. I needed to get this done as quickly as possible for I had serious doubts about leaving Reginald to manage Lord John's estates.

The knowledge that he had my mother to help him gave me little comfort. She would hear no wrong of him, and doubtless all his wild schemes would win her approval. Since our father's capture, Reginald and his men had brought fear to many of Lord John's tenants but Mother always defended him. He had a difficult start in life, she would remind me. He had been a poor sickly child with little hope of survival, was her favourite excuse. It had taken all her skills of mothering to raise him. The fact that he had survived to reach manhood was only down to her devoted care. She kept that one for the worst excesses. I sometimes asked myself if it had all been worth the effort.

The smell of roasting capon rose from a courtyard below. My inn was in the rue Duras, a street not far from the home of my benefactor. If you want the truth, it was more of a narrow alleyway, cool and dark, the overhanging balconies almost touching each other and offering shade against the heat of the midday sun. The inn's kitchen opened on to a smaller side alley. I hung out of my window and peered down on it. The ovens were already working hard, great clouds of steam and smoke billowing out into the morning air. I succumbed to the temptation and decided to stay. At least till something better turned up. That proved to be sooner than I expected. Something turning up, I mean. Only Lady Fortune knew whether it was for the better.

I left the inn and followed the noises of early morning trading. I found myself heading down towards the river along the main street, the Grand'rue, which ran the length of the city. I had no idea what I would do next but the thought of gainful employment entered my head. I had to exist in this strange city until I had the means to travel west. Much as I wished to serve my country and my liege lord, King Edward, I had no doubts that his generosity towards my family was commensurate with the information I could send him of the French king's plans. These were best known or to be discovered in the lands around Bordeaux.

The Grand'rue was busy, for it was here that the most important shops of Cahors were to be found. Each house had doors at street level where a trader had installed his wares. There were the usual trades you would expect to see: shoe repairers, candle makers, barbers, bottlers, soap makers, carders, but some shops were quite new to me, selling goose feather mattresses with fine flax covers, jars of sweet apricot and fig jam and great barrels of deep red wine. I saw products there I had never seen before in my country village: ginger, cloves, mace and nutmegs. Most expensive of all were the tubs of black pepper, brought by sea traders who travelled the roads from Montpellier.

This indeed was truly a sophisticated place. Most of all I marvelled at the trestles where the moneylenders plied their trade and where the many pawnbrokers were carrying out a brisk business notwithstanding the early hour.

Passing an entrance off the Grand'rue I caught a glimpse of the cathedral that dominated the main square of the city. Outside the door of a building near the cathedral, I saw a crowd of people pushing and jostling each other. Interested in what was going on or, as some would say, just plain nosey, I turned into the narrow alley. As I approached the crowd, a tall fellow stepped quickly backwards and caught my arm. It was now back in its socket but still painful enough. I stepped to one side, caught my foot in a pile of rubbish stacked against a wall and measured my length in the street. The fellow who had caused the problem hauled me to my feet and dusted me off.

'Sorry, mate,' he said. 'Didn't see you behind me,'

I tried to salvage a bit of dignity by dismissing the fall with a cursory gesture.

'No harm done,' I replied. But out of curiosity, I added, 'Why the crowd?'

I hoped my French was up to the mark but the man gave no reaction to my accent. I supposed it was normal in this city astride routes for pilgrims and travelling business men to be thankful that any stranger spoke something approaching words that could be understood.

'Usual crowd,' he said, 'when there's work in the offing. Not that this lot stand much chance.'

I tried not to look too interested. 'What sort of work?' I asked.

'Oh you know,' he replied, 'the usual sort of thing. Bon Macip's expanding all the time. Got to be a lot of money in the travel business.'

I pricked up my ears at that. Travel had a nice ring to it.

'Trust a canny old Jew to see the possibilities of guided tours,' the fellow went on. 'Still he won't want this rabble. The job calls for a bit of talent. You know the sort of thing: manners, the gift of the gab, a good head for direction. In other words, a little sophistication.'

He preened himself slightly. He had obviously been practising his CV.

'What's the exact job then?' I asked.

He looked at me a little more closely, perhaps recognising the newcomer that I was. Too late he perceived another contender for the post. He probably regretted his bonhomie. 'Tour guide,' he said in a less friendly tone.

'I think I might hang around then,' I said. 'You never know, he might have two vacancies.' I didn't want to look too pushy and I didn't think that I seriously had any chance of getting the job.

Well, that's where I was wrong. I waited till the end, then knocked at Bon Macip's door. He was almost packing up. He'd had enough of interviewing no-hopers.

My new acquaintance had come out smirking. As he passed me he raised his right arm. His elbow was bent and his fist clenched. It was a gesture I knew well. It said, 'So I told him,' or something a little ruder. It meant he hadn't got the job but had given himself the satisfaction of telling Bon Macip where he could put himself and other members of his race.

For myself, I cannot judge how the meeting with Bon Macip went, having no experience in the matter of job applications, but I do know that at the end, to my surprise the old man said he would give me a trial. And he was as good as his word. The very next day I was given the task of escorting a group of ladies and their children to the shrine of Our Lady Salve Regina at Pradines just outside Cahors. A mad dog had been seen in the hills around the city. A visit to the sanctuary to ask for the Virgin's protection had been organised by the city's mothers. Not exactly a grand tour, but for me, who had no idea where I was going, it was hard enough.

The old Jew was avaricious and crafty. It hadn't taken me long to learn that, nor of his contempt for most of his clients. In one sense, however, Bon Macip was a good employer. He gave me all the directions and advice I needed as a tour guide. Or so I thought at the time.

When he had finished giving me the benefit of his expertise, he summed up the rules of Penance Way: 'Always agree with the customers, dear boy, admire their choice of destination, watch out for stragglers and keep to the beaten track.' I thanked him and was about to leave. 'There's one final piece of advice,' he said, clapping me on the back, 'never explain, dear boy. Whatever happens, never apologise and never, ever explain.'

For my first excursion with the group of ladies, I was to cross the city and take a bac at the port Valentré. There was no bridge on the southern side of Cahors and travellers had to cross the Olt by means of a ferry to reach the paths that followed the lower banks of the river.

At the port Valentré, we discovered that there was a long queue. The bishop had recently raised the charges for the crossing. A dispute was taking place at the barrier for entry on to the bac. A farmer refused to pay the four deniers now being charged for transporting his pigs across the water. A fight was about to break out. I feared my employment as tour guide was about to end before it began.

Strange as I found my new situation, I knew a little about pigs. We had many on our estate and in our present state of crisis with Lord John absent, I often worked with the villeins on the demesne lands. I called the lead boar forward with the whistle I used at home. The animal had no problems with my accent and walked on to the bac with the rest of the swine following. The queue surged forward preventing any chance the ferryman had to stop them. A compromise was then reached. The ferryman agreed to let the pigs pass for the old rate with the promise of a side of pork on the farmer's return from the markets in the city.

I learned from one of the matriarchs in my party that the queues at the port were a source of constant dispute. They caused many an argument between the city consuls and the bishop. Business was the lifeblood of the merchants of Cahors, of whom the lady's husband was one. There were only two bridges in Cahors, she explained, the ancient Roman Pont Vieux and the Pont Neuf and they were situated to the north and east of the city. Travel along the road to Toulouse was dependent on the swell of the river and the good services of the ferryman.

Some ten years later a fine towered bridge would be built across the Olt at the port Valentré. But that was only for the good Lord to know at the time when we crossed. Or perhaps the devil, for later, it was said, he had played a part in its construction.

I was very polite to the ladies and used all my skills of chivalry to handle them carefully on to the ferry and disembark them on the other side of the river. I also looked with a fair appearance of admiration at their children. At the end of the trip I received a glowing report.

The next morning when I appeared in Bon Macip's office, he told me that my trial would continue that day with a slightly longer excursion. My second commission was to accompany a group of citizens to Puy L'Evêque, where the bishop was staying in his country retreat, the very one I had passed on my way to Cahors.

A smirk passed over Bon Macip's face as he informed me the bishop often fled there for a break from his problems in Cahors. Not that he used the word 'fled'. He was too much of the businessman to take obvious pleasure at the parlous state of the church.

'Our clients will be carrying a petition,' he said. 'The Olt apparently is in a dreadful state.' I swear the smile lingered, as he went on, 'A log has stuck under the bridge at Castelfranc. Our good citizens are taking their grievances to the bishop. Their boats cannot get past and business is suffering.' He added, for good measure, 'It's the bishop's responsibility to keep the river clear.'

It was obvious where the old Jew's sympathies lay. If he had any, that is. Early on in our acquaintance he had told me of the importance of the Olt and its junction with the Garonne. It gave the

51

merchants of Cahors a connection to the sea and all the trading opportunities which followed. I couldn't help feeling a pang of sympathy for the bishop. As if he didn't have enough problems looking after the faithful, he had to keep the river clear as well.

The canny citizens of Cahors didn't need me to show them the way to Puy L'Evêque. They made enough visits there to harry the bishop. My duties were only to keep them together, to arrange luncheon at a riverside inn and generally to listen to complaints. The fact that I didn't know much about the local situation just made it more interesting, especially for the more garrulous amongst them. They recounted at tedious length the difficulties they faced in their volatile city.

My admiration for Bon Macip grew. He was making a good living by arranging excursions that anyone with a bit of local knowledge could arrange for himself. But as I was to learn many times, that's the nature of the travel business.

The two trial excursions must have gone well for I had only been with Bon Macip a short time when he called me in to lead the group to Rocamadour. At the time I'd thought that news had got around that I was working for Penance Way. I could understand that my rescuer, Jacques Donadieu, hearing of my employment might call in a favour. But this was some favour. It was going to be something different from anything I had experienced before. Still how could I refuse? Jacques had helped me at a time of misfortune. The thought of the gratitude of all those pretty daughters was pleasant to contemplate. Little did I know then of French maidens, particularly those raised in Cahors.

Bon Macip explained that he had easily assembled a group of pilgrims anxious to spend a few days at the sanctuary of Rocamadour. There were fifteen in all, sixteen including myself. Some were the usual sort of tourists, eager to see a bit of the world, experience a little adventure, and take a break from usual humdrum affairs. Others were the real thing, pilgrims who had come down from Le Puy on the Via Podiensis. These members of the group were keen to make a short excursion to Rocamadour before tackling the main route down to Castile. And then there was a last minute addition to the party.

As I have said there were fifteen clients in all. Two nuns, a Knight of the Temple, three students from the cathedral school, the convicted heretic I had just acquired, a Franciscan monk, a morose looking businessman, a couple with their son and a woman with a withered arm. Finally there was a silent fellow who arrived on a black horse. That made fourteen pilgrims if I had counted correctly. I soon learned to my dismay who the fifteenth member would be. Marguerita, Jacques' eldest daughter, was joining us.

She was not a welcome addition. I had real doubts about taking her along. Don't get me wrong. Any other time I would have jumped at the obvious delights of getting to know her better. Now all I could think of was being held responsible for her safety. She might hinder my style when it came to dealing with the relic thief in my little band.

I said as much to her father. I had been called to meet him the day before our departure. I found him in the Place du Change. This was the square close to the cathedral where the important businessmen of Cahors carried out their monetary transactions. It was busy as usual. There was always a steady stream of citizens ready to pledge their property for a bit of the ready. It was said that the bishop was a regular customer. It seems half the goods of the church were pledged against financial help to keep the spiritual head above water.

The tables were laid out with the coins already stacked. A large instrument called a trébuchet was being used to sort out coins which were too light. I had to wait my turn while Jacques consulted with what looked like an important client. He then greeted me with some courtesy. The previous transaction had obviously gone well. He asked if I had fully recovered from the blows I had received upon my arrival in his fair land. I thanked him for his concern and assured him that my head was well used to a knock or two. He seemed much more relaxed than when I had first known him. I put this down to being back with his family and having proper treatment for his kidney complaint.

To my surprise, he quickly dismissed my concerns concerning his daughter. 'I am entrusting Marguerita to your care,' he said. That was what I was afraid of. Before I could protest further he went on with some resignation in his voice, 'She is determined to go. She has always pledged herself to visit Our Lady, the precious virgin in her sanctuary at Rocamadour.'

I marvelled at his air of calm when he told me of his daughter's plan. I would have put him down as a devoted father unable to contemplate allowing his fair offspring any freedoms which might compromise their well being. But then what do I know about bringing up children on your own, especially feisty French girls.

'I have no son,' he reminded me, 'to defend the family's honour. I would accompany you myself, but I believe Bon Macip has explained the problem to you. It is my duty to help the sacristan of the cathedral and regain the Sainte Coiffe. These wretched relic thieves, however, must not suspect that I am aware of their plans. Marguerita will be accepted as just another young wealthy pilgrim. You will find her help invaluable for she knows the route and is proficient in the local dialects.

Well I couldn't argue with that. Reluctantly I accepted his proposal. It wasn't really for me to lay down the rules. All I wanted to do was get this project over with as soon as possible, pick up my wages and get off in search of my own father.

Bon Macip had arranged that my group would meet outside the cathedral at dawn. Sharp. There were a good few already there when I arrived. I hoped they were going to stay an obedient bunch. It was one thing to listen to the advice the old Jew had given me regarding my position as group leader. It was another thing to exercise it. I didn't have authority here. Well not yet.

At the forefront of the first arrivals was the woman with the withered arm. I hadn't charged her too much, the sight of her arm hanging thin and shrunken by her side had got the better of me. I should explain that I set the charges for the trip. To encourage me to head up this crazy enterprise, Bon Macip had agreed that I would keep a percentage of the takings, and it was up to me the profit I made.

Overall I had charged according to the clients means, although I didn't tell them that. I had come out with a good sum for my father's ransom which I had entrusted to Jacques Donadieu for safe keeping. When I say entrusted, you can be sure that I had reservations on that score, but I reckoned that the coffers of a merchant who valued financial transactions might be a safer bet than a drawer in the desk of my erstwhile employer.

I soon learnt to keep sentiment out of financial negotiations. The woman, whose name was Huguette set me straight on that.

'Young man!' Her tone, despite her dejected demeanour, was demanding. I could see that I might have trouble with her. I wondered how she had recognised my position as tour guide. Then I recalled 'Penance Way' was inscribed on the badge Bon Macip required me to wear. There was nothing wrong with her eyesight.

'At your service, madam,' I doffed my hat as I said it, in what I hoped was a flamboyant gesture. I had plenty of experience handling difficult old ladies. They were often visitors to my father's house. The hours spent in their carriages tested their tempers as well as their old bones.

As usual it worked. Her tone softened somewhat as she said, 'A hand with my bag, if you please, when we set off.'

'Naturally, madam,' I replied, 'all part of the service.' I assumed that one of the carts lined up by the fountain in the square was hers. Only later did I learn that she was cadging a lift with the nuns. She calculated correctly that their vows of charity wouldn't allow them to let her walk. With the reduction in the fare I had charged, she was travelling for next to nothing. It seemed the ladies of Cahors were as astute as their men folk. Now at my words, she managed a weak smile. I anticipated less trouble after that.

I had seen that there were a good number of carriages and several mules lined up by the fountain in the square. Obviously most of my clients had decided not to walk the distance. Well if you've got the means why make heavy weather of it. Mind you, given the terrain we were going to cover, it would take a miracle from St Amadour himself for the transport to arrive there intact.

On Bon Macip's advice I had arranged a cart for myself as well. I had included it in the price. That way, we would all make reasonable time. If the old nag that arrived with my transport and the ancient cart stayed the course, that is.

It was a misty morning. The river below us was masked by a soft golden haze as the rising sun started to burn its way over the horizon, the trees on the banks pushing their heads into the first streaks of blue. It was going to be a hot day. The cathedral still stood as a massive dark shape to the north of the square. Night or day it was an impressive sight.

I'd not seen anything like it before but then I'd not travelled much. It did not have a beautiful facade like our cathedral at Exeter or much decoration either, come to that. In fact, to me, it looked more like a prison. It had two great cupolas, huge rounded roofs which covered the vast nave inside. They had been added by a previous bishop. He'd seen them on churches in the east while on a crusade with some local notables. They'd cost a fortune. No wonder the church was in debt.

As I have mentioned, I learned this on the crash course Bon Macip had ordered as a condition of my employment. He'd called out a retired guide to fill me in on the interesting parts of the city. Well I could see the point of that. Some of the pilgrims were citizens of Cahors. I couldn't have them knowing more about the place than I did.

I now knew about the Roman origins of Cahors when it was called Divona. I'd seen the magical spring, La Chartreuse, which provided the city with water. I learned of a great warrior named Lucterius, leader of the local Gauls called Cadurques, who defended the city against the Romans and only surrendered when they cut off the water supply. I was up to date in my knowledge of St Didier, the saviour of the city in the days of the Vandals. Most importantly I knew of the church's stand against the heretics of Toulouse which had got one of my present clients in such trouble.

The rest of the pilgrims soon arrived. I had a quick head count. Thirteen were waiting to depart. I couldn't see Marguerita. Trust her to be late. My mind was working overtime as I surveyed the group who were going to be my companions for the next few days. Among this lot was a relic thief with whom I would have to negotiate on the road to Rocamadour. What lay before me when we reached the sanctuary I tried not to contemplate. For the present I had to concentrate on the thought of bargaining with a scoundrel.

The problem was they all looked so decent. Well I suppose I ought to substitute the word 'harmless', for one or two looked like they had scraped together their last *sou* for the trip. No one had thief emblazoned on his surcoat. I supposed he would approach me to discuss terms. I assumed that the point of the theft was to gain some inexplicable favour as money seemed to be a last resort. I realised rather late in the day that there were many more questions I should have asked Bon Macip. I would just have to be ready for the thief's first move.

I looked around for Marguerita. I assumed that her carriage would already be here. One smart affair had arrived with a liveried servant. Then I recognised the passenger. It was the convicted heretic I had signed up a few days before. He was obviously pretty well breeched. I wished I had charged him more. Despite the yellow cross he was wearing he had an air of authority. Obviously the trauma of the conviction was wearing off. I hoped I wasn't going to have trouble with him. I was concerned to see the servant. I hadn't bargained for an extra member. But I noticed with relief, that having given his master a leg up on to the front seat of the carriage, the man took his leave and headed off.

Most of the pilgrims were dressed in long-sleeved tunics made of coarse wool. Nearly all had a hood which covered their head and shoulders. Each one carried a sack. Most had a pouch attached to their staffs. It seemed to me a sort of uniform but I learned it was standard gear for the holy tourist.

I knew that they had all been to confession the previous day. They had stated their intention to be pilgrims, taken mass, and had their possessions, such as they were, blessed by the priest. In this way they put the property they left behind, as well as their families, under the protection of the church. It was a brave man who dared the wrath of God to interfere with these until the owner's return. Too late, I realised that one pilgrim had not complied with the usual rules. But then I did not consider myself a pilgrim.

I still couldn't see Marguerita. I was sure I would recognise her. There were five women in our party. She would have stood out from the others for they were old crones by comparison. I hoped she wasn't going to hold up our departure. I could do without a poor timekeeper.

A well-dressed lad approached me. He was a fair looking fellow, still young enough to lack any growth on his chin. He had an air of determination.

'When are we going to depart?' he asked. 'The sun is well up. We ought to be off.'

I had no idea who he was but I determined to put him firmly in his place. I was the tour manager. It was my job to decide the timetable. As I looked him full in the face he gave me a friendly wink. Then he laughed. 'Oh come on,' he said, 'lighten up.'

I peered closer. It was Marguerita.

'What in the name of all that's holy are you doing? I demanded. I think I stuttered slightly. This annoying habit seems to strike me at moments of stress. 'Why are you dressed like this?'

'Didn't my father inform you? I am coming with you.'

'He said nothing about disguise.' I was still spluttering but managing to get my voice under control.

'Disguise!' Marguerita had the scathing note in her voice I would soon come to recognise. 'This is no disguise. I travel often like this when I accompany my father on his business trips. I am the daughter of a merchant. It is my usual attire for the stony paths and dangerous waters we traverse.'

I obviously had a lot to learn; especially about French ladies, particularly about the ladies of Cahors. Then I remembered that Marguerita was also the granddaughter of a talented business woman, famous in her own right. They were something else, these independent-minded women.

My mother had warned me about foreign women before I left. 'I've heard,' she said, 'that they are no better than they should be.' I have never understood the exact meaning of this remark but then again, I never disagree with my mother. Her knowledge of foreign ladies, however, whether French, Castilian or Provençale was limited. It existed solely of tittle-tattle from the royal court by way of serving maids who accompanied my father's frequent noble visitors. Mother's final piece of advice had been to keep my wits about me. I was certainly going to do that.

'Are you sure your father knows of this?' I questioned Marguerita. The last thing I wanted was to mess up twice on this perilous journey.

'Quite sure,' she said in a tone which meant, 'that's the end of that.'

I gave in. 'How are you travelling?' I asked. I could not see her carriage.

'With you,' she replied. You've hired a cart, haven't you? I hope it's a decent one with good wheels. Our road is steep and rocky.'

She waved her hand dismissively towards the smart carriages lined up in the square. 'They won't be of much use,' she went on scathingly. 'I hope you are good at repairing wheels. You'll need to be.'

I didn't reply. It was a tactic I came to use quite often where Marguerita was concerned. Instead I decided to call my group to attention.

The fountain in the square was ornamented with nymphs blowing on shells. I rather rudely climbed up on one. It looked sturdy enough to take my weight. I was taller than most of the pilgrims and with this added height I soon got their attention.

'Fellow travellers,' I shouted. There was no point rubbing home the fact that at least one was a convicted criminal, if heresy is an offence that is. On that one, I kept my thoughts to myself.

The pilgrims raised a head in unison. I glanced up at the sky. The mist was lifting well. 'It's after daybreak,' I said. The time was obvious to everyone but it's a good idea to take the first steps slowly.

I told them that I hoped to get to Rocamadour later that evening.

'I have arranged lodgings at an inn there,' I announced. 'If we keep up a good pace we should be there by dusk.' I said this with as much authority as I could muster. In truth, in case of delay, I had made a provisional bed and breakfast booking on the route, but I saw no point in telling them that.

'My assistant will lead the party,' I went on with somewhat less confidence. I indicated Marguerita as I spoke. She gave me a black look but luckily did not dispute her new role. I felt I had gained a little authority. Well that's what I thought. Also there was no point in mentioning the fact that I had need of her as I had no idea where we were going.

'I shall follow at the rear,' I went on. 'So if anyone has any problems I shall be around to lend a hand.' I realised that this meant I should be on foot but I calculated correctly that the pace would not be fast. Anyway when everyone was settled and well en route I planned to take a seat on the cart even though it meant riding with Marguerita.

I recalled at that moment that Bon Macip had said something about assistance. Surely he hadn't counted on Marguerita's decision to join the pilgrimage. I had no time to give this further thought for there was a sudden loud clatter in the square. All heads, including mine, turned towards the commotion. A Knight of the Temple had arrived on a huge white stallion.

He was a magnificent sight with his white tunic emblazoned with a large red cross on his left shoulder and his long grey beard. Like all the travellers I stood and gawped. I had heard tell of these soldiers of the cross who braved the infidel and took tours of duty to guard the holy places in Jerusalem. Their exploits were the stuff of legend. The stories about them told of deeds of valour, generosity in victory and courage in defeat. There were also darker rumours which talked of greed, ostentation and even sodomy but then there are always those who spread nasty rumours. All I knew was that they were considered very rich and the new arrival did nothing to dispel this thought.

This Knight of the Temple was a man of about fifty years. I learned later that he had not seen battle in the Holy Land for many a year. He was stationed in the commanderie at Cahors mainly engaged in training new recruits.

He dismounted from his horse and approached the fountain. Even standing there he looked me straight in the eye. 'You are the travellers to Rocamadour?' he enquired. I nodded my head. Speech had left me for the moment. Then I gathered my wits. 'We are about to depart.' I didn't mention that he was late. Somehow it seemed inappropriate.

'Good,' was all he replied and with that he remounted his horse, turned to the north, and with Marguerita following behind in the cart, he moved out of the square leaving the great shadow of the cathedral on his right.

The rest of the pilgrims hastily clambered in to their carts and carriages and followed suit. There was a general jockeying for position and then the line moved forward. I saw the nuns helping Huguette with her pilgrim's sack. I scampered behind trying to look as if I was organising the rear.

I checked behind the fountain just to make sure that nobody was having a last minute pee and then I ran along the length of the line of carriages and carts counting heads. It was an action I was to learn to do often on the journey as the line of pilgrims became more and more spread out.

After some minutes scurrying about, I managed to get to the front of the line and hissed at Marguerita. 'Do you know him?' I indicated the Templar who was now riding comfortably in front hopefully out of earshot.

'Not personally,' she replied. Then added, 'but he has had dealings with my father.'

'Why has he joined this group?'

'I've no idea,' she said. 'Does it matter?'

Then she favoured me with one of her imperious glances. 'Oh, I see he's cramping your style.'

I protested but it was obvious she had scored a point.

'I just hope he doesn't cause any trouble,' I countered. I had no idea what a forlorn hope that was going to be.

We started our journey passing the great carved door of Cahors Cathedral. Even in the mist it was an impressive sight. It showed the ascension of Christ in a perfect mandorla. He was accompanied by his apostles and the Virgin Mary. St Stephen was also there enduring his martyrdom and giving his name to the mighty place. I mention this for I noticed that most of the pilgrims turned to give this pious scene one last look before they left the square, as if the sight of Christ would give them comfort on their journey. I wondered about the thoughts of the one who secretly carried the sacred relic taken from the Cathedral crypt.

Me? I looked as well, but not for heavenly support. For what I was to face, I preferred more earthly accomplishments.

Passing from the square we hugged the side of the bishop's palace, the official residence where he was obliged to live when in the city. The present bishop was called Raymond. He was going to have a hard time of it explaining where the missing Sainte Coiffe was if I failed to negotiate its return. Still he was used to that, hard times that is. It was no sinecure governing this troublesome city.

I had learned that quickly enough from my benefactor. He was not only a rich merchant but also a consul of the city. He and some other merchants assisted the bishop in ruling Cahors. More often than not they were at loggerheads with each other, the bishop usually getting the worst of the encounter. The consuls could always remind the bishop that he still had a huge loan to pay off. This was a bit of a shame, for the debt was not Raymond's doing The money the church owed had been borrowed some eighty years before to pay for the crusade against the heretics of Toulouse. Successive consuls had been too canny to wipe the debt out. With the threat of making the bishop bankrupt, they could usually count on getting their own way. I think our King Edward would have sympathised with the bishop there.

At the end of the palace walls we came into the Place du Change where all the moneylenders had their stalls. It was situated right next to the bishop's town house. I could imagine what Raymond thought about that.

It was still early but several local bankers were getting ready for a day's work. I was glad to see Marguerita's father was not amongst them. I hoped that I would never have need of his services. I wanted to raise my father's ransom by means other than borrowing. I had little desire to spend a lifetime trying to redeem some pledges.

Moving out of the Place du Change we had a choice of roads. To the left of the square was the start of the large straight thoroughfare which led through the city. I had walked it a few days before on my tour of acclimatisation. It was a very impressive road. The houses were very grand. Most had beautiful wooden pillars enclosing handsome bricks made locally at St Cère Lapopie, a fine town which guarded the Olt to the east of Cahors. The houses all had huge ornate arcades opening on to the street from where I caught glimpses of the courtyards behind great iron gates. The upper two or three storeys had handsome windows with colonnades, while below I was just able to make out the huge stone stairways inside. Every courtyard was ablaze with colour for the citizens here seemed to fill their living spaces with flowers. At street level each arcade was occupied with the wares of a trader, reminding me again of the business of buying and selling that supported the good life of Cahors.

The alley which formed the exit to the right of the Place du Change led down to the Port Bullier. This was not the smartest part of town. At the port the butchers of Cahors plied their trade. There were stalls for the cattle and pigs waiting to be slaughtered. Steps led down to the Olt where the carcasses were washed and the useless bits thrown away to float downstream. I didn't consider this the direction for high class pilgrims.

I pushed my way to the front of the line and indicated that we should turn left. But the Templar pointed positively to the right and the pilgrims dutifully followed his lead. I turned to the cart which Marguerita was driving.

'Why take this route?' I hissed at her. I should have asked who was in charge here but we were moving too quickly for my words to have any effect.

'Why not?' was Marguerita's reply. 'This is the quickest way out of the city for the road north.' There was no arguing with that so I waved my arm as well, to show my authority but few noticed.

I needn't have worried about the Port Bullier. At this hour no slaughtering had yet taken place and the blood from yesterday's butchery had been washed away from the quay. We passed by without any sideways glances.

We negotiated the Tour des Balmes and made for St Catherine's gate. By now we were hugging the bank of the river. The great citadel that protected the northern part of the city soon rose before us. We showed our travelling papers and went through the Porte del Mirail. At the furthest edge of Cahors I saw again the great tower of St James and I pondered on the fate of the relic thieves should they ever be apprehended.

By now I had given up indicating the route we should take. The pilgrims trusted the powerful arm of the Templar as he waved the little band forward. I followed at the back making a big noise of keeping the group together. Already spaces were beginning to show marking out the pilgrims who were finding it difficult to keep up. I groaned inwardly. This was not going to be a journey like the one I had made getting to Cahors. But eventually without mishap we left the barbican behind us and took the route to Larroque des Arcs.

CHAPTER 4

We made quite good time for the first part of the day. At that hour, the weather was mercifully cool.

The whole group was full of anticipation. For most it was a real adventure outside the experience of humdrum life. Even the convicted heretic was looking forward to completing a penalty and getting back to his usual routine. The full-time pilgrims, those continuing the journey to Santiago de Compostela, looked on this as a small excursion, a short side tour to enrich their faith and to acquire the sportelle of Rocamadour. For me it was a chance to see something of the new countryside and to earn a few sous to put towards my father's ransom.

Don't think, however, that I ever forgot the real reason that I was leading this band of travellers. I continually scoured their faces for any signs that someone with a relic was ready to negotiate terms. We passed through the last gates of the city without any comments from the guards. All the pilgrims' papers were correct. Bon Macip had explained that would be the case.

'These are no amateurs,' he said. 'These are relic thieves who know how to work the antiques trade.' I had no idea how they had done it but it was plain that something had been arranged. Bon Macip had made it clear to me that I must retrieve the relic without making any payment. I wasn't sure what they wanted in return for the Sainte Coiffe. I could talk myself out of most situations. But that was back home with the local ruffians. How I was going to fare with crooks of this calibre was another matter.

On leaving Cahors, the path we followed was stony but quite flat. The sides of the track were heavily wooded with chestnut trees. Though we hugged the river and the early mist was clearing, it was often hard to keep sight of the fast flowing waters. Every so often we heard the cries of the boatmen as they brought their flat-bottomed sapines downriver to Cahors. They were carrying flax and grapes and goat's cheese from the markets on the upper reaches of the river. I'd heard that these boatmen were some of the hardiest men around. They coped with the changing moods of the Olt and the hazards of its sandbanks and rocks. They faced the dangers of floating debris:

branches and dead animals which had perished in the winter gales. Most of all they were toughened in their encounters with river pirates who were a plague of the region. I had been warned to be wary of ambushes on the towpath and I was glad when after about five miles the track pulled away from the river.

The carts trundled along at a good pace. That's to say the pilgrims did. For my part I was soon worn out with the task of running backwards and forwards to each end of the line which became more strung out as we went along. It became increasingly difficult to keep the pilgrims together. I did my best but the front ones seemed to make a better pace and were often lost to view on a turn of the path while I tried to chivvy the ones at the back.

At one stage I caught up with Marguerita. 'Slow down,' I hissed at her.

'I am,' she retorted. 'I could go much faster than this.'

'It's still not slow enough,' I pleaded. 'Think of the carriages at the back.'

'I'm keeping my eye on the front,' she replied rather haughtily. 'I thought you were looking after the rear.'

Not for the first time I wondered if she had some knowledge of which I was unaware.

'The knight of the Temple?' I looked round. 'Where is he?'

'Oh, him,' she answered casually. 'He's gone ahead to make sure the road is clear.'

'Is that a good idea?' I didn't want to alarm her but the words were out before I thought.

'Why not?' she asked. 'Don't you trust him?'

'I trust nobody,' I replied. I could have added, 'not even you', but politeness or temerity managed to keep these words unspoken.

My worries were eased when we approached a clearing and I saw the Templar on his great warhorse standing astride the path. He looked arrogantly around as we approached as if to indicate that there was no difficulty he could not face and overcome.

Earlier I noticed he had dismounted and walked by Marguerita's cart. He had taken it upon himself to indicate views and sights worthy of comment. There were many of these. The path turned as it rose from the banks of the Olt revealing the distant hills to the north. The red and gold beams of the sun caught the craggy edges of the Causse. This was the land of hidden streams and clear rushing springs which flowed suddenly from the ochre rocks. In summer they disappeared but for now they cut blackened courses into the limestone rock and fed the rivulets which crossed our path.

I thought it was time to assert my authority. 'I think we should stop,' I said to Marguerita.

'Is the pace too much for you?' she responded cheekily. But with that, she glanced back to judge the distance of the line from front to rear. At the end of the line should have been the carriage of the two nuns but it was now nowhere in sight. Marguerita reined in the horse and jumped lightly from the cart on to a boulder by the side of the road where the Templar stood.

Standing there in her surcoat, soft woollen tunic and hose, she looked every bit the fresh-faced youth. I saw the Templar give her a sharp glance. The meaning of it I could not tell, but either way I promised myself to keep a close eye on him.

'Good folks,' Marguerita called. 'What say you to a break?' Mindful belatedly of my position, she asked archly, 'If that is all right with our leader?'

I nodded quickly as if the very words had been on my lips. For good measure I added loudly, 'As my assistant has said it's time for a short break. But not too long,' I warned, 'for we still have far to go to reach our destination.'

Some of the pilgrims looked towards me but I hadn't yet got everyone's attention. 'I must ask you to be vigilant,' I added, at the top of my voice. There was no harm in putting the wind up them. Perhaps they would come to appreciate my position. A few more faces turned towards me. 'We are entering the country where robbers lurk. Your belongings must be kept carefully hidden,' I warned. 'Keep together, there is safety in numbers.' Now everyone was looking at me.

The Templar walked over to where I stood. He looked straight at the raised faces. 'Care when travelling. Remember this advice,' he said. His words were simple but his voice thundered out as if commanding a new squad of recruits. It was irritating to see how they all nodded in agreement. But at least they were back in the semblance of a group.

Marguerita appeared by my side. 'Tell them about Larroque des Arcs,' she mouthed at me. 'We shall be reaching it soon. You are the tour guide.' She might as well have asked me to acquaint them with the mysteries of Cathay for all I knew about Larroque des Arcs.

I had to fall back on ingenuity. 'My assistant,' I said, pushing Marguerita forward, 'will advise you of the itinerary.' Marguerita gave me a frosty look but launched into a description of the road ahead. I learned a lot in the next few moments. Larroque apparently stood at the confluence of the Olt and the Francoulès rivers. It took its name from the great aqueduct the Roman conquerors of this region had built to carry water down to Cahors. They were too clever to rely on a fountain that could be cut off. It was here, Marguerita explained, we would turn away from the Olt and head northwards towards Rocamadour.

A short time later as we drew nearer the town I saw clearly what she had described. The massive stone arches of the aqueduct were an impressive sight. To me at least. Some of the pilgrims were obviously well acquainted with the remains of Roman building projects for I noticed that the sight of this great monument did little to excite them. I found them quite stunning but then, when the Romans had visited my fair west country, it was not to build aqueducts but to tramp over the hills to mine our tin.

Larroque was the first town we encountered but I was concerned how long it had taken us to get there. I had hoped to be further along our route. I had done some homework before we left and had calculated the distances involved. But I had not taken into account the slowness of the pilgrim party. The rocky road caused problems for the carts and carriages. This and the pace of the slow walkers had quite thrown my calculations out. I hadn't realised that some of the pilgrims would decide to walk but then I had forgotten the point of the journey. These pilgrims were travelling for their soul's comfort and it would not do to make the path too easy. Some had decided to walk as part of their penance, only choosing to ride when legs began to flag or we reached a place where the carts could move along more easily.

Also I was not familiar with the terrain. The hills seemed to merge into one distant barrier and the paths had a terrible similarity. For all I knew we might be retracing a route we had already passed.

I said nothing of my worries but perhaps my concern showed in my face. We had stopped where the path rose above the valley below. While some of the party seated themselves to admire the view, others went to visit the chapel of St Roch to pay their respects. Some disappeared behind rocks for private matters.

The Templar approached me. He looked as fresh as the moment we had started. Despite his years he had the air of one who could cope with any crisis.

'We're heading for the main route which passes the town of Labastide Fortaniere? It is there we have lodgings?' His tone put it as a question but I detected a note of sarcasm in his voice. He always managed to annoy me.

'I have provisionally reserved rooms and a meal at the house of the Dominican fathers,' I replied rather frostily.

'A good choice,' he commented, 'although I should bargain the price. The holy gentlemen know the value of a sou and will charge accordingly.'

'It's been paid in advance,' I said, wondering if this fact should be divulged. Bon Macip had advised me to get the lodgings sorted out before we set off. It was not unusual for the clients to refuse to pay afterwards if the board and lodging did not come up to scratch. I had arranged with a Dominican monk visiting Cahors to prepare the rooms for us when he returned to his monastery. I had secured the agreement with a deposit. The balance I would pay when we arrived. He had not quibbled and I had congratulated myself on securing the first night's lodging. Of course if we didn't need the lodging I would hold the fees against other eventualities.

'Well then, we should be well placed,' I heard the Templar comment, and with that he swung himself into the saddle and cantered up to the path we would soon take. With his height and huge horse he commanded a good view of the roads.

As if a signal had been given, the party rose from whatever mound they were on and fell in behind him. Marguerita sprinted to our cart and took up the second position close behind the Templar. I wondered not for the first time if he had been commissioned by Marguerita's father to care for her.

Once again I felt marginalised, but comforted myself that when there was a really serious decision to be made I could be forceful enough.

As we moved off northwards in some semblance of a group, I took the opportunity to ask myself if the thief with the Saint Coiffe would soon show his hand. We were well away from Cahors now, and handled surreptitiously there was no need for any other member of the party to be involved.

I surveyed the pilgrims. There was no point in looking at the items they had brought with them. A small sweat-stained piece of cloth would fit easily into any pocket or sleeve. For all I knew it was being worn brazenly around the thief's neck.

No, I had to wait for the blackmailer, for such he was, to identify himself and approach me. I looked at them all again. In truth I had no idea what to expect. In their way almost all looked equally innocent or guilty. They were a very mixed bunch. If I had to make a wild guess, I suppose, at first I would have gone for one of the three young men. They were from the cathedral school in Cahors. I have little experience of students but if they were anything like Reginald they could run up huge debts. His attempt at education hadn't met with much success. My father never spoke of it, but mother was a different matter. 'Have you ever heard an ass play a lyre?' was her comment when Reginald was sent down by the monks at Exeter. My mother had an adage for most occasions but whether this was her opinion of my brother's unsuitability for further education or her verdict on his general abilities she didn't explain. To my mind both applied to Reginald.

My own schooling was the basic sort: reading in English and Latin, some arithmetic, scripture and music. I managed most of them but my best progress was in the skills of the tournament. I had avoided further education by proving myself able at estate management.

Now I wondered if one of these students had got into financial difficulties and jumped at an opportunity to make a quick sou. They had all the signs of study: white faces, long fingers and bent backs. Two of them looked right wimps. The third was taller with red gold hair. He had the air of a spoilt child. I reckoned they would all be a pushover in a fight. Not that I expected to put that theory to the test. My brief was negotiation or wily trickery, not fisticuffs.

They had plans they said to go to university: Orleans or Toulouse or if they made the grade, Montpellier. They had ambitions or perhaps their parents did, to become lawyers or doctors. After thirteen years at Cahors' best seminary they were taking a year off. The short trip to Rocamadour was but the first in a programme of pilgrimages which would take them to the shrines of St Thomas at Canterbury and St Jacques at Compostela. They had hopes of making it to Rome. After some minutes listening to the merits they had achieved in their studies and their prospects for the future, I was ready to erase the students from my suspicions.

I considered the pilgrim in the cart behind. He was a sad looking fellow, as morose now as when the journey had begun. He was older than the students and did not have the pale look of years of book learning. Rather his complexion was coarse and dark as if he had spent much of his time on the road. He had told me he was a businessman. That information really enlightened me. It covered practically all the inhabitants of Cahors. Bon Macip had informed me that he had recently been widowed, and was making the journey on behalf of his dead wife. It struck me that it might have been more helpful to go while she was still alive. I looked at him as he sat hunched on the cart I had provided. His clothing did not speak of riches, but then I couldn't assume every businessman made a good profit. It may be that a trade in relics had been called for to make ends meet.

Amongst the others, there was the Templar who, though I disliked his arrogance, I could not envisage as a robber or blackmailer; Marguerita, whom I dismissed, of course; and the convicted heretic. I studied him carefully. As usual he sat erect in his carriage. Despite the trappings of a rich man, it was hard to ignore the yellow cross on his back. An air of depression had taken hold of him. Had he the energy to go in for a bit of theft?

Behind him came the carriage of the couple with their son. The boy was a pimply-looking fellow. It was difficult to judge his age. He was tall and well built but his manner was childlike. He mooned about a lot and seemed generally preoccupied with his hair. Still I didn't exclude him from my suspicions, for there's an age when most boys are up to no good. I have to admit I speak from experience there. His parents seemed pretty ordinary although they had the means to bring their own carriage. On one occasion as we rested, his mother announced that she and his father were celebrating the anniversary of their marriage.

'This is a sentimental journey for us,' she said. 'We met at Rocamadour some eighteen years ago. It was love at first sight. We married soon afterwards.' A haze of romantic recollection passed over her face. I glanced at her husband as the nuns offered their congratulations. He had the air of a man not given to contradiction. Their son looked embarrassed. I felt for him there. I knew all about mothers who could let you down in public.

For myself, I didn't know whether to be pleased or worried when I heard that. They were familiar with Rocamadour, which might help if I had problems finding my way around. On the other hand, they might discover my lack of knowledge about the place and cast further doubts on my powers of leadership. I would have to watch my step with them.

The next cart carried the remaining females in the group. The old woman with the maimed arm was now quiet enough. From time to time she had a few words with the nuns. She had taken it for granted she would share their cart. I didn't doubt that the poor withered arm which lay by her side was the reason for her visit to the miraculous Madonna of Rocamadour. I couldn't help thinking she had left it a bit late in the day. Whether she had other motives for this pilgrimage was difficult to imagine. She was tougher than I had thought, however. If there were times when I wondered if she would survive the journey they were soon dispelled.

Sitting with her were the two nuns. They said little, occasionally politely answering a direct question. They spent most of the journey whispering to each other and holding hands as if to warn any molester that he would have two of them to deal with. Their high wimples were still fresh and hid their faces as they leaned forward to carry out their inaudible conversation. Occasionally I heard ripples of quiet laughter coming from them. It was my first but not last experience of the fun and mirth that sisters could extract from their simple life.

That left two pilgrims. One was the Franciscan monk. He was tall and athletic and wore the grey cloak of his order well. The knotted rope hung loosely around his slim waist. He too had a tanned complexion but his features were finer than those of the businessman. Furthermore he had an open friendly manner. This was probably one of the tools of the trade for a travelling churchman. I had heard tell that the followers of St Francis were well received wherever they went. He travelled in the cart but well away from the three female occupants. Occasionally he read from a manuscript he had brought with him. He wore pieces of glass in a frame on his nose. This caused much amusement to the sisters who giggled at almost nothing. But when he showed them how the eye glass made the letters of the manuscript larger, they were full of wonder and considered him from under their veils with awe and admiration.

Finally there was the stranger on the black mare who refrained from communication with anyone. He had very little hair on his head, which he brushed with his hand from time to time. I noticed that they were good hands with long slender fingers. The nails were not broken. They were not the white hands of the students, however, but hands that looked as if they had seen service. I reckoned that he might be a musician or a doctor. I considered him as the relic thief. As a negotiator he seemed a poor choice. He had said barely ten words since joining the tour. To arrange terms he would have to communicate with me and that was something he had no desire to do.

Marguerita approached me just before we left Larroque des Arcs. 'We'd better get going,' she said.

'I know, I know,' I replied tetchily. I was getting fed up with being reminded of the obvious.

Still she was right, and we moved off and followed the narrow path that hugged the Francoulès river. We followed the track as far as Valroufié, and then we struck across country to Labastide Fortanière.

CHAPTER 5

We reached Labastide Fortanière at about four of the clock. It was quite late and the company was tired. Now I had a real dilemma, as the Templar had expected. We could push on and reach Rocamadour late in the evening and chance problems travelling in the dusk, or we could take an early rest and seek the bed and breakfast I had secured on deposit, in the Dominican priory.

If I'm honest, it was the pilgrims who had paid the deposit although they didn't know that exactly. Bon Macip's first rule of travel was to avoid itemising the costs of the tour. 'Remember, dear boy, to keep the financial arrangements to yourself,' he warned. 'That way you can cover any changes in the travel plan.' I was beginning to see what he meant.

Still I didn't like to fleece people. Well not all of them. I had almost made the decision to stop when the Templar turned his great horse and rode down beside me. At this time I was hitching a ride on Marguerita's cart, my legs having grown weary of dashing about along the length of the line. The pilgrims had now become used to the route and the procedures we followed. It enabled me to have a short rest. Very short that is, for the Templar broke into my brief moment of reverie, to ask, 'Where exactly is the lodging?'

Of course I had no idea but I wasn't going to let him know that.

'Here,' I replied, confidently waving my hand towards the buildings of a town which was now in view, Marguerita having reliably informed me it was Labastide Fortanière. We had approached it from the south after a short stop at St Martin de Vers. Now we dropped down on to Labastide as the sun was lowering in the sky, sending its long fingers to dance on the sea of roofs which lay before us and bathing the church tower in a ruby glow.

The Causse here was rugged with a low covering of scrub oak, maple and juniper. The sweet smell of thyme and fennel filled our nostrils as the carts moved slowly along, crushing them underfoot. It was late spring and honeysuckle was already trailing in confusion and binding the scrub at the side of the path. As we passed, we disturbed grasshoppers and crickets. Sometimes a lark flew up around our feet and soared into the sky. Now hawks hovered overhead, searching for their last meal before giving place to the owls in the darkening sky.

This was the sort of terrain I knew well for it reminded me of my beloved Dartmoor. Not for the first time, my heart grew heavy at the fate which had brought me here. I determined to fulfil this obligation as quickly as I could, find my father, and return home.

I knew enough about the Black Friars to realise that their house should have been obvious. The Dominican brothers always built their friaries outside the walls of the towns. It was said they had the ear of the pope. There were few priests who welcomed them in their parish.

From our viewpoint, the huge walls of the monastery should have been apparent. I hoped that perhaps it was hidden from sight by a turn in the path but the Templar soon disabused me of that idea.

'Are you certain there is a house here?' he asked. It was a simple question but I detected the sarcasm in his voice. He knew for certain there was no Dominican priory at Labastide.

I was about to protest that I had paid a deposit when I understood what he meant. The black cloaked monk in Cahors had been a scoundrel dressed to deceive the unwary. I had fallen for his disguise and parted with my clients' money to no avail.

The knight perceived my discomfort. To give him his due he made nothing of it. He said simply, 'There is a commanderie near here, a little to the south-east at Soulomès. I am sure the knights there would put their guest room at your disposal.'

It was probably a well intentioned suggestion but somehow I still managed to resent it. Hastily I turned down the offer. Mindful of the manners mother had drilled into me, I thanked him for his concern. 'I appreciate your offer,' I said, 'but I do not wish to turn south. I think we should push on,' I continued, more positively than I felt. 'I am sure that with a bit of effort we can reach Rocamadour by nightfall. Our rooms are reserved there.' I wasn't sure of that as he probably well knew but the knight said nothing. Luckily for me Marguerita for once backed me up. 'Come on then,' she encouraged. 'I'm sure we can get there this evening if we keep up a reasonable pace.' I did not know at that time that she had another motive for urgency, one that concerned her own plans, not my support.

74

With that, we continued the route although I have to say there were groans and comments from the pilgrims. I reminded them that tiredness and discomfort in the bones was part of the point of the pilgrimage. I'm glad to say that no one argued with that.

Even so I was beginning to grow very concerned. Without stopping, how was the relic thief to go about his business of negotiation, and who was he? So far I had kept my wits about me but the lack of action was beginning to wear me down. Perhaps that was what the thieves were counting on. All I could do was wait and be as vigilant as I could.

Deciding to continue on the road to Rocamadour was not the best decision I ever made nor was it the only mistake on this venture. But then, as I have said, what do I know about the tourist business and pilgrimages in particular.

As Lady Fortune would have it, the road past Labastide Fortanière grew very steep and rocky. The mules were tired and had trouble keeping to the centre of the path. We had just turned off towards Carlucet, a hillside town built on two levels, when Marguerita's prediction came true. The carriage of the convicted heretic broke a wheel and deposited him unceremoniously on the ground.

My heart sank. I had experience mending cart wheels. I had done enough on my father's estate, but I was not familiar with these carriages and it would hinder our progress if I took too long. Nevertheless I tried to sound positive. 'Stand aside,' I shouted. 'Leave it to me.'

But with that the Franciscan monk hurried forward. Rolling up his cloak he waved me aside. 'My department I think,' he said, and, with that, did an excellent job of restoring the wheel to its axle. I thanked him well but all he said was, 'Part of a day's work.' I had seen friars before as they trudged the streets of towns with their begging bowls, preaching the path to salvation. I had never seen one mend a wheel. My opinion of the church was changing.

Later, he told me that he had been a wheelwright before finding his calling with the friars. His wife had succumbed to the traumas of childbirth many years before and with his two grown daughters well married, he had lately taken the vows of St Francis.

The stop to mend the wheel, however quickly accomplished, inevitably slowed us and permitted more complaints from the weary travellers. We carried on until Couzou, a long straggly village high in the Causse, came into view. By now the pilgrims had grown almost aggressive and demanded a rest.

The Templar once again was to the fore. 'We could camp here,' he said. 'The village is not far away and this path can be guarded by one person. We all have carts or carriages.' He did not include the quiet man on the black horse, but I assumed he would step up on Marguerita's cart and rest with me for the hours of darkness.

I knew the horses and mules needed to rest. I had bought some items of food in the last village, goat's cheese, some pickled beans, the dark, heavy bread of the region and two flagons of wine. We would not go hungry. I knew his suggestion, as usual, made sense.

I called the line to a halt by standing up on Marguerita's cart. I was about to inform them of my decision but they too had come to the same conclusion. The pilgrims reined in enthusiastically and needed no second bidding to make camp. They did it with an expertise that made me realise I should not underestimate my clients.

Needless to say the Templar had the wherewithal to make a fire, and I have to say that we passed a pleasant enough evening. The night was warm and after the rigours of the trail, the simple meal was good. As the sun sank below the hills and the shadows of night filled the sky, I could have thought I was enjoying one of my adventures back home.

The two nuns ate very little and refused any offer of the local wine. When the flames of the fire grew lower, they bid us good night and hands clasped tightly together, they walked quietly to their cart, settling themselves into a corner as if it were all the comfort they asked. For all I knew it was home from home to these sisters of the cross.

Marguerita and Huguette followed shortly. I noticed that the old woman joined the nuns, anxious no doubt to secure her place for the morrow. I heard the married couple organising the sleeping arrangement for their son. Then they wandered together, for a few moments, over the moonlit grass, before joining him in their cart. The Templar moved off to check his stallion was safely tethered. I took the opportunity to see that the ladies were safely settled for the night. Doubtless he would do the same.

When I returned I found the students, the Franciscan and the heretic gazing into the glowing embers of the fire. A little apart sat the businessman looking rather depressed. The silent man on the black horse was no where to be seen but that didn't surprise me.

I sat down beside my clients. It was a good time to get to know them better. It had been a harder task to keep them together and get them here than I could ever have imagined. I realised I knew very little about them save the meagre facts given by Bon Macip. I needed to find out more if I was to fulfil my duties as a guide and discover who had the Sainte Coiffe.

If I harboured some idea that by clever questioning I would get the culprit to reveal himself, I was sadly mistaken. Not that I had much experience. My knowledge of the criminal mind was limited to some of the thugs that hung around with my brother. I was pretty green in combat save for assisting in the lists. Nor had I been involved in theft. Well not serious theft. I didn't count a bit of poaching on our neighbouring estates.

I engaged the students in conversation. That was easy enough. They talked at length of their studies and their ambitious hopes for the future. Two of them did, at least. After a good half hour of listening to the syllogisms of St Thomas Aquinas, I was beginning to nod off. One of them, called Hubert, did mention the natural history of Albertus Magnus but that, too, was above my head. I was interested enough but the young man had the academic habit of making everything very dry. I judged he would have a good career ahead of him lecturing at some university.

The third student, the tall one with red gold hair, said very little. I learned only that his name was Bertrand.

I couldn't see any one of them as a relic thief. They didn't have the wit to organise anything that did not involve great peroration. Being a criminal was just not in their line.

I gave up the unequal task and turned my attention to the Franciscan, the heretic having disappeared soon after my return to seek the privacy of his carriage. The friar had an open air about him that encouraged confession, a useful characteristic for his calling. He may have learned at some seminary how to be a good listener.

Perhaps it was natural to him. Not that I confessed anything. I hadn't learned to keep my mouth shut anywhere special. That was just natural to me.

It was he who started the conversation. The moon was now a yellow orb in the starry sky. Looking upward he said, 'The Lord's in his heaven tonight.' I didn't disagree, having little knowledge of where else God might be.

'You are glad to be here?' I asked. It wasn't the cleverest response but I had no stomach for a lengthy theological discussion.

The friar answered with his usual charm. 'I am happy to be at one with this world and I am prepared for what the Lord asks of me in the next.' So he liked the job he'd got and seemed to have a secure future.

I tried again. This time I brought the conversation round to the subject of relics. 'Tomorrow we shall visit the holy virgin in her shrine,' I said. 'She is said to be a wondrous sight.' Too late I realised that as a tour guide I should have a better knowledge of such a well known object of veneration.

If the friar noticed my unease he gave no indication. 'This is my first visit to Rocamadour,' he replied. 'I am blessed that God has granted me this opportunity.'

He glanced round as the Templar returned and seated himself on a flat rock. His presence still dominated the group. 'I have checked the others,' he announced. 'I think you will find all is in order.' There was a pause while I swallowed the words of annoyance which rose immediately to my mouth and found the ones to thank him for his concern.

'All part of the service,' the Templar replied, acknowledging the duty of care rules which governed his brotherhood. We weren't exactly visitors to the holy places in Jerusalem but perhaps a pilgrimage to Rocamadour was a poor second best. As if to underline his point, he addressed the Fransiscan. 'We share a concern for those in need, do you not agree?' he said. 'Though I am a servant of God's holy army while you offer blessing of a different kind. The blessed Saint Francis, however, did not shirk the dangers of the east. I have heard of his journey to the Holy Land and of his meeting with Sultan Melek al-Kamil.'

The friar made no reply but bowed his head in acknowledgement of the honour paid to his founder by a seasoned campaigner. He stood up and his smile seemed to encompass everyone. 'I think, if you will excuse me,' he said, 'I shall spend some time in silent prayer.' He moved off slowly, his hands clasped in front of him. After a short time the Templar went too. I saw him later fondling the mane of his great white horse.

The businessman, the widower who seemed always preoccupied with his own thoughts, remained, silently looking into the dying coals of the fire. I remembered that Bon Macip had told me of the death of his wife. 'Are you finding comfort in this pilgrimage?' I asked him as politely as I could. You may consider that rather bold in the circumstances but time was running out. I had to start somewhere.

At first he did not reply, but when nobody else answered he looked up. He mumbled an apology. I rephrased the question. 'Are you enjoying this wonderful experience?' I enquired. He looked as if he found it hard to enjoy anything, but I was well briefed in the jargon of the tour leader.

'Make sure they realise they've got value for money,' Bon Macip had advised. They hadn't, of course, and he knew that. The only person who had a good return on investment was himself. 'Your tip will suffer, dear boy, if they don't see the benefits of spending this much money on a pilgrimage,' he warned me. 'Grateful pilgrims are the most generous,' he added, 'especially if they receive God's forgiveness for their sins.' The old Jew was clever. I knew that. To convince clients of God's blessing was one of his skills I had yet to learn.

The businessman looked around as if wondering to which wonderful experience I referred. He looked back at me with a strange look in his deep brown eyes. I found it impossible to read his thoughts. 'I come to experience the good of mankind,' he replied, and with that enigmatic comment I had to be content.

'And your wife?' I asked. My mother would have reprimanded me for impertinence but he seemed to have forgotten the real reason for his pilgrimage. 'You will pray for her soul?'

'I shall pray for all who deserve it,' he remarked. I could but hope that the good lady was included in that.

I gave up. I had drunk plenty of the wine and my head was now quite light. I decided to make for my own bed, such as it was. I did the last rounds and exhorted everyone to sleep well and rise early in the morning.

The knight of the Temple took it upon himself to do guard duty and the last I saw of him as darkness drew in upon us was his outline as he patrolled the path. His horse grazed at the side although what the huge stallion found to eat I am not sure, for the grass on the Causse was scarce enough. Still it was not my concern. These animals were used to the region and obviously were accustomed to finding herbs and plants that satisfied their hunger.

I am a quick sleeper. By that I mean I sleep well but not too long. I have learned to wake early. As I have confessed already, I was used to sleeping in the open after some escapade in the villages around my father's estates and usually had time to reach my own bed before the sun rose. This day, despite the dark red wine I had enjoyed the previous evening, I woke as usual, when the sun was still well below the horizon. It was time to relieve the Templar of his guard duties.

As the last cool fingers of night faded from the sky, I stretched myself and looked around the other carts and carriages. All was quiet except for the general snores and grunts that sleepers give out. Marguerita was lying still at one end of the cart. The strange silent man had refused my offer of a space on our cart and was stretched out on a bank of moss beside his horse.

Without any noise I climbed down over the wheel of our cart and made my way around our makeshift camp.

No one had approached me that evening and I had learned nothing from my conversations. I had begun to wonder what this was all about. I didn't know whether to take Marguerita into my confidence. Did she know about the theft of the relic. Knowing her better now I would have thought she did, but she had given no hint of it. I did not want to divulge a secret that perhaps her father had confided only to Bon Macip. I cursed myself that I had not found this out before we departed from Cahors.

Now with everyone asleep I thought of searching some of the baggage. Perhaps I could cancel some of the pilgrims from my suspicions. Despite constant warnings, there were various pouches which lay unguarded as their owners dreamed away. I had no idea really what the Sainte Coiffe looked like, but it would be helpful to identify any bit of old cloth that was hidden in a corner of someone's possessions. I dismissed that idea, however, as quickly as I had it. Doubtless the Templar, vigilant as ever, would spot my undercover activities.

The hour of dawn was nearer than I thought, for the first streaks of greyish blue were moving across the sky. Behind was the pink and gold that heralded the dawn in this region of beautiful mornings. I stopped for just a moment where the path rose slightly, to survey the Causse and look for the Templar.

As I gazed about me I saw a boulder to the right of the path. I had not noticed it when we had arrived and I peered more closely to make out the outline of the shape. It had a formation unlike the yellowed stones of the Causse. With the dawning light I could soon see the colour, a dull white. As my eyes grew accustomed to peering through the first weak rays of the sun, I saw to my horror and fear that I could make out the shape of a leg. Gradually the whole form of a man appeared before my eyes.

I almost flew down the track. I knew, however, with a strange sickness inside me what I was about to discover. The body of the knight of the Temple lay there. I touched his face and hastily withdrew my hand from the cold skin. I should estimate he had been dead at least several hours.

At first I thought that his age had overtaken him. His heart was no longer young. I did not know what life he had led. He had the air of a strong man but the exploits of his youth might well have told on his ageing body. Drawing much closer to him however I could make out the reason for his lifeless form. A dagger with a handle fashioned into the form of a strange greenish brown tusk was sticking out of his neck. Someone had felled him like an ox.

If you must have the truth, I almost panicked. Bon Macip hadn't given me a rule to cover this eventuality. Here I was in a foreign country, amongst people I did not know, going to a place I had never visited before and now with a dead body on my hands. I breathed in deeply. I thought of mother, of my adopted father, of King Edward, and finally of my brother Reginald.

I think it was the thought of the mess he was probably making of my father's estates that pulled me together. Lord John was Reginald's father too, not to say his natural father, but that didn't stop me despairing of my brother.

I covered the face and neck of the knight with his fine woollen kerchief. I wiped away what blood there was. A little had drained from him and splashed the leaves of some scrubby plants with flecks of brown. I bent these down and held them with a limestone rocks. Before leaving the lifeless body I did one last thing. I removed the dagger which had been the cause of his death and hid it in my boot. I had no wish to frighten the clients more than was necessary. Also I had some thought that to discover the owner of this deadly weapon would be my next move.

As I took one last look at the Templar's face, grey in death, I felt a pang of remorse that I had not felt more kindly towards him. He had more than likely been commissioned to look after somebody. If it wasn't Marguerita, I had a faint suspicion it might have been myself. Now for his reward he had been murdered. Only I knew of the real purpose of this pilgrimage. Had he stumbled upon the thief? Had he realised that the precious relic was amongst some baggage? If the thief was prepared to kill then the journey became quite different. This was no joking affair. I had taken the theft of the Sainte Coiffe almost lightly, believing I had only to discover its whereabouts or negotiate terms for its return. This was serious. How would I explain the knight's death? Would the thief show himself for the murderer he was? How could I protect my clients? I did not know them well but I had grown accustomed to them. I couldn't let another die.

As far as any explanation was concerned, I need not have worried. Waking the others I reported the awful news to them. To my amazement they took it in their stride. They were shocked and saddened, but most accepted the death with an equanimity that underlined the faith which had urged them to make this journey. 'The hazards of the road,' was all they really said. It seemed that they believed he had succumbed to the rigours of undertaking a pilgrimage at too advanced an age.

The word 'routiers' was also on some lips. I did nothing to dispel the idea. Let them think that the Templar had died while guarding the camp. That might be the explanation. They could be right, but I knew what they didn't know. We had a thief amongst us and now it looked as if we had a murderer as well.

Even the problem about what to do next was taken out of my hands. The Franciscan friar came forward. 'Did I hear talk of a Templar commanderie near here?' he asked. I remembered what the knight had told me. There was one to the south-east of Labastide Fortanière. It was some miles back at Soulomès. We couldn't leave the poor knight here and I nodded in agreement when it was suggested that we should go back to inform his comrades. I was in the process of deciding how we would do this when the Franciscan offered to go. 'I can ride fast,' he said, 'and get help.' With that he saddled the knight's horse and sprang on to its back. Once again I wondered at the prowess of this lately professed friar. Before I could say 'Godspeed' he had gone, galloping over the rocky terrain with an expertise that defies description.

Naturally we had to wait until he returned. I did my best to keep the pilgrims away from my grim discovery. The nuns insisted on keeping vigil by the body and this helped to prevent the curious from getting too close. I encouraged the pilgrims in their belief that his heart had just given out.

You might have thought that the next hour hung on our shoulders with a heavy weight but that was not so. I called all the pilgrims together and gave them a makeshift breakfast of bread steeped in wine. I had watered the wine from a spring. The rush of water from the rocks was for me evidence of its purity. At least I hoped this to be the case. If not I would have a few more dead bodies to deal with.

Little was said as my clients ate. Each was wrapped up in his or her own thoughts. After the makeshift meal some of my pilgrims sat quietly in deep reflection. Some moved away from the carts and walked amongst the purple orchids which were lately pushing their heads through the tangle of thyme and saxifrage. Marguerita for once had little to say. She stayed close to me, and once or twice gave me the comfort of her hand in mine.

It seemed, therefore, that little time had passed before we heard once again the sound of hooves ringing on the stones of the Causse. Four men came into view accompanying the friar. With great solemnity they dismounted and looked in reverence at their comrade's body. The friar informed me that they knew him well. Some of them he had trained. Their grief was evidence of the great esteem held for him by the brotherhood of Templars.

With tender care they lifted the dead body and placed it on his horse. They had brought a cloth of gold to cover him, and if they saw the wound where the dagger had penetrated his neck they said nothing. Tying him carefully so that he would not fall, they all remounted and slowly and silently descended the rocky path for the journey back to their commanderie. As I watched the party leave I could have thought that our knight was just enjoying a stroll home.

The friar assured me the departing knights would deal with the appropriate authorities to report his death. Like the rest of the pilgrims, they appeared to put his demise down to the misfortunes of travel. The friar advised us to stick closely together and not to spend any further nights in the open. The knights also urged us to seek the safety of an inn or the guest house of a monastery. 'Even then,' they warned, 'you must be vigilant. There are those who choose to do their misdeeds under the guise of hospitality.' There was no need to remind me. I had learned that one for myself.

By the time we set off again the sun was climbing in the sky. I encouraged the party along. We had the time to reach Rocamadour that same morning but I was tiring of this journey and thought the sooner we got there the sooner my problems would be over. That was another mistake.

We left Couzou just after nine. It was a short journey to Rocamadour but a hazardous one. The road was steep and winding. As it rose the land fell away to left and right until we grew weary of looking down. By now we were all on foot, for here the path was too hazardous to remain in our carts. Even the heretic deigned to step down from his carriage. One large jolt would have sent him plunging to the valley below. Our party moved slowly. The mules were weary and trod carefully on the slippery shale of the narrow path. We pilgrims had much to think about. The sadness of losing one of our band, mixed with the anticipation of the destination ahead. Little was said and we all took care to keep together.

I travelled now with a heavy heart. I was sure that the death of the Templar had been no act of a highway ruffian. It had been difficult enough imagining that any one of the pilgrims was a relic thief. Now I had to search out a murderer from amongst our band. I found it hard enough to concentrate on the road that we followed. A hundred questions entered my head. What was his motive? Would he strike again? Who else was in danger? Was the thief also a killer or was I taking two criminals with me to Rocamadour. Did Bon Macip have any idea that this would happen?

Not for the first time, I questioned my own part in this pilgrimage. I could abandon these people here and now. Surely I could find my way to a path that led westwards. Time was short. I was far from Gascony. Even in King Edward's lands I had no idea where my father was. I should be making my way back there to seek out his prison and redeem him with a ransom.

The thought of the money I would need to raise brought me to my senses. I needed to fulfil my obligation to Bon Macip to get the final part of my pay. Explaining to him I'd lost a client was bad enough, admitting I had returned without the Sainte Coiffe would no doubt cancel any thoughts of remuneration, let alone the bonus he had promised me.

I have given you the thoughts that filled my mind. I have not yet mentioned the new Marguerita. Since the death of the Templar she had stayed close to me. She drove the cart without sharp comment or she walked quietly by my side. At times she placed her hand upon my arm. Once she laid a friendly arm around my shoulder.

I'm not saying what counted most in strengthening my resolve but I reached a decision. I would carry on to Rocamadour and see this pilgrimage through. One way or another I would search out the relic thief and avenge the death of a man who had done me no wrong and had lost his life while in my charge.

Chapter 6

Nothing prepared me for my first sight of the sanctuary of Rocamadour, suspended, as it seemed, from the heavens above. I'm not a seasoned traveller, you must remember, when I confess I forgot my position as tour guide and stared open mouthed as the saintly city came into view. I had only ever given scant attention to the prayers of our family confessor. Now surely I was seeing proof of our Lord's miraculous power. The rumble of our transport eased as the pilgrims reined in their mules and horses and like me gazed in wonder at the sight.

As I forced my eyes from the marvellous walls of the great fortress which reached into the skies, I saw that Rocamadour was clinging to cliffs which rose sheer above the floor of the valley. The outline of the houses and chapels above us was softened by trees that grew all around the rocky ledges on which the city was built.

We were approaching our destination along the bank of the Alzou. The paths here were well worn and we had taken to our carts, which now moved easily along the track. Despite the steep path we had made good time from Couzou. The wild scrub of the Causse had now given way to forests of birch and oak. The long fingers of the sun filtered pleasantly through the soft young foliage. Our spirits lifted as we now contemplated the end of our journey.

I was riding at the front. The pilgrims were following in an organised line. I say organised. It was as good as I could get it after much chivvying. The nuns' carriage was still at the back but I'd insisted it remain in view. Bon Macip would have approved of my progress as a tour guide.

'You've got us here,' announced Marguerita, who had reluctantly given the reins to me. It wasn't much of an accolade but I took it as a compliment.

'What a place.' It was all I could manage for that moment. I soon pulled myself together. I had fourteen pilgrims, their mules and horses to shelter for the night. It was my responsibility to see them fed and bedded before any thoughts of sightseeing.

I stood up on the cart while Marguerita steadied the tired old mare. 'Fellow travellers, the sacred city is a feast for the eyes but we must move on and find our shelter,' I instructed. With that we moved forward and my weary band of pilgrims dutifully followed suit.

After the arid and craggy Causse of Gramat where we had passed our first sad night, the comforting sight of the houses and the sanctuary clinging to the rocks above gave a sense of hope that filled my whole body. There's many a pious soul, my mother included, who would say that the holiness of the site had overtaken me. For that I cannot judge. It's certain my loneliness eased as I saw the crowds who thronged the paths. The death of the Templar had caused me more grief than I liked to admit and yes, it's true, I was homesick.

Whatever the cause, I felt a thrill of warmth and joy as I saw the sanctuary of Rocamadour that first time. Little did I know that the place would bring me small comfort and that my worries and responsibilities were only just beginning. If I thought that the journey to get here had been hard, I would soon wish that I was back on the stony paths of the Causse.

As our carts trundled over the meadows below Rocamadour, I was amazed to see the arrangements made for the pilgrims. This was truly a great tourist centre. On the sides of the Alzou which was but a stream at this time of the year, was an assortment of tents, monastic outposts and wooden inns equipped to offer accommodation to all purses. Naturally the rich stayed in the city, but I assumed correctly that our lodgings would be out here on the grassy slopes below Rocamadour.

Bon Macip had told me to look out for a hostelry called 'The Little Swallow'. Marguerita took it upon herself to make enquiries as to its whereabouts from some likely-looking pilgrims. After much waving of arms and gesticulations new to me, we located the hostelry. It was situated close to where the Holy Way left Rocamadour and wound its way to the hospital of the Knights of St John on the hill across the valley of the Alzou. In one of his rare moments of conversation, the businessman, whose name I now knew was Guillaume Dellard, had told me of the welcome the knights gave to weary travellers. They offered superior accommodation and medical care thrown in for those who needed it. It was too much to hope that Bon Macip had made a provisional booking there.

A battered sign, hanging precariously from a post, attracted my attention. It depicted a small crudely drawn bird. It was certainly small but that was all the resemblance it bore to the beautiful birds which arrived each year to nest in the stables and cowsheds on my father's estate. A wooden structure, its walls of wattle showing holes where it had been too hastily constructed, stood nearby. There was a rough bit of grass fenced off for the horses and mules. Our carriages would have to take their chances by the side of the track. I might have known this would be the lodgings Bon Macip had in mind. You didn't become a rich man by treating your clients with too much generosity.

I indicated to the line of following carts to halt. A makeshift door hung in the entrance. It swung noisily on its hinges as I pushed my way through an outer porch and peered around. A hole in the wall gave enough light for me to see our accommodation. The inn, for such it claimed to be, consisted of a single room with several cubicles off. It was very basic. I couldn't imagine this hovel had gained many stars with the tourist office run by the monks of Rocamadour.

I didn't know how to put it to my clients. I needn't have worried. In the spirit of accomplished pilgrims they accepted the refuge for this night. I would have to wait for the morrow to hear their complaints. As yet they hadn't the energy to find fault but I suspected correctly that would soon take place.

The proprietor of The Little Swallow, a fat fellow with his belly overflowing towards his knees, approached me. He looked as if he had got rich on the proceeds of pilgrimages. I found that he was expecting us. It was clear the inn was well known to Bon Macip from previous pilgrimages to Rocamadour. The canny old Jew had told me that no firm bookings had been made. This proved to be correct, for the rooms had been secured only on deposit. I had to stump up the difference.

Trust Bon Macip to negotiate something just about habitable. The proprietor made no comment that our party was one member short. We had been allocated three cubicles, one for the men, one for the women and one for the heretic. His money told, even here. He quickly ensconced himself in his private room.

Marguerita blamed me for the accommodation. It was no good defending myself by telling her I hadn't made the arrangements. She had less experience of Bon Macip than I did. She was slightly mollified when she learned that I had secured the rooms for only one night. Although I wondered how we would all fit in, I have to admit it was quite clean. The pilgrim trade was important to the city and there were severe rulings from the monks about unsanitary beds. They inspected the inns on a regular basis. Bedbugs were acceptable but not mattresses soaked in previous guests' urine or vomit.

I asked about food and was relieved to discover that a meal had been laid on for later that day. When I heard the price I shuddered, but when I put it to my clients they all seemed prepared to pay. Within the sacks they carried they obviously had the wherewithal to make their journey comfortable. I was not so fortunate, but was pleased to find that the guide's meal came free of charge if he persuaded his clients to eat in.

I realised later why this rule was in force. As the afternoon progressed the valley became ablaze with fires and the smell of roasting pig filled the air. It was possible to eat to your heart's content at the stalls and tables that were quickly erected along the banks of the river. There was something for every purse: black puddings, carp in aspic, patties of beef marrow, pickled ox tongue, fatted goose liver paste, various small birds on sticks, not to mention heads of artichoke, green beans, wafers of apricot and almond junket and a choice of cheeses such as I had never before seen. I would need a long parchment to record all the dishes I saw that evening. I witnessed some of my clients having a second meal before the day had ended.

Me? I ate quite sparsely having learned in my life that the emptier the belly, the quicker the get away in times of trouble. Despite the ease of our arrival I had not forgotten that the thief had not yet made his move and that the murderer of the knight might well be amongst our company.

As soon as my clients had worked out their sleeping arrangements for that night, I called them together to outline the programme for the visit. I fished in my pocket for the list of activities. Bon Macip had drawn it up. If his choice of lodging was anything to go by, however, I dreaded to think what lay ahead. The main purpose of the pilgrimage, a tour of the sanctuaries in the holy city, was scheduled to take place the next day. Friday was set aside for a visit to the rue de la Mercerie. It was there, that the sportelles, Rocamadour's badge of pilgrimage were manufactured. There would be time to marvel at the work of the smiths and to buy souvenirs which proved my clients had reached their destination. Tonight there was the enjoyment of a travelling play. This had been arranged by the monastic tourist office to entertain the pilgrims during their visit to Rocamadour. Meanwhile, I informed them, they had some free time to recover from the journey and enjoy themselves.

Bon Macip had advised me to get the pilgrims sorted out as soon as possible. 'Left to themselves for too long,' he warned, 'they will wander about, missing all the sights of the tour and blame the company for negligence.' His face took on the pained look he reserved for moments when he pretended his good name was in question. Whatever good name that was. 'For all we know, dear boy,' he said, 'they might even demand a refund.' I didn't think, on that score, my employer had any worries. Penance Way, from what I'd heard, had never been known to part with a single sou in recompense.

That day, nevertheless, I was happy to follow his orders. I needed an afternoon to familiarise myself with the sanctuaries of Rocamadour. I had decided my first task was to find a helpful guide and had earmarked the tourist office for a visit.

It was not difficult to encourage my pilgrims to take the afternoon off for their own enjoyment. On any other day I would have done the same. The meadows we had passed through became a field of colour as they were prepared for the afternoon's entertainment. Tents of blue, gold and red were erected in front of the cottages which lined the Holy Way, the sacred path which led from the meadows below the holy city to the hospital of the Knights of St John on the hill above. We could hear the clash of drums and gongs and the strains of the lutes being tuned for the musical display. Jugglers were already performing miraculous tricks with flames. To keep the crowds happy, actors appeared dressed as demons with horns and forked tails. There were screams of laughter as they ran between the stalls scaring the ladies. Others, got up as village fools with masks of lolling tongues and rolling eyes, danced and tumbled causing great excitement.

The travelling play visiting Rocamadour had already arrived. The wheeled platform was being put in place, and artificers were preparing the stage. Pentecost was approaching, as I knew all too well. Jesus would need to rise into heaven and the pulleys were being assembled. There were howls of mirth as a light breeze caught at the robes of the actor practising the ascent, revealing his bits and pieces underneath. Fire throwers were honing their skills in preparation for the descent of the Holy Spirit and the rush of heavenly fire. Several small children were in danger of going up in flames before the drama had begun.

Further along the valley men with hawks displayed their prowess to an admiring crowd. Along the grassy banks of the Alzou, ball games were taking place. There were screams of delight as a thrower scored a hit on the painted butt. Passing between the crowds were jesters with monkeys and actors dressed as old witches luring the tourists to booths where their fortune could be told. Minstrels made their way amongst the trestles delighting the pilgrims with songs of their own true love. Everywhere, there were countless souvenirs for sale.

I reminded my pilgrims to be vigilant at all times, to guard their pouches well and to return at a reasonable hour to be rested for the next day's programme. I have to say that I was a bit nervous about leaving the nuns to the merriments taking place around us. Marguerita informed me, however, that the sisters were well able to take care of themselves. They would stick together, probably spending the afternoon in prayer. There were many temporary wooden chapels built in the meadows offering refuge for the ladies of the cloth. I had seen a house for the Poor Clares and another for the sisters of the True Cross. My ladies were from the church of the Daurade in Cahors. I hoped they would find a sister house of the Benedictine order to give them shelter. Their habit gave then some protection. It was a very brave scoundrel who would chance the wrath of the vigilant monks, not to mention God as well, by attacking daughters of the church. Nevertheless I particularly warned the two nuns to take great care. They giggled as usual and hid their faces behind their hands. But they thanked me sweetly for my concern and promised to take careful note of what I said. Before he rushed off, the boy travelling with his parents asked eagerly what else was planned for the next day's entertainment. 'That's for the morrow to show,' I told him. I made it sound exciting. There was no point in admitting I had no idea myself.

Before I departed, I had a last look at my clients. I wanted to know what they would do with their spare time. This was the first occasion I had left them to their own devices since we had set off from Cahors. Now was the best time for the thief to approach me. Or the murderer for that matter.

The heretic, his air of despondency even more pronounced, was sitting on a rough board which passed as a seat outside the door of our inn. Perhaps he was pondering on his act of penitence which would take place on the morrow. For all his money, that was something he had to do for himself. I wondered if it would be a first.

Glancing around, I spotted the friar weaving his way amongst the crowds. He had his hands folded in humility and he smiled upon the many poor pilgrims who touched his cloak. I trusted his blessing would bring them some comfort. I could do with some of that myself.

As usual I could see no sign of our silent friend but I saw the married couple, Guy and Jeanne, walking towards the Holy Way. They had left their son, Arnaud, behind to enjoy the entertainment. I observed him jeering and whistling as two men on a greased barrel poked at each other with pointed poles. Two of the students, Hubert and Gaucelin were already seated at a stall enjoying a plate of salted beef. I had fears that they were blueing all their pocket money on the first afternoon. They needed to keep some back for a badge each to prove their arrival in Rocamadour. No point in coming all this way with nothing to show for it. The third student, Bertrand, was not with them.

I looked around for Guillaume Dellard but he was not there. Still, although he had said little enough on the journey, he looked well able to care for himself. I assumed that he was investigating the toilet facilities and decided to leave him to it. He had complained of a pain deep in his entrails. The last thing someone with bellyache needed was a busybody enquiring what he was doing.

Marguerita also was nowhere to be seen. She had said nothing of where she was going. Not for the first time, I dreaded the responsibility of looking after her. Now, however, I had greater worries. I had to check out the sacred city towering above us while keeping my eyes open for an approach from the relic thief.

With that heartening thought, I set out for the city of Rocamadour. I made my way across the river Alzou which, as I have said, barely flowed at this time of the year, and headed for the Porte du Figuier. This was the great gateway surmounted by a tower which guarded the eastern entrance to the holy city.

I was stopped by the guard on duty who roused himself from a lunchtime nap. He had to be seen to do his job. It turned out to be the bare minimum. Doubtless if he had suspected banditry or seen evidence of a brandished weapon, he might have reported me. As it was I answered a few perfunctory questions establishing myself as bona fide pilgrim, and he passed me through into Rocamadour.

I hurried along a narrow street under the cliff towering above. Small houses lined the road clinging to the rock. The clamour of voices and noisy drunken shouts filled the air as well as the smells of lunch being enjoyed inside. Every home here offered board and lodging to pilgrims who could stump up the necessary.

Soon I came to another gate, the porte Salmon which gave entrance to the central part of Rocamadour. Above it was a fortified tower, the dungeon of the city. The guard here barely glanced at me. The movement of pilgrims took place night and day. It was a zealous duty officer who checked everybody. A few prisoners in the cells were enough to impress the abbot, there was no point in creating unnecessary work.

I now found myself in the rue de la Couronnerie. Here were the shops and taverns which catered for the crowds of penitents who sought the great stairway which rose to the sanctuaries in the holy city above, the final destination of the pilgrimage. Up there, the wounded and the sick and the pious asked for the blessing of the Holy Virgin. Here, in this busy street below, thousands of pilgrims ate and slept and bought their souvenirs. I was about to join them. I hoped I was up to the challenge.

The inns and taverns I passed looked very smart, and I resolved on the morrow to make better arrangements for my clients. They had paid for a luxury excursion and an expert tour guide. So far both had been lacking. I couldn't do much about the latter, but I could arrange more salubrious rooms for their second and third nights, rooms which gave the customers their own bed and a curtain for their ablutions. I would make the offer of an upgrade. If they could afford it, which I suspected was the case, they could move up here during the day.

As I've explained, my first stop was to find the tourist office for a bit of up-to-date information. The time had come to impress my clients. I hadn't done much of that. Certainly not with Marguerita. I looked around for a sign board or a helpful mark which would indicate the direction to follow. It was difficult to make out anything which wasn't right under my nose. Rocamadour seemed to consist of one long street punctuated with small squares, and that street was crowded with pilgrims. Everywhere people pushed and shoved, ducking and manoeuvring to find a path through the mass of bodies. Baskets were held high as customers forced their way to the entrance of the many emporia. Stallholders showed off their wares to admiring tourists, adding to the general crush. Ladies in jewelled gowns and ermine cloaks brushed shoulders with the wretched barefoot poor.

I saw one masked maiden riding astride a pure white palfrey stepping her way towards me. I moved aside before the four knights guarding her decided to do it for me. I learned later she was the daughter of the Duke of Burgundy. You could certainly mix with the cream of society in Rocamadour. Other maidens were hurried past, in the charge of black-gowned sisters. Brave young men in their best clothes ogled all the talent. I saw also the injured and the deformed, hobbling on wooden staves or carried on makeshift stretchers. One young man was struggling under the weight of the man he carried on his back whose lifeless legs dangled uselessly below him. Monks patrolled the places under the trees where beggars gathered, moving along these unfortunates. Some they arrested, but most were directed to the bureau which sorted out lodgings for the most needy. Everything was available here. Rocamadour catered for all pilgrims. Or at least that's what I hoped.

As I looked around to get my bearings, a figure caught my attention. Amongst the crowds of tourists, he stood out. His head of red gold hair drew admiring glances. It was Bertrand, the third student in my group. I thought at first he was looking for me but I soon realised that his path lay in a different direction. Intrigued, I decided to follow.

It was difficult to keep him in view. He walked quickly, dodging around those who blocked his way with an energy I had never seen on the journey here. Once I lost him altogether but then I saw him again. This time another had joined him, a dark-haired man of some thirty years. Together they pushed on through the crowds who were thinning now. I had no idea where I was going but I hurried after them. There was some mystery here and I determined to find out what it was.

We passed through the Porte Hugon and continued down the rue de la Couronnerie. From the rough plan of Rocamadour provided by my employer, I guessed we were heading towards the Porte Basse. This fortified gate guarded the western end of the city. As we neared it I saw that its folding doors were bolted and two great beams had been placed across the wooden posts. The guards on duty were occupied with checking a newly arrived party of wealthy looking tourists. They weren't having anyone sneaking in while their backs were turned.

Here the houses were smaller and close together. Narrow alleyways connected the lower part of the city with the small streets above. Some of these rocky passages led upwards to a dizzying height. They were used by the monks to avoid the crowds as they climbed to their priory overlooking the sanctuaries. Up there also were the small isolated cells providing shelter for the many hermits who came to Rocamadour for a life of prayer.

All of this, you understand, was what I learned later in this strange city. For the moment I was taken up with following my student and his new companion. They had now slowed to a steadier pace and were looking to the left and right. I had drawn nearer to them. I nipped behind a wall jutting out to the side of an entrance and watched them closely.

Suddenly the door of a narrow dwelling, with a low tiled roof almost obscuring the window as if emulating the overhanging rocks above, opened and the two men dashed inside. The door closed as quickly as it had opened and the last I heard were bolts being shoved into place. I was locked out as securely as if I had approached the Porte Basse.

No doubt you will believe me when I tell you that a hundred thoughts filled my head. I was just the tour guide. My clients had no obligation to inform me of their reasons for this pilgrimage but in view of the theft of the Sainte Coiffe and the murder of the Templar, each one of them was now a suspect. I had taken Bertrand for an effete student. It was obvious I would have to revise my opinion. It was quite possible he had the holy relic. Perhaps the plan to negotiate with me had been abandoned for a richer prize. It was also possible that he was a murderer, or at least in league with one.

I soon gave up my first idea of hanging around to see what would happen. For all I knew Bertrand would be there all afternoon. If I knocked at the closed door what would I say? Bertrand would not admit anything which implicated himself. His new companion looked well able to take of himself. Bertrand too, for that matter. I was up for a challenge but where would it get me? This undercover commission was proving pretty hard indeed.

In the end I trudged back to the centre of the city. I saw a spare table at a pavement café and I sat down. I needed time to think clearly. I was about to order a flagon of ale when I heard a familiar voice. Approaching me across the square was Marguerita.

'Come on,' she ordered. 'Why are you sitting there? This way,' she went on. 'I must show you something.' I had long since given up answering any particular question she may have had. I waited for the general idea. I soon gathered she had had the same plan as me. An upgrade to a more salubrious inn.

I followed Marguerita who had set off towards a line of upmarket hotels. We entered a grand-looking hostelry within sight of the Porte Salmon. It was constructed out of the yellow stone of the region. The windows had glass, beautifully edged with lead. The fine open door had a huge knocker fashioned in the shape of an eagle. The owner was nowhere to be found but a maid was vigorously shaking the mattresses for the comfort of the evening's guests. Here in the land of geese, everyone expected to have a feather bed. Linen sheets, woven from the flax of the region, hung over the rails of the terrace. Wealthy tourists certainly got the best.

The young maid disappeared into the back and soon emerged with a red-faced woman. She was prepared to negotiate a price for two nights' stay. The rooms were only available at this reduced rate, she was quick to explain, because the rush of the real pilgrim season had not yet started. I couldn't imagine what that would be like if this was low season. Even so the price was high, and I'd added a bit more when, later I put it to my clients. This was to enable me to have a room. I'd already booked the places in this comfortable inn when I explained it to them. I was confident they would accept the inconvenience of moving given the chance of such comfort and the fact of staying inside the city itself.

There were one or two grumbles at the cost but they dug into their pouches and eventually agreed that they could afford the rooms. I had reserved a room for the nuns and the woman with the withered arm. They seemed to have struck up a friendship. The couple with the son had their own room. The students had a room with the Franciscan monk. That left the businessman, the heretic, the chap who rode the black horse, Marguerita and myself. The heretic enquired about a single room. One was found for him at an extortionate supplement. He didn't bat an eyelid and paid up without a murmur.

Marguerita shared with me. Now I know what you are thinking. It doesn't sound very suitable for a maiden. The problem was she was taken for a youth and my assistant at that.

'Are you sure you're up to this arrangement?' she asked in her haughty manner when I put it to her. And then added quickly, in case I had thoughts above my station, 'I shall be taking the feather mattress and you may sleep on the boards.' As it turned out I was to spend no time in the room.

The other two men were a problem. I had put them in together although I was not sure that was a good idea. Still they needed a bed for the night. At least that was what I thought.

So it was that six rooms were reserved for the following two nights The owner's wife noted the fact on a slate and I paid the usual deposit. In truth Marguerita paid. I was fiddling in my pouch to check I could raise the sum required when Marguerita held out her purse. There was sufficient there to close the deal.

When the business was concluded, I made to descend again to the valley. I had given up on Bertrand for the time being. I wanted to get back to the other pilgrims to find out exactly what they were doing. I had left them to their own devices. That was a mistake. I was getting used to that. Making mistakes that is.

Marguerita did not fall in beside me and I looked back to see what she was doing. I had resolved to keep her in my sight. I had done nothing as yet to find the Sainte Coiffe. I could not go back to Cahors with that mission unaccomplished and my benefactor's daughter's honour compromised into the bargain.

Marguerita was looking along the street towards the square where the stairs rose to the sanctuaries. Despite the hour there were still many pilgrims about. Some were making their way up the great stairway. I was told there were two hundred and sixteen steps and I verified that painfully for myself the next day. The pilgrims climbed on their knees stopping on each one to say their rosary. Some crawled up almost prostrate. Others I noticed had chains around their necks. The stairs sloped at a good angle so this was indeed a formidable penance.

There was fresh blood on some of the steps and dark stains from previous penances. Loud groans and wails and laments filled the air as this was taking place. I saw a monk emerge from one of the sanctuaries above and strike a particularly noisy pilgrim with this staff to quieten him. The monks held regular services in the sanctuaries and they weren't having their prayers disturbed by the whingeing of the faithful.

I went back to Marguerita who was still peering about. Having second thoughts?' I asked. In the next instance I regretted my facetious tone. Her face half-turned towards me, and to my concern, I detected tears in her eyes. It was the first time I had seen this feisty lady so affected and I was moved to place my hand around her shoulder. She took no notice but continued to look into the distance. A tear trickled down her cheek.

'Tell me,' I said as gently as I could, 'what troubles you?' With that she turned towards me and clung on to my arm. I was taken aback at this demonstration of familiarity and rightly assumed that her worries had made her forget her attire and the fact that we scarcely knew each other.

'Where is he?' she asked.

Naturally I asked to whom she referred. It might sound a bit pedantic but I was getting out of my depth.

'Ridolfo,' she replied. 'He said he would be here.'

I didn't like the sound of this at all.

Before I could ask her anything else she let go of my arm and darted in front of a strange man who was gazing into the door of a souvenir shop. He turned as she approached him and I saw the look of disappointment on her face as she stepped back into the shadow of the doorway. I went quickly to her and took her hand. I didn't care a straw about our lack of acquaintanceship. This was a young girl in turmoil and it was up to me to take care of her.

I led her to a pavement café near to the great stairway. It was getting quite late but they were still serving sweetmeats. I ordered a plate of quince pies and begged her to tell me what troubled her so much.

What she told me horrified me but explained her desire to come on this perilous journey. The Sainte Coiffe was far from her mind. I was not sure that she even knew of its disappearance or cared. I wondered what reason she had given her father for her desire to join this pilgrimage. Mercifully he was unaware it was to rendezvous with this Ridolfo.

'We met in Cahors,' she told me. 'He came with his uncle. He's a merchant from Lombardy and had business with my father.' I groaned inwardly when I heard her next words. Not for myself you understand but on behalf of all infatuated young men. 'He said he loved me,' she sobbed. 'We agreed to meet here in Rocamadour.' The tears flowed more freely as she told me of the plan. She would make the journey under the guise of a pilgrimage. This would arouse little comment. No one, least of all her father, would know of their liaison. On his part, Ridolfo would suggest to his uncle that he go to Limoges for the summer. Some of the best silver was fashioned there. The profit his uncle made in Cahors could be turned into luxury items and sold for further profit in his native Lombardy. Marguerita confessed that she had sent a servant to inform Ridolfo of our visit to Rocamadour. He was to leave Limoges and get there as soon as he could.

I offered Marguerita my kerchief. It was the least I could do. Maiden's tears are always a difficult proposition. The final part of the plan, which I learned through the folds of material as she wiped her eyes and nose, was for him to stay each evening by the great stairway. That way, whoever got their first would wait for the other.

'Well then,' I said in my most avuncular way. 'You obviously have arrived here first and there is no need to worry.' I'd got that wrong as well.

'But there is,' protested Marguerita, tears now flowing freely again down her face. I wondered what the other customers would make of this 'youth' who cried so easily. But no notice was taken. With the wails and shouts of the ascending pilgrims a few more tears aroused no comment. Marguerita explained that the servant had returned telling her that Ridolfo would leave immediately and would be waiting impatiently for her arrival.

'Well,' I said trying again, 'anything could have held him up. I shouldn't worry yet.'

'But he is here,' she countered. This was all getting too much for me. I asked her quite sharply how she could know that. Through her sobs Marguerita confessed that the inn where I had booked the rooms was not entered by chance. She had guided me there for that was where Ridolfo was staying. While I negotiated the price, she had asked the maid servant if a young Italian had made an appearance.

Apparently he had, although it turned out that the maid had not seen him for the past two days. I began to appreciate Marguerita's concern, but I hoped it did not show on my face. I gave up my idea of checking on my other clients. This one presented enough difficulties. Anxious to relieve her mind I said we could make further enquiries together. With that Marguerita fell on my neck and kissed my cheek. What visitors to the holy city thought of two youths kissing I hope I shall never know.

So it was I located the monks' tourist office. As with all major well organised pilgrim centres (which I was to discover later in my journeys), there was a bureau where you could gather all sorts of information. We found it near the porte Hugon. Naturally, the brother on duty was expecting the usual questions: the time of the services in the sanctuary churches, the places with rooms available in the height of the season and the cost of the souvenirs for sale. He was a good enough fellow, however, and accepted my question about missing persons with an equable look on his face.

'It's not easy,' he opined. 'There isn't the usual crush here yet, but there are enough pilgrims to make your task difficult.' Still he said, 'Leave it with me. A young handsome (as Marguerita had declared) Italian tourist should show up somewhere. I'll make some enquiries.'

With that, for the moment, Marguerita had to be content. I vowed to return the next day with my own questions. The ones that any good tourist guide should ask. Meanwhile I persuaded Marguerita to return to the valley. I wanted to check on the party before dusk fell. I promised her we would find her Ridolfo in the morning. What I was going to say to him, I did not inform her.

CHAPTER 7

When we got back to the Little Swallow I found most of the party eating the last of the meal provided in the bed and board. Marguerita had lost her appetite and ate nothing. She put it down to her worries about Ridolfo. I wondered if it was more to do with the quince tarts she had scoffed not an hour before. As I've told you I was keeping a lean belly, but I accepted the offer of some spiced lentils. They tasted surprisingly good. I remembered I had eaten nothing since our meagre breakfast that morning.

Some of the party declared themselves well stuffed. Considering the food stalls they had visited, it was to be expected. Still I had fulfilled Bon Macip's first rule of tourism, to keep the clients happy. The old Jew had many first rules but this one did the trick that evening. The festivities on the meadow were drawing to a close. The gaily coloured tents were being taken down until the morrow. I wondered at the effort of erecting and dismantling these each day but I learned that this was a rule laid down by the tourist office. The innkeepers in Rocamadour would have little trade if these tents remained up all night. The man who told me this was a burly fellow with a bare chest and bulging muscles. I had little doubt he could have deterred the most determined squatter but then, as he said, rules are rules, the abbot's rules. The lord of Rocamadour certainly kept the place in order. I was beginning to appreciate the problems of catering for the thousands of pilgrims who made their way here each year.

Some of my pilgrims announced that they were ready for their bed. The night was still young but all that had happened had worn them out. Huguette led the two sisters to their small cubicle while the heretic retired to his single room. Two of the students, Hubert and Gaucelin, looked the worse for merrymaking and staggered to their mattresses clutching each other around the shoulder and mouthing silly rhymes. Freed from the confines of the classroom and from parental control they were making the most of this holiday. I enquired after Bertrand. Even if they knew his whereabouts they were not saying. All I got were blank stares or guffaws of laughter. I stood well back. The ale and wine they had consumed was enough to convince me I would learn nothing from them.

The boy was mooching around kicking some stones. He had been sick behind the back wall of our lodging house. Doubtless without his mother's watchful eye he had overindulged on the salted beef pasties. I said nothing. I'd been there myself. I did question him, however, about his parents. Apparently they had gone into the city. Although we were making the formal tours of the sanctuaries the next day, they wanted a quiet moment to themselves to revisit the places where they had first pledged their love. Their son informed me of this with some embarrassment. The idea of true love was far from his mind. I could have wished the same applied to Marguerita. I accepted what the boy told me. I saw no point in informing him I had seen his parents making their way to the path leading to the hospital of the Knights of St John on the hill above. The opposite direction from the sanctuary where they claimed their romance had begun. I advised him to lie down on his bed and await his parents' return. I pointed out a gap in the wall of their room in case any more beef pasty decided to make a hasty exit.

Guillaume Dellard was still missing. I had seen nothing of him since we arrived. The silent man on the black horse was nowhere to be seen either but that didn't surprise me. I had come across him earlier, in the long grass which bordered the Alzou, tending to his horse. He had nodded and waved his hand but as usual he had said nothing.

That left just Marguerita and the Franciscan. I haven't included myself. I had my own plans. I wanted time to wander on the paths alongside the fields below Rocamadour. With the cover of night I hoped the thief would approach me. There were many of my party unaccounted for, Guy and Jeanne, Guillaume Dellard, Bertrand, our silent companion. Surely it was the time for whoever had the sacred relic to make a move.

A brazier had been lit outside our inn. We sat around it. At first Marguerita attempted some conversation. Obviously primed in small talk by her father, she was able to speak of many things to the Franciscan. I joined in. This was my first chance, since the few words I had passed with him on the journey, to get to know the friar better. For one who had been quite open before, he was now rather reticent. Asked about his former life he said nothing beyond what he had confided to me. It seemed he was concentrating on his present calling. I persevered but to no avail. Marguerita nudged me to cease my questioning. I gave her what I hoped was a severe glance, but took the meaning of her elbow.

After that we all fell silent. What thoughts passed through the mind of the Franciscan I cannot say, but Marguerita and I had much to ponder. The glowing embers of the fire faded away as the evening grew in upon us. The lights in the city were flickering in the deepening dusk. The chants of compline hung on the air. It was very peaceful and I must confess quite holy. Despite the old Jew's cynicism, I understood what brought pilgrims to Rocamadour, and what it must mean to those who had a favour to ask of the Blessed Virgin.

The stallholders packed up for the night and the flaps of the tents went down. I stood up. 'Well I am away to my bed,' I said. 'We have a busy day in the morning.' Marguerita showed no sign of coming with me, rather she looked somewhat disconcerted. Dressing as a youth may have worked well when she toured on business with her father. Here it was not so easy. She solved the problem by declaring the bedroom too small for all the men and promptly settled herself against the wall of the kitchen near the dying fire. As the men's cubicle only had the sick boy in it at that time, it was difficult to follow her argument. Still there was no one to hear her explanation, save the friar and he declared himself in need of some silent prayer. The last I saw of him he was making his way to the temporary shelters in the valley set up by the mendicant orders.

I saw Marguerita back into the lodging. I explained I was going to do a final check on the whereabouts of my other clients and left her sitting by the kitchen hearth. The innkeeper had long since gone, probably to one of the stylish houses that lined the main street of Rocamdour. Once outside again, I doubled back to the path that bordered the Alzou. This was now the first chance to walk on my own. I thought of the dagger I had concealed in my boot. Would I need it? Could I use it? As I've told you, I'm just a country boy. Negotiating the return of the Sainte Coiffe was enough to contemplate. I had no desire for any strong arm stuff, let alone stabbing. I hoped the relic thief would approach me soon. If indeed he was a member of my group. On that score I was beginning to have my doubts.

I followed the path beside the river. As I have said it was but a trickle at this time. In summer it often disappeared altogether. The tents on either side were full of sleepers, judging by the snores emanating from them.

The strangeness of it all struck me once again. Was this really me in this famous place with a group of people I didn't really know? I thought of my dear adopted father and wondered what he was doing at this hour. The thought gave me courage and determination, and I quickened my pace telling myself I was able to tackle anything fate should throw at me.

It was a good job I had made that resolve, for with a turn of the path I came upon a sleeping figure. There were always pilgrims who slept in the open. I had learned this from the proprietor of our inn. Whether he meant it as a threat to encourage my party to accept his below-standard accommodation, I cannot say, but it had done the trick. Every one of my pilgrims had paid for a bed for that night.

One, however, was not yet making use of his. I recognised the rider of the black horse. The animal was grazing near by, its tail slowly moving over its back to disturb the night midges that swarmed by the water's edge.

I approached the man to bid him goodnight and remind him he had a bed inside if it pleased him to go to it. I must confess that until now I had spoken few words to him. It was soon apparent that I would not have the chance. Not in this life, that is. The wretched man looked as if he were in a deep sleep, but when I peered more closely I saw the pool of blood oozing into the ground beneath his head. Horror once again caught hold of me. I knelt down beside him. He was recently dead for his flesh was still warm. It made me shudder more than the cold flesh of the Templar.

He lay among some sharp rocks and his head was close to a jagged corner that protruded from a boulder ready to trip up the unwary. I told myself that was what had happened. I didn't wish the poor wretch dead but if it had to happen, an unfortunate accident was to be preferred to the other thoughts racing through my brain.

An empty flagon lay by his side. He had enjoyed the dark red wine of this region and then missed his footing while under its influence. The other alternative did not bear thinking about. To have two fatalities within as many days was difficult to explain. I tried to tell myself a pilgrimage was one of the most hazardous experiences of life. What with the robbers and villains on the routes, the wild animals in the forests, the dubious wine and food, the contact with all sorts of maladies. It was far safer to stay in one's impious home than make the holy journey to find peace with God. Pilgrims were not concerned with this life, however, but the next. My mother had often warned me that I should concern myself more with the comfort of my soul but I had put aside asking God's forgiveness until I had a better catalogue of misdeeds to confess. Losing two clients surely now came sorely high on the list.

I looked around. There was no one about. I saw, however, that the man's bag had been tossed to one side. I picked it up carefully. It had been turned inside out. Nothing remained. My thoughts raced. Robbery was the obvious motive. Had this poor man been killed for the sake of some money or the Sainte Coiffe? If it were the latter what was the point? The plan was to return it after I had made the negotiations. Unless the thieves had fallen out and one of the gang had different ideas. I tried to dismiss that thought. The relic's return had been agreed. At a price. Or so I thought.

I decided to return to the lodgings and say nothing about my discovery. I left the man's pouch by his side and retraced my steps. I entered the inn quietly. Marguerita was still by the hearth but now she was asleep, her head resting on a cushion she had found from somewhere. I had to pass what was left of the night. I could not sleep. Guilt overcame me and I sat with my back to one of the worm-eaten wooden posts that formed the walls of this makeshift building. When dawn streaked the sky I was still awake, wondering what the new day would bring. The Sainte Coiffe did not seem so important. I would do my best to get it back but now my chief concern should be to keep the rest of my party alive. It wasn't the usual job of a tour guide but then I wasn't the usual man for this post.

I had not long to wait to see what the morning brought. The monks who patrolled the encampments, checking on the pilgrims, soon discovered the dead body. Luckily they assumed what I hoped they would, that the poor fellow had missed his footing in the dark, fallen over the rock and bashed his head in. I learned later that they also thought he had bled to death which did nothing to make me feel any better. Still I comforted myself with the thought that by the time I found him there was nothing I could do to save him.

I was amazed by how casually the monks seemed to take the man's death. But it was obvious with the thousands of tourists who thronged the sanctuaries every day, there were bound to be accidents and fatalities. There were also many births which took place at Rocamadour. The hospital of the Knights of St John offered a complete range of medical care.

I made quiet enquiries as to where bodies were buried at this place and learned that the knights had their own cemetery. This housed not only monks who had quitted this life for a better place, but also patients who had not responded to their ministrations. Occasionally, as now, a burial place would be found for a pilgrim who encountered death while on a visit to the holy city. A pilgrim who had the occasion to meet his maker while in one of the sanctuaries was buried in the crypt of St Amadour. Those who went to meet God in the valley below were usually taken to the hospital cemetery of the knights.

I left it to the monks of Rocamadour to oversee the funeral of my client, promising myself that I would visit his grave later. That morning I had other urgent business. Well, at least Marguerita did. She reminded me as soon as she rose that we were finding out the whereabouts of Ridolfo. Luckily most of the party did not know yet about the death of another member. The man had so distanced himself from the rest of us that most of the pilgrims hardly noticed that he was missing.

The Franciscan did, however, and asked after the man. In his case, being a holy man, I divulged the happenings of the previous night. The Franciscan took the news with an equanimity I would have expected. He lowered his head in respect. 'I shall pray for his soul,' he said. 'Today in the sanctuary I shall ask the holy mother to look kindly on him and intercede on his behalf with the good Lord.' I thanked him warmly. I hadn't had the wit to think of doing the same.

Marguerita was up early. Doubtless she was eager to get back into the holy city to continue her enquiries. First I had my pilgrims to organise. This was their big day. The visit to the sanctuaries would take place later that morning. Huguette rose early too. I found her outside the inn taking the morning air. She was waiting for the two sisters. They had been up before dawn. Where they had been they didn't say but their cheeks shone with a bright glow. With most ladies I would say a good man was the cause, but I'm hoping it was the good Lord who had more to do with their air of happiness.

The heretic remained in his room. He had become something of a recluse. I determined to get to the bottom of this later. I didn't want an unsatisfied customer on my hands. The two students slept on. For now I left them. There would be two sore heads when they woke. The married couple had returned. Jeanne was awake when I peeked in the women's room. Her husband and son lay asleep next door. I decided that they also should account for their disappearance yesterday. Guillaume and Bertrand were still missing. So too I realised was the Franciscan. Keeping my party together was proving to be as much of a nightmare as finding the Sainte Coiffe.

Marguerita was now pressing me to leave. Finding Ridolfo was foremost in her mind. It was best to get that out of the way. The sooner I could show her the libertine that he was, the better for this maiden. I put Huguette in charge. I can't think why. Possibly she reminded me of another redoubtable lady, my mother. I asked her to get the pilgrims together and remind them to be at the great stairway by noon. She told me to leave it to her and I was pretty sure I could.

Marguerita and I set off. She hurried me along and we were soon heading for the information office. We both hoped that the brother there would have something to tell us. We had to wait for his bureau to open, for dawn had only just cleared away the night clouds when we arrived.

He had some news, we discovered, when he turned up, but it was not very comforting. Ridolfo had been in Rocamadour but no one had seen him for two days. He had not returned to the lodgings he had booked. We were informed that the landlord was quite miffed for he could have rented the room twice over. Marguerita offered to settle up but I stopped her. We were not certain that this was the truth. I had learned enough of the citizens of Rocamadour to know that, however holy the sanctuaries might be, this did not extend to all the innkeepers and stallholders.

It was apparent now that I had a multitude of tasks ahead of me in the next few days. Besides guiding my clients safely to the blessed Madonna in her sanctuary and making sure they lived long enough to get there, I now had to locate the missing Ridolfo, not to mention negotiating the return of the Sainte Coiffe.

In a moment of madness, I wondered what would be the reaction of Bon Macip if I returned with none of these accomplished. That was easy to answer. I wouldn't return. Then I thought of Marguerita. Of course I must go back if only to restore her to her family. She had been entrusted to my special care, and however brave she might be she was still vulnerable to the darts of love.

I had a private theory, as I've told you, that Ridolfo had grown tired of waiting or had found himself another lady. There were rich pickings here and any merchant lad who could woo a lady in Cahors could do the same somewhere else. It was in the nature of his trade to be constantly on the move. However attractive Marguerita might be, I couldn't believe he'd not met other beauties along the routes he travelled.

However, I breathed nothing of this to Marguerita. She was anxious enough and close to tears for much of the day. She believed wholeheartedly in Ridolfo's love for her and his faithfulness for their tryst. We arrived at our new lodgings. While I checked out the inns in the main street, Marguerita found the maid we had seen the evening before. I left them deep in conversation. Marguerita was interrogating her about what she knew of Ridolfo. It turned out to be very little.

I drew a blank with my investigations. Marguerita had obviously done the same. She looked round expectantly when I returned. My heart sank. I had been looking forward to some time on my own, but I could see that she had other plans.

'You're back,' she said rather unnecessarily.

'It would seem so,' I replied. I bowed with my arm across my chest in the true manner of chivalry. 'And how may I serve you my lady?' I shouldn't have teased her. It was not the moment for light-hearted conversation.

'I want you to search every lodging house in the town,' she snapped at me. 'Apparently there was an altercation with the proprietor and Ridolfo left in a huff. The maid does not know where he went but she saw him around the town after he left.' Then her voice softened. 'He must be somewhere,' she added hopefully.

Me? I didn't feel so sanguine but them I'm a fellow. I'm afraid to say I have broken a heart or two. Or so I have been told. For the truth of that, I cannot be sure.

I felt sorry enough, however, for Marguerita. I agreed to fall in with her plan. There was some time to spare before the visit. Some of my clients had not taken long to follow us into the city. I saw them sitting in the shade of awnings in a square bordering the main street. The temptations of the sweetmeat stalls, however, were calling them. I reckoned I should have an hour or two before I was needed.

'Where shall we start?' I asked Marguerita, and she looked at me for perhaps the first time with a kind light in her deep brown eyes.

'I have made a plan of almost all the best hostelries,' she informed me. I should have guessed that she would have done her research well. She was a very organised and practical young lady. I could see why her father trusted her on his business trips. Following in the footsteps of her illustrious grandmother, she might well take over the reins of the family firm in due course.

'We shall start here in the city itself,' she went on. 'I don't think that Ridolfo would have stayed down there.' She cast her arm around to indicate the tented village that had arisen on the banks of the Alzou river. Our inn of the previous night was one of the few permanent structures in the valley. I agreed with Marguerita. It seemed unlikely that a smart boy like Ridolfo would have taken lodgings there. He was obviously out to impress and that would be far easier in the comfortable establishments that lined the Grand'rue of Rocamadour.

Under Marguerita's direction we started the search straight away. Much good it did us. Ridolfo was nowhere to be found. At noon we admitted defeat. At least I did. Marguerita was disappointed naturally but remained in good heart. 'We shall find him,' she said positively, but the words rang a bit hollow in my ears. I felt that he had left this lady in the lurch and I did not relish the moment when the truth would dawn on her.

For the time being, I left Marguerita to rest for an hour or two and I went to find my clients. I must say they were proving a well behaved lot. I had arranged to meet them at the foot of the great stairway and I was gratified to discover that most had listened to my orders and were waiting there for me when I arrived. In fact they were all there except for the Franciscan friar, Guillaume Dellard and the married couple. I was told that the friar had gone on ahead. I suspected that he was fulfilling his vow to make a special plea for the soul of our departed friend. Guillaume's whereabouts were a mystery to all. Myself included. Guy and Jeanne's absence worried me. Their son was waiting with the students. I don't know who looked more fed up with the arrangement, them or him.

Arnaud was showing off, jumping up and down on the first four stone slabs of the stairway. I had only just arrived in time before some monk arrested him for defiling the sacred steps.

'A word please,' I said, with as much authority as I could muster. It wasn't much. The nuns kept their eyes down, but I detected a slight smile on their lips.

Arnaud eventually twigged I was addressing him. He slouched over, clicking his fingers.

I softened my tone. It couldn't be much fun. I wasn't sure which was worse. Going on a pilgrimage with your parents or going with them and finding them never there. Not that I could voice a definitive opinion, seeing I would have avoided any outing with my mother. Not that she had ever offered.

'Are your parents coming soon?' I asked.

A sort of expression passed over Arnaud's face. I understood it. I'd used the same look myself when questioned by my mother over my own whereabouts. It meant, either he didn't know or he didn't much care.

Huguette helped out. 'They've gone ahead,' she called out. 'They want to visit the place of their first meeting on their own.' I could appreciate Arnaud's reluctance. He'd had to give the same embarrassing explanation once before. He wasn't doing it again. Not that I believed the reply. I'd heard it once before, too, and then it hadn't been true.

I looked hard at the red-haired student who was now waiting with his two companions. He dropped his gaze but when I asked how he had enjoyed yesterday's festivities he answered boldly enough. 'I missed them,' he replied. 'I had an errand here in the city.'

'We must stick together,' I admonished. 'The company cannot be responsible for your safety if I do not know where you are.' I tried to sound stern. In view of the non-appearance of Guillaume Dellard, it was a pretty poor attempt. Also I couldn't imagine Bon Macip caring what happened to his clients if they got lost or even murdered. As long as they had no opportunity to sue. My attempt to elicit where he had been also fell on fallow ground.

'Sorry, it won't happen again,' was all he said.

I had no time then to interrogate him further, as my pilgrims were becoming restless. The visit to the sanctuaries was all they had in mind. Most of them had already eaten, for the attractions of the food stalls were hard to resist. I myself had found the time to buy some thick slices of goose which I ate on a fatted trencher. The stall holder had scooped the grease of the goose on to my bread, and I must say I have rarely tasted anything so delicious. I washed this down with a strong red wine. Afterwards I treated myself to some gingerbread which I ate as I hurried to the meeting place.

The hour of midday was a good time to ascend the stairway. The heat kept all but the most serious tourists away. I encouraged my party with the claim that it added to the value of their penance. The sun fell directly upon us as we struggled to the top. I say 'we' for I felt duty bound to accompany my clients in their efforts.

It was a great struggle for Huguette, but she was not going to let anything stop her. 'Tour guide,' she called. I looked around for a split second until I remembered that was my job. 'Give me your arm.' She grabbed hold of me with her good but ancient hand and we went up together. I dragged her up if the truth is known. We did not go on our knees but we might as well have done, the number of times we stumbled together and missed our footing. Several times we collided with other pilgrims struggling to climb the steps.

I apologised as best I could even though it was not always my fault. Even so, the incidents drew forth words which I am sure were not suitable to that blessed place. Insults were flung around as the tempers of the pilgrims became more frayed. It was a relief when we reached the top and the shade of a great fig tree which dominated the square.

We were the last to arrive. The old girl had said her rosary so many times while we climbed it seemed to have taken forever to get there. I noticed as we stood under the welcome leaves of the tree that the other members of the party had already passed us and moved on.

As we emerged from the first part of the stairway we found ourselves in the place des Senhals. There were several stalls here selling the badges which vouched for the fact a pilgrimage to Rocamadour had been completed. It was no good going to all this trouble if you had nothing to show for it. I had noticed other brooches and tokens sewn to the hats of my pilgrims. Each one depicted a successful pilgrimage, a tour accomplished. Some pilgrims here, I noticed, had so many they filled their hat and most of their cape. I saw penitents with the shell of St James of Compostela, and one or two with the badge depicting the keys of St Peter in Rome.

The sportelle of Rocamadour was pretty impressive. It was shaped as an almond with six small rings around the edge. These I soon saw were used to tie the badge to a prominent place on the customer's hat. The badge itself displayed the blessed Madonna seated on her throne. I saw she had her infant Jesus on her left knee. In her right hand she had a sceptre, its end fashioned like the flowers of the lily. In case there was any doubt both the Virgin and her child were encased in a halo with the words Sigillum Beate Marie de Rocamadour. The stalls were doing a roaring business. There was a fine selection of lead, pewter and copper badges to suit every purse. The crush of tourists grew as guides brought their parties into the square from the rue de la Mercerie. They had been to see the sportelles being made by the smiths who had their workshops there. It was all part of the grand tour and produced many a backhander for the best operators. I couldn't include myself in that company. Not yet.

As the crowds in the square grew, I lost sight of my pilgrims. Huguette left me to find the other members of our party. She had regained her breath and wanted to find her friends, the nuns. I'm glad to say she'd had enough of my helping arm. My clients were now well into their visit. Luckily no one had yet asked me for any information. I decided to leave them well alone for the moment.

I climbed the remaining steps and found myself in the parvis of the sanctuaries. Here the tourists were forming an orderly queue which wound its way back from the entrance to the Madonna's shrine. Any pilgrim who wailed too loudly was admonished by the monks on duty. Many of those emerging from their worship of the holy lady staggered in a daze of reverence overcome by the Virgin's forgiveness. They were helped down into the square by lay brothers who draped them over the railings to recover.

I looked around the square. It was time now to get my bearings. I'd managed to avoid my clients for the moment but I couldn't make that last for too long. To the left of where I stood was the chapel of St Michael. Outside the door of this sanctuary, the cliff face was adorned with frescoes. It was but a short distance past these to the entrance which stood raised above the other sanctuaries. This was where the queue was entering the chapel of Our Lady where the miraculous Virgin sheltered.

On its other side, St Michael's sanctuary was connected to the monks' priory. This in turn led to the palace of the abbot, which rose above me. Across the square was the great church of St Sauveur. A tower stood by its side with the two small chapels dedicated to St Anne, the mother of Mary, and St Blaise. Underneath the church was the crypt of St Amadour for whom this place had been named.

This information I gleaned from a helpful monk who kept the queue moving. He saw my badge indicating I was a tour guide and filled me in on the details. Doubtless he hoped for a tip. This was not permitted by the abbot but then, as the monk said, with a quick glance over his shoulder, he wasn't looking.

I didn't oblige but thanked him and descended the steps into the crypt of St Amadour. Before I joined the queue and met the Madonna, I might as well become acquainted with the saint who had started all this.

I gazed around in wonder at this simple sanctuary which clung to its place on the edge of the cliff hanging over the town below. I had already seen the four enormous buttresses which held it there; now I saw rough-hewn walls around me and above a great transverse rib at least seven-feet thick with huge diagonal arches supported by columns set in the walls. A gentle light bathed the sanctuary. There was no strong sun here, just peace and calm.

Behind the altar were further rooms. For the moment I was alone, save for the monk on duty. He woke himself from a reverie of stupor when I approached. I gave him a quick nod and prepared to pass the time of day. His boredom level was surely low that day for once awake he launched into his set talk.

The rooms, he told me, had long served as a prison but were now stocked with provisions for needy pilgrims. I replied that had I known that before I might have put in a request. My humour was lost on the monk. His expression told me he had heard this poor joke too many times. He contented himself with saying that only true beggars who made the journey were served from this special store.

I could see slabs in the floor of the crypt. These were where the devout had been buried. The sacred remains of St Amadour were here, having been removed from the rocky grave where he had first been interred. My guide was now becoming pretty garrulous. Having once found a tourist prepared to listen he wasn't going to let up in a hurry. Indeed I was listening. Very carefully. I was going to impress my clients with my knowledge of the saint who gave his name to the city of Amadour set on a Rock.

His remains, my guide informed me, had been found intact in the rock face at the entrance to the oratory many years before. The saint's bones were then re-interred close to the altar and soon afterwards many miracles began to happen. Rocamadour became a place of holy pilgrimage.

Lunchtime was a slow period for visitors. My guide had obviously recognised an ignorant tourist. He spread beyond the usual details of his standard talk. St Amadour, I learned, was a servant of the Virgin Mary. He had journeyed far in the world arriving finally in the fair land of France.

I felt I had had sufficient instruction for the day and looked hopefully towards the door. My guide, however, had not finished. St Amadour, he told me, had settled in a hermitage in the rocks at this place. At that time it was the refuge of wild animals. The inhabitants, I was further reliably informed, had never heard the word of the Lord. St Amadour taught them of the love of God and built an altar to the Virgin. It was, the monk told me in hushed tones, the most sacred part of this most revered place.

It was all pretty impressive. Some of it may have been true. Such was my ignorance of Holy Scripture that much of it was news to me. I cannot vouch, therefore, for the truth of the story. I must confess I have since heard many tales like this in my travels, especially at great tourist centres.

On that day, however, I felt the holiness of this sacred place and the genuine reverence in which it was held. I allowed myself a moment's quiet reflection. If this brother also had hopes of a tip, he, too, was unlucky. Some other pilgrims entered the chapel. While he was repeating his story to them, I took the opportunity to leave and moved on to the shrine of St Sauveur above.

I emerged alone into the square. I stopped for a moment's reflection of all I had just heard. Suddenly a figure appeared from nowhere and in his hurry he barged against me. Now you may realise already how clumsy my feet are, always getting me into trouble. I dodged sideways, tripped over my own foot and went down on one knee. I think it was this which saved my life. For as the man went by, his arm struck out and I could see the gleam of the knife directed at my neck. I was now below the villain and the rush of the knife cleaved the air but did no damage to me. I rose with the thought of defending myself, but the attacker kicked me hard in the stomach and was gone as quickly as he came. I bent double trying to get back my breath, for the encounter had sorely winded me.

When I was able to stand upright again, Guillaume Dellard was there. He stood in the shadow of the crypt but I could make him out. He said nothing to me nor did he enquire how I was. He just stood and looked at me. I moved towards him. He had some explaining to do. Where had he been and what was he doing here. Before I could advance more than a pace, he turned on his heel and disappeared. I was left wondering if he knew who was behind the attack.

Two of my party were dead. Was I meant to be the third? It was a sobering thought but what could I prove? There were notices everywhere reminding pilgrims to be on their guard against thieves, pickpockets and assassins. The whole business shocked me but, with all the warnings around, I had reason to think this could be an occurrence which often took place. With all these unsuspecting tourists there were really rich pickings here. I rested for a while to recover my breath. I had been very lucky. According to the warnings put out by the monks, some pilgrims were robbed as they knelt in homage to the Virgin. Most, like my attacker, got away. The miscreants who roamed the streets and stairways of Rocamadour were much too clever to be caught.

My clients were now nowhere to be seen so I entered the upper church of St Sauveur. It was also a wondrous place. It lay under the rock face of the city. The church had two equal naves and these were divided into bays by two huge columns. Poor pilgrims, I was told, could spend the night here. The janitors went in early to clear the church of any mess and to send the nightly residents on their way. I looked around for spiritual comfort but found none. The holiness of the site had evaporated for me, at least for the time being.

Leaving St Sauveur I spent a moment looking around the square. Above me was a high cliff face. A small oratory with a roof and an altar showed where St Amadour's simple sarcophagus had been carved into the surface of the rock. There was also a rough-shaped iron sword driven into the rock. This was the sword Durandal, the weapon of Roland who had fought the Saracens. It was the one piece of useful information Marguerita had given me.

At last I turned towards the shrine of the Madonna. Unlike my clients I had hesitated to enter this most holy place. The Holy Virgin was there. Only I knew that there were thieves who dared to consider stealing her. As you have realised I am not the most pious person, but at that moment I feared to approach her in case she found me wanting.

At last I plucked up the courage and went towards the entrance to the Virgin's shrine. Outside the rocks were covered in pictures which were part of an enormous fresco. I had never seen the like. The dazzling blues and reds and gold told of the angel announcing his message to the Virgin Mary and her visit to the blessed Elizabeth to tell her what had happened.

Inside, however, I was immediately plunged into candlelit darkness. The warmth of the place from the bodies of the faithful and the flames of the candles enveloped me. For a moment I could not breathe, but whether that was from the smoke or from a reverence that took hold of me I cannot be sure. I could see the rough stone walls in the flickering light and the many votive offerings fixed to them. I could hear the prayers and cries of the pilgrims. I could feel the weight of suffering and the urgency of hope. I have never been as moved as I was that moment. I could scarcely raise my eyes to the shrine where the Virgin sat.

Her seat was a marvellous sight, covered in silver which gleamed in the half-light of the chapel. She glowed as well from jewels which shone around her neck, but it was not those that held my gaze. I looked at her and saw a beautiful, noble face so calm and strong. It seemed that she was smiling at me. She had her son with her. The little man was seated on her knee and I could not tell who was more proud, the child Jesus of his saintly mother or the Virgin of her holy son.

I did not stay long. There were monks to urge us along. Other pilgrims were pushing through the entrance. Those who lingered, held immobile by the inspiration of the Madonna, were led out to continue their prayers in the light of the square. Me? I had other worries to think about. The safety of my clients, the Sainte Coiffe, two deaths. I soon fixed my thoughts on these concerns, but the images I saw that day in that holy place stayed in my heart for a long time.

My pilgrims had already moved on. They were looking at the sanctuary of St Anne dedicated to the mother of the Virgin and the chapel of St Blaise. This saint protected travellers in dangerous situations. I said a silent prayer to him as I passed through his sanctuary. I had need of his assistance now.

This chapel, I saw, had once been part of the defence system of Rocamadour. Now, with the great gates below, the monks had dedicated it as another place for prayer. The rewards of the pilgrim trade were more beneficial to the city than a lookout post. They did not say that of course. It is what I surmised. But taking into account the souvenir stalls and the number of inns, not to mention the monks who acted as tour guides, I think I have told you the truth.

I could not dawdle, however, for my party was moving on again. It surprised me that having come all this way the pilgrims should walk by so quickly, scarcely glancing at the marvels inside, before excitedly looking at something new. But this was the early days of my knowledge of tourists. Later I was to learn that they were always the same, apart from a few who really appreciated what they saw on their travels. Still this lot had another day here. I assumed correctly that some would come back for a further look, having been unable to take it all in on one visit. I climbed upwards to find them. I did not want to leave them alone in this dangerous place.

My clients had approached the chapel of St Michael. I caught up with them there. Luckily, they were occupied, listening to a brother who was pointing to the sanctuary situated on high, near the top of a bell tower almost buried in the rocky face of the cliffs of Rocamadour. These great walls of rock were all around and above us. One was covered in a huge fresco like the one I had seen on the walls above the Virgin's shrine. I was tempted to enter but I had other concerns. I bade my clients farewell for the time being. I warned them to take great care before reminding them to assemble by the tourist office when they had finished their visits for the day.

CHAPTER 8

I nipped back to our new lodgings. Marguerita was not there. I found the red-faced woman in her little cubicle by the door. She had seen Marguerita leave not a few minutes since. She had not said where she was going, but according to our hostess she had a determined look. As that summed up Marguerita's normal expression it didn't give me much idea of her plans. I guessed she was either renewing the search for Ridolfo or she was making her way to the sanctuaries. It wouldn't do to return home with no knowledge of the sacred Madonna she had been so keen to visit.

I checked with the innkeeper's wife that all my party had taken up their rooms. I asked to inspect them, and with some reluctance she directed me to some rooms upstairs. They were obviously the cheaper end of the market, for they had no view and overhung the street below with all its noise. Still they were a vast improvement on our beds of the previous night. I found the room taken by the three students. A quick search brought no result. If I had thought Bertrand would leave any incriminating evidence of his strange visit the previous day I was mistaken. The room was bare of any possessions. These clients at least had heeded my warnings and kept their pouches and the contents safely with them.

When I got back to the centre of Rocamadour, I found most of my clients waiting for me. They had assembled by the door of the tourist bureau as I had instructed them earlier. Obviously some had been there for some time for there were groans of relief when I put in an appearance. I said nothing. Cultivate an air of authority, never apologise and never explain. I recalled another of Bon Macip's first rules. It was easier said than done. Of course he hadn't expected death to overtake two of his clients. Penance Way didn't have a regulation for that eventuality. I would leave it the old Jew to apologise to their relatives if that was the correct procedure in the circumstances.

It was now early afternoon. The usual festivities were being set up in the valley below. Each day brought a new set of pilgrims and a new clientele for the stallholders. I wanted some more time to myself. I had found out where Bertrand had gone when he left the group although I was none the wiser what mischief might lurk behind his disappearance. Now I needed to know the reason for Guy and Jeanne's departure, perhaps with them I would have more luck. Guillaumme Dellard had not been around since we arrived. I had to discover why he had witnessed my attack and said nothing. Marguierita was still absent. I was beginning to worry about her. It wasn't the time to be occupied with my duties as guide whatever the tour programme had laid down.

I informed the pilgrims that the visit to the workshops making the sportelles had been brought forward. When they had eaten lunch they should make their way to the rue de la Mercerie, where another guide would take them through all the processes. After that they were free to look around the souvenir shops or join in the fun in the valley before returning to the inn for the evening. I hadn't arranged another guide, as you can well imagine, but I reckoned that the fabricators of the Rocamadour badge would be well versed in a running commentary, especially if it produced a good tip at the end. Most tour guides pocketed the tip but foregoing that pleasure was the least of my worries.

My party nodded in agreement with the new plan. Like me they were finding the tourist services offered by the monks more than helpful in locating places of interest. Doubtless Bon Macip knew this already. Once again I marvelled at the charges for this trip. Not that I had any complaints. It all added to the money I needed to raise my father's ransom.

I watched my group mooch off to find suitable taverns for their lunch. Bertrand was still with his fellow students. Guy and Jeanne had made an appearance. I saw them with Arnaud. They led their son to a hot food stall. A large crowd had gathered around it. A strong smell of seasoned savouries filled the air around. They had no trouble settling him there. I saw them pay the stallholder's assistant. They then said something I couldn't hear and left Arnaud to enjoy his food. Remembering him from the previous afternoon I hoped he wouldn't overdo it.

The married couple then made off in the direction of the sacred city. According to Huguette they had already made an early visit to the sanctuaries. So early no one had seen them there. With the crowds thronging the many chapels and portals, however, it was possible we had missed each other.

Why go back now? Either they had missed some chapel the first time or they had other business there. I decided to follow. I know. I was making a habit of this but I'd come to the conclusion that spying involved a lot of footwork. I was certainly getting in training for my services to King Edward.

It was a simple job to keep my sights on Guy and Jeanne, for they never looked back. Soon I was climbing the great stairway again. I tried to imagine what they were doing. If they had the Sainte Coiffe, why had they not approached me? They'd had many opportunities. They had had no trouble avoiding their son, if it were he who had made contact difficult. I asked myself if Guy was a murderer? He certainly looked a fellow able to take care of himself but that didn't make him a killer. And if he were intent on murder, why would he keep his wife at his side? Was she in fact his wife? Was Arnaud their son? Were they perhaps a family who had made relic theft a speciality? A hundred thoughts raced through my head. It was difficult to imagine the three of them a band of villains, but Bon Macip had warned me that the relic was in the hands of experienced robbers. I remembered also his last comment about the fate of the Madonna. I hastened my steps behind them as we reached the first of the sanctuaries.

To my surprise the couple did not stop there but hurried on, passing the entrances to the chapels, until they reached a small opening between the rocks. I had noticed it earlier but then it held no significance. Now I saw it was the entrance to a stony path. Steps cut into the cliff led upwards. Guy and Jeanne went up these hardly breaking their step. Me? I followed but more slowly. Looking back I saw the height we had reached. It was enough to make any fellow feel somewhat dizzy.

At the top, the stony stairway came to a flat rocky plateau. The trees here were small, and scrub mainly covered the ground. It reminded me of the Causse. I didn't like to recall what had taken place there. Guy and Jeanne now stopped and looked around. I hid behind a tree. Not that they were aware of me. Their attention was caught by a hole cut into the cliff. They walked towards it slowly. As they approached, they called gently, 'Brother Martin.'

They waited beside the entrance to the cave for several minutes. Then slowly, very slowly, an aged man appeared. He was so old that his back was bent almost double. His white beard reached almost to the ground. He stood there saying nothing, not looking at Guy or Jeanne. They went towards him speaking in low voices. The hermit held out his thin hands. The veins stood on them like knotted rope. The two pilgrims knelt before him and he reached for their heads to bless them. I realised that he was blind.

Jeanne raised her head and whispered something to the old man. He nodded his head in agreement. With that she broke down sobbing on her husband's shoulder. I crept away. Whatever this meant I doubted that it had anything to do with a stolen relic or a murdered man.

I returned to the main street of Rocamadour. I had eliminated three pilgrims from my suspicions. The relic was still missing, as well as Ridolfo. Time was running out. As I passed a pavement café I saw Marguerita sitting at one of the tables. She was tucking into a plate of saffron tarts. Her melancholy at losing Ridolfo had not affected her appetite.

I was pleased to see her. It was one worry off my mind. I have to report that she showed equal pleasure in my appearance. Not for my own charms I must confess. They've worked well in the past but Marguerita had only one young man on her mind. She begged me to start the search again. As I couldn't quickly think of a reason why not, I agreed. I have to say I was beginning to wonder myself where he had got to.

And so we set off again, Marguerita and I. We went everywhere searching every square and alleyway. We looked behind and in front of all the stalls. We inspected the faces of all who passed us. I had no idea what Ridolfo looked like but Marguerita told me to watch out for a very beautiful Italian man with long black hair and the sweetest smile. He would be dressed in the latest fashion, she also informed me. Now why didn't that surprise me.

I have to report that we didn't find him. Evening approached and once again we returned to the inn with no progress made. Some of my clients had taken to their rooms. Others, I was informed by the innkeeper's wife, had returned to the valley for some evening entertainment. The travelling play was still there. There was no telling what excitement would take place. A pulley might break, the holy spirit might fall off the stage in his efforts to bring the word of God to the disciples, the tongues of fire might get out of control, anything could happen. It would be a shame to miss a real disaster.

Marguerita declared herself worn out. She would go to our room. She didn't want her tears to be seen by all and sundry. I saw Marguerita into the lodgings. I did not climb the stairs with her. I simply told her I was making a final check of our clients. Then I exhorted her to bar the door of our room.

'How will you get in?' she asked.

I told her that I had seen a space in the tiles of the roof. It would be easy on my return to remove a few and make my entrance. I did not inform her that my business that night might not allow me to come back before day break. She accepted my lie without question, which was an indication of her preoccupation with Ridolfo.

I had not told Marguerita what I now planned to do, for I did not want her to know my next move. I had decided to visit the hospital of the Knights of St John and find out where they had buried our companion, the poor soul who had lost his life the previous day.

I sloped off towards the Gate of the Fig. As I went, I saw the Franciscan monk making his way along the other side of the street. His arms were folded and he seemed deep in thought. I did not hail him, and he turned into an alleyway and disappeared into the gloom.

I thought also I caught another glimpse of our surly businessman, Guillaume Dellard, but I could not be sure. What business he had in Rocamadour was for me to find out. It didn't seem to involve the Sainte Coiffe.

From the Porte Figuier I descended into the river meadows that bordered the Alzou. This time I didn't cross the stream but directed my steps to the Holy Way, which rose up to the hospital of the Knights of St John. It overlooked the Alzou valley. I skirted the field where the entertainment was taking place. I could hear the howls of merriment and hoped that my clients were having a good time. My mission didn't offer the same possibilities of enjoyment.

I walked as quickly as I could. You might think it was rather late to pay a visit but the hospital was open night and day. The knights took it in turns to offer hospitality, succour and medical care around the hours of the clock. Pilgrims arrived at Rocamadour at all times, and however late it was they were certain of a welcome.

At the end of the Holy Way, I arrived at a fortified gate which gave entrance to the square in front of the hospital. I passed through with little trouble. I fancied I had the look of a needy pilgrim. The hospital of the Knights of St John was an impressive affair. The door of the guest house was shut, but a bell stood beside the huge walnut edifice. A board below it offered refuge to the weary traveller. That was me. I rang it as gently as I could for I had no wish to disturb the sleeping sick. I should not have worried. The screams and pleadings and admonitions coming from the wards were enough to deafen anybody.

A lay brother answered the call of the bell, and I was taken with little ceremony to the room of the knight on duty. He was surprisingly young. Surprising, that is, to me, because my last contact with a knight had been the Templar. This man had still the air of youth and had obviously risen up the ranks through his own prowess.

The knight rose from the seat beside a great window that gave upon the rocks outside. From there he had a view of the holy city. What a position that was. A man could spend a lifetime never tiring of this wonderful sight. Perhaps that was what he planned to do. Spend a lifetime here in the care of the sick and needy. Surely God would reward him for his endeavours.

I told him simply of my concern. That I knew almost nothing of the deceased, but that he had been put in my care. I said I would like to see his grave. I could then inform any who enquired in Cahors that he had received a good burial in a sacred place. I hoped that would give some comfort to his family.

The knight replied that he understood my concerns but there were no facilities for visits to the cemetery. The place was private and revered. If he allowed one visitor to march amongst the tombs he would have to open the place to all and sundry. With the volume of visitors in Rocamadour that would prove impossible. He was sorry but there could be no further discussion on the matter.

I pleaded my case, putting forward every argument I could think of. I have a reputation for slick conversation. It's got me out of many a tight corner back home. My fair words have been known to move the heart of the most implacable. Not this time.

The knight listened politely and renewed his apologies but repeated that there was no exception to the rule. I took my leave. I was going to get nowhere here. I was shown out with courtesy but little ceremony. I thought little of it. The knights had their work to do. Valuable work. Greater than anything I could contribute.

The great door closed behind me and I made to walk back down the path I had just climbed. But something made me turn. I saw a monk dressed in the habit of the Benedictines cross the path behind me and head in the direction of a path behind a row of trees. I don't know quite what made me follow but follow him I did. I slipped in and out of the shadows behind the monk and I am sure he had no idea that I was there. I soon realised that he was heading for the chapel. Beyond that, was the burial ground of the hospital.

As we approached the cemetery where countless knights and pilgrims had found eternal rest, I realised that there was activity taking place. A torch burned and there was the noise of spades ringing against the hard earth and rocks. Three or four lay brothers were digging a grave. I hid myself behind a tree to take in what was happening. The monk I had followed approached the group of diggers and spoke quietly to them. I was unable to make out what he said. But I could see the tallest one nod his head. Then a body in a winding sheet was carried from beneath a tent which had been erected there. The shroud covered the whole head and body, but as the corpse was placed on the ground beside the hole that was about to receive him, one of the diggers removed the sheet that covered his head, and the monk made the sign of the cross on his forehead.

The moon was up that evening, and with the light of the burning torch I could see clearly what was taking place. I could also see clearly the face of the dead young man. For such it was. A young man with black hair and a sweet face. Marguerita had described Ridolfo well.

I was shocked and saddened by this discovery. What in God's holy name had happened here? Who had killed the young man? How was I going to break the devastating news to a heartbroken maiden? I thought of disclosing my hiding place and challenging the group burying Ridolfo, but I soon thought better of that. I did not want the same fate to befall myself. I had every other man's instinct for survival, and the added responsibility to my mother of securing the release of my adopted father.

I slipped away from that grim place and made my way down the hill. I thought I might be too late to re-enter the city. The entertainers had packed up and the tent flaps were down. I had no worries, at least, on that score. Late revellers were making their way back into Rocamadour. I kept out of sight. I had no wish to meet one of my pilgrims.

There was a night guard on duty at the Gate of the Fig. I showed him the pass I had received on our arrival. He accepted that and let me in. I did not return to the inn, however. I had seen something terrible that evening. I needed time to reflect before I saw Marguerita.

I decided to seek refuge and comfort in one of the sanctuaries. There was always a welcome there for late arrivals. According to the helpful monk I had met earlier that morning, there was a snack of bread to be had and a pile of straw for weary bones. I would shelter there while I thought about the third dead man I had seen in as many days.

I climbed the stairway again that day, but this time I ran up as quickly as I could. I don't know what the pious would have thought of my haste but luckily there were none to see me. I sought the sanctuary of St Michael's chapel. I had marvelled at it earlier that day set high at the top of a great bell tower standing like a watch post over Rocamadour. Like all the buildings of the holy city, the sanctuary seemed to cling to the rockface, its high perch fashioned from the overhanging cliff which formed its wall and vaulted roof. I passed through an entrance gate and found a small stairway also cut into the rock. There was an opening in the north wall through which the entrance to the sanctuary of Our Lady could be seen.

The whole chapel of St Michael was filled with colour. A huge fresco at the entrance shone in the glow of the candles inside. A beautiful mosaic covered the dome of the apse. The figure of Our Lord shone forth surrounded by a huge halo. His hand was raised in benediction for all who made the ascent to worship him in this glorious place. Four evangelists were with him, seated at desks, as well as a seraph and the archangel Michael for whom this chapel was named. St Michael was holding a scale for it was his task to weigh the souls of the dead and negotiate with the devil for the souls in purgatory. I hoped that Ridolfo's soul would do well in this heavenly business, and that he would soon find a place with God.

I sat inside the sanctuary for some time. The hours of night passed and I think I dozed some of them away. But suddenly I awoke with a start for I heard voices and the sound of footsteps. I shrank into the shadows so I was not seen, for I had no certain knowledge that this sacred chapel was a permitted refuge for a night's sleep. My helpful monk had told me hospitality was extended in most sanctuaries to the most needy pilgrims. Scruffy as I appeared, I wasn't sure if I fell into that category.

I had not planned to listen to the conversation of those entering the chapel. I'm no eavesdropper, particularly where the gossip of monks is concerned. For that was who these new arrivals must be. Monks doing the rounds to check that everything would be suitable for the next day's pilgrims. The abbot took this tourist business very seriously. The younger monks cleaned and swept while others organised the visits to make sure all went smoothly. Some brothers were overzealous and moved people on before they had time to pray, I had observed a young woman being shepherded quite roughly out of the sanctuary of the Virgin because the monks felt she had overstayed her time there. Her family were arguing. It seemed the poor soul had not heard the call to move forward. She was afflicted with deafness and was praying to the Madonna to restore her hearing.

Anyway, as I have said, I did not plan to eavesdrop. Not at first that is. Then I saw that only one of the two people entering the chapel was a monk and no ordinary brother at that. From his robes, I recognised an abbot. The abbot of Tulle, as he turned out to be. The other, to my consternation, was the businessman, Guillaume Dellard. I knew little of the man but I already suspected that there was much about him I should like to know. I leaned forward in my hidden corner to listen carefully to what they had to say. The conversation was clear to hear but nevertheless I was undecided what it meant.

The first words I heard came from the abbot. Surprisingly, he had a deferential tone in his voice and much warmth. 'I am eager to hear your thoughts on this matter, my friend,' he said.

'It is very early to say,' responded Guillaume, for that is what I shall call him, although I now know that was not his real name.

'But you must have some idea,' the abbot persisted.

'I would say that that there is a good possibility,' Guillaume replied.

'That will suffice for now,' said the abbot. 'Come, my friend, a nightcap is called for I think.' With that they descended to the level beneath the chapel. I decided to follow. The little I had heard had left me mystified. But that was no surprise. I was getting used to mysteries. Time was running out and I had to make some progress.

The two men walked ahead of me deep in conversation. We passed along a narrow passage. I stopped and hid as they entered the calefactory. This doubtless connected to the abbot's palace where I presumed Guillaume would be entertained. If I could discover what lay behind this puzzling friendship, I would tackle the businessman the next day.

The thought had barely entered my head when I discovered I was going to learn more about Guillaume much sooner than I expected. Two huge arms enfolded me. I struggled to turn my head but two other hands gripped me around the neck. They pressed so hard I could barely breathe. My legs were still free. I kicked upwards with my right foot but the assailants had predicted my next move. Moving quickly out of the reach of my foot, the first man kneed me hard. I stumbled and lost my footing. With that I was lifted bodily from the floor and deposited roughly on the ground. My assailants were two burly lay brothers. Once again I took my hat off to the organisation of the church.

I realised by now that killing me was not the object of this attack. With my arms pinned behind me, I was dragged to my feet and marched, stumbling and cursing, to a small room which acted as my prison. I have no idea how long I was there but long enough to reflect on the further ignominy of my efforts as a tour guide. I had lost two pilgrims, failed to discover Ridolfo alive and now got myself imprisoned for an offence which was not yet clear to me.

The room was not lit and, as there was no window, I had no hope of discovering where, in this complex of small rooms clinging to a cliff face, I had been taken. I was to find that out in the next few minutes. A guard arrived to escort me. I was taken without ceremony along a passage under a series of great arches to a terrace which ran along the side of the cliff. We then entered through a gateway into a vaulted hall. The two guards knocked discreetly on a fine oak door. When the signal to enter was given, they pulled open a smaller entrance set in its frame and thrust me inside. We had reached the study of the abbot, spiritual and temporal ruler of Rocamadour.

I can do respectful as well as anybody and this seemed a good moment to put my skills to the test. With my hands still bound, I bent one knee and gave what I hoped was a deferential nod of the head. It did the trick for the abbot indicated to the guard to release me, and then to my surprise drew forward a stool and invited me to sit. I had hopes that my misdemeanour would not prove too grave.

I took the seat offered slowly for it gave me time to look around the room. It was far grander than the study of Father Richard in our abbey at Torre. This was a place of comfort. Tapestries woven in carmine, indigo and gold hung down the stone walls to the long wooden settles underneath, which were covered with thick woollen spreads. A fine bureau ran along the outer wall, its intricate carving lit by three great beeswax candles held fast on silver spikes. In the soft glow I could make out the ropes of grease that dripped on to circular dishes of beaten pewter.

The room was warm. At the far end, a fire burnt well, the massive log on the grate held wide on andirons carved in the shape of eagles. The smoke from the flames disappeared from sight through the stone wall which overhung the hearth. Comfort of this sort I had only ever seen once before and that was in the great chamber of Lord Gilbert de Clare. These monks of Rocamadour knew how to look after themselves. At least, the high-ups did.

This was a room to welcome the most important visitors. It had been well prepared for the abbot of Tulle, Lord of Rocamadour, who was on one of his rare visits. I had discovered this from my helpful monk in the sanctuary of St Amadour. I'd gathered from his words that however boring guide duty might be it was better than the cleaning fatigues reserved for the newest recruits.

The brothers in question had done a good job. There weren't many blackened cobwebs and the silver plates were well wiped. The floor had been swept and sprinkled with trails of sweet woodruff and petals of lavender and balm. An urn with two madonna lilies stood by the side of a massive oak chair. From what I had discovered that night, it came as little surprise to see Guillaume Dellard seated there.

The abbot, for I had presumed correctly it was he, stood an imposing figure in his robes of scarlet silk lined with ermine. No black mantle for him. He had a cloth of gold around his thick neck almost to his mouth, whether in readiness for Pentecost or to keep himself free from the acrid breath of those he blessed, I couldn't say. A fine leather belt studded with red and green stones was hanging beneath his ample waist, its long prayer rope of stitched fleur-de-lys reaching almost to the floor.

I waited. I wasn't sure, as a tour guide, what rule I had broken. I decided Guillaume Dellard must have lodged some sort of complaint. He obviously had a good deal of clout to have the ear of the abbot.

With that, Guillaume Dellard, for such I still took him to be, stood up and approached me. I stood up too. I was ready to defend myself and the whole tourist guide fraternity. I may not know what crime I had committed, but I was prepared to present a good case. The widowed businessman suddenly appeared taller and had acquired a distinct air of authority. I saw that he was now wearing insignia, a badge with a strange device I didn't recognise.

The abbot wasted no time. Extending his hand in a gesture of acquired deference, he said, 'This is Signor Tommaso Cavelli, captain at arms in the service of his Holiness Boniface VIII.'

You may like me now to relate what I said in reply, but in truth it was nothing. I was new to the diplomatic world you understand. No clever answer, no sensible question, not even a word of politeness broke the silence which followed. I was finding it impossible to collect my thoughts. It was difficult to think of the sad depressed figure I had brought to Rocamadour as an officer of the Pope. It was even more worrying to imagine what papal regulation I had breached.

Guillaume, or Tommaso, as I must now call him, didn't wait for any more formalities. He already had the measure of me from the days we had spent together on the road here. He dismissed my concern regarding any offence I may have caused his holiness, the Pope. He had something much more worrying to put to me.

He returned to the great oak chair he had recently left. He spoke slowly, choosing his words carefully, as if taking me for some sort of dunce. He was right there. Only a fool could have fallen into the trap prepared for me. When he finished, the great log had burned to dying embers and the first golden streaks of dawn were piercing the leaded panes of the high window.

The thought entered my head that he suspected me of complicity in the disappearance of the Sainte Coiffe. If I had thought he would start by warning me of the penalties for relic theft I was mistaken. Instead, to my surprise, he reminded me of a sad day many years before.

'You were young,' he said, 'but you may recall the day when reports reached Christendom of the fall of Acre.' He was right. I had passed then but thirteen summers by my mother's reckoning but I remembered well. The news had fallen very hard on the ears of my father. Though his age and increased girth had diminished his skills in battle, Lord John had always been a fine warrior. In the days when King Henry ruled our land, he had taken up arms and followed Edward on a crusade to the Holy Land. All who served him knew the story he told of how he had left his estates the companion of a prince and returned the subject of a king.

I cursed myself now that I had not listened more carefully to the tales of that city which often followed a banquet for visiting guests. As the wine flowed, so had my father's reminiscences. The crusaders, I knew, had landed at the huge fortified port at Acre. Now I had only a vague recollection of talk of lemon and peach orchards and gardens of asparagus and artichokes fed by irrigation ditches, and of banquets where the crusaders were served with crane and quail and sides of ibex and wild boar. There had been tales of fabulous towers, magnificent churches and underground passages, which my father claimed defied description. Like most good hosts he had not allowed that to curtail his anecdotes.

I had been in the meadow assisting with the lambing when the messenger arrived. It was the meanest employment. I preferred hunting with the hawks but my father had ruled that I must learn to manage his estates by working first on our demesne lands. My mother warned, on my return at dusk, that father was distressed. The loss of Acre struck at the heart of every crusader, and none more so than Lord John.

I sought him out in the solarium.

'The great glory days of King Richard are over,' he said, tears glistening in his eyes. 'I fear the Holy Land is lost. The knights of the Temple and St John for once fought side by side but they were driven back.'

'The Arab forces were too strong?' I commiserated. I was an uneducated boy, you understand, unversed in holy war.

'Arab forces too strong!' Lord John repeated with some vigour, shocked at my ignorance. He thought for a moment and then said, 'No, it's the squabbling Christians, I blame. Warfare is always ruined by politics.'

I had no more time to recall that day for Tommaso was speaking again.

'I see by your face you know of our great stronghold at Acre,' he said, 'and its fall to the forces of al-Ashraf.' I hadn't heard of the Arab leader's name but, of that, I made no comment. No point in confirming him in his opinion of me.

'I know the news of its loss caused my father much heartache,' I replied. I hoped my reply was non-committal.

'When the city fell,' Tommaso continued, 'there was time for some to seek the harbour and the safety of the galleys waiting offshore. Not all were successful,' he went on, 'and many died that dreadful day.' I hope I looked suitably sorry. For all I knew he had lost a dear friend. It was difficult to tell where all this was leading.

The abbot noticed my attention was wandering. On that count he was correct. The night was passing. Soon it would be a new day. I wanted to get this over. My thoughts were turning to how I would break the news to Marguerita of Ridolfo's death.

Also, although I readily admit my shortcomings as a tour leader, I did feel a sort of duty to my pilgrims. I hadn't had many scruples about charging them well for the trip, but I wanted to give them some value for money. This was their final day at Rocamadour. It was the last opportunity to enjoy the festivities before preparing for the journey back to Cahors.

'Some did escape from Acre,' the abbot interrupted. I changed my look to one of relief. 'Despite the danger,' he went on, 'one of our brothers left the doomed city and made his way to Greece.' For a wild moment I thought he was referring to his family. Then I remembered he was a man of the church.

Tommaso again took up the account. 'This brother,' he said, 'carried with him a sacred text from the great library at Acre. He rested for some months in Greece and then continued his journey west. We believe that he was making his way here, to Rocamadour.

Impressive as the city was, I wondered what made the monk choose Rocamadour. What's more, why had he taken so long? It was many years since the news of Acre's defeat had reached my father.

As if he had read my thoughts, Tommaso came to the real point. 'The monk's life was in danger from the moment he left the shores of Outremer,' he said. 'al-Ashraf was determined to recover the manuscript and his spies were everywhere. The monk remained hidden for much of the time and only travelled west when he believed the path was safe. He could never rest for always there were rumours spreading of his journey.'

The pope's army officer failed to mention how he had come to learn all this. His network of spies was obviously as good as that of the leader of the Arab forces.

'Sometimes we heard talk of him,' Tommaso continued, 'then for many months we would hear nothing. Finally messages came to us from Fréjus. The monk had reached the shores of France and was making for Le Puy. From there we believed he would follow the Via Podiensis, the pilgrims' road to Cahors and make the final part of his journey to Rocamadour. That was the last we heard.'

I still had no idea why I was hearing this story. The words pilgrim, Cahors and Rocamadour, however, hung in the air. No one moved. I began to suspect they were waiting for me to speak. Naturally I obliged.

'Why are you telling me this?' I asked. No one answered. One of the fat candles on the abbot's desk sank on to the pewter plate and flickered in the melted tallow. 'What's it got to do with me,' I added for good measure.

Finally Tommaso answered. 'The manuscript is missing,' he informed me. 'We need you to find it.'

I laughed. I did. I couldn't control myself. The two men waited for my howls of mirth to subside.

'So the Sainte Coiffe isn't enough,' I said as soon as I could speak. 'Now I have to find a missing manuscript as well.'

A strange smile passed between Tommaso and the abbot. They both looked at me. I realised an explanation was needed. 'It's why I'm here.' I said. 'I have a commission to secure the sacred relic of the cathedral at Cahors and return it before the day of Pentecost.'

I shouldn't have divulged my enterprise, I know. Bon Macip had warned me never to give out any information. Now I dreaded to think of the consequences if rumour reached Cahors that the sacred relic would not be there for its ceremonial outing. The citizens were turbulent at the best of times. Disappointed pilgrims were known to riot. I had heard tell of priests being jeered and chased with bows and arrows, and worse, churches being set on fire. Damage and looting often followed. I regretted my words as they left my lips.

It was Tommaso who spoke. He made nothing of my confession save to ask, 'Penance Way, this tour organisation, what do you know of it?'

'Nothing much,' I replied. 'I've only worked there for a week.' Given the accuracy of my answer, it was fortunate that Tommaso was no longer a bona fide tourist.

'The pilgrims you are escorting,' he continued, 'what do you know of them?'

I looked around the study. Not for a means of escape. Much as I wanted to free myself from this situation I suspected that the two hefty monks who had conducted me here were still on duty outside the door. Rather I needed time to think. This was turning into some sort of interrogation and it was already looking as if I would come off the worst. I realised also a bit late in the day that I knew almost nothing about my clients. I had been so preoccupied, first with guiding them and later with my worries about safeguarding them, there had been no time to get to know them, let alone understand them. Save, of course, for Marguerita. I'd made a little headway there. Or so I hoped.

I thought of Reginald. When he found himself in a spot of bother he always gained my mother's support with the excuse that attack is the best form of defence. Although in Reginald's case there was a lot of attack and not much need for defence.

'Why do you ask?' I challenged Tommaso. 'You were one of them. 'Why do you not know the answer to your own question?' I thought of the two clients no longer in my group. 'Why did you not assist when the knight of the Temple died or the pilgrim who rode the black horse?'

'It was very difficult,' replied Tommaso, 'but I could not reveal myself. Untimely death must be investigated by the local authorities. My duty is to protect the safety of Christendom.'

'And now it seems to be mine as well,' I replied. 'This manuscript, the one you have lost, how am I supposed to find it?'

Needless to say, Tommaso had the answer. 'We lost track of the monk,' he said, 'after he left Le Puy heading for Cahors. At first we believed he would make for Rocamadour in disguise, but later reports suggested that someone else carried the manuscript. Either the monk was too ill to travel or he feared that his disguise had been penetrated. We looked for a pilgrim group heading for Rocamadour. A lone traveller would be too vulnerable. Penance Way was the only company with an organised tour.'

Despite myself I was becoming interested. 'What did you discover?' I asked. I wanted to learn some tips. I needed help if I was to make any headway in this business of gathering information.

'Nothing,' he replied. 'I doubt very much that the monk is one of your party. As for the manuscript, I have found no trace of it.'

I thought that a bit rich. He was an army captain, paid to keep the pope's peace. If he couldn't find this missing manuscript, what hope did I have? I said as much. Then I stood up. I was tired of this questioning. Despite the heavies on the door I intended to leave with as much dignity as I could muster. 'This manuscript,' I said, 'it has nothing to do with me. I've told you my concern is to retrieve a stolen relic and return it to its rightful place.' If the truth were known its rightful place was probably somewhere in Outremer, but Cahors would do me for now.

With that Tommaso also stood and confronted me.

'And have you retrieved it?' he asked. 'The Sainte Coiffe, I mean?'

I had no answer and I gave none.

His question, however, lay between us. It made me think as he had intended it would. I hadn't found the Sainte Coiffe. No thief had approached me. I was as far from finding the sacred relic as the day I left Cahors.

I was more than a fool, I told myself. I answered his question with my own. 'So you think Bon Macip set me up?'

'In truth,' Tommaso replied, 'it was not Bon Macip.'

I'd had enough of this conundrum. He knew something and I wanted the truth. I went towards him. I don't know what I intended, but in my haste I managed to knock over the urn of flowers and crush underfoot the great white petals of the lilies. The water spread over the floor soaking into a richly embroidered rug.

I stepped closer, ignoring the bishop who put out a hand to restrain me, and pushed my face close to this agent of the pope. 'Who, then?' I demanded.

'It was the king.' Tommaso spoke deliberately, 'King Edward I of England.'

I pulled myself back and stood up straight. His words had stunned me as he knew they would. Finally I found my voice. 'King Edward!' I sniggered, but I knew by his expression I had heard aright.

'How do you know?' I demanded. 'What has my liege lord to do with this?' I might be taken for a simpleton, but I would hear no false words spoken of the king.

Tommaso did not answer my question. Instead he said, 'This manuscript is a great prize. All the rulers of Christendom seek it. Your King Edward is no different. He covets this for his halidom. What is more, he believes it is rightfully his for the monk fleeing from Acre is an Englishman. At least,' he added, 'he has an English name. The maiden who bore him named him after his father. He was probably a craftsman who accompanied the crusaders and stayed to work in Palestine.'

My thoughts turned to the girl. She had found herself in the same situation as my mother. The monk and I, at least, had something in common. These thoughts made me long for my home at Torre.

'I'm just a country lad,' I said. 'Why am I involved in this?'

The abbot interrupted at this point. I think his patience was wearing as thin as mine. 'To answer that,' he announced, 'I suggest we introduce the young man to Maimonides.'

CHAPTER 9

Before I could gather my wits and ask who this Maimonides was, the abbot had summoned the two heavies. We left the room in a procession. The abbot led the way, engaging Tommaso in close conversation. I followed a poor third placed between two strong arms. We passed through many passages. They were obviously built against the rock, for in places they narrowed so that the three of us could barely pass. For all that, they were well decorated and hung with fine woven tapestries. The magnificence of the abbot's quarters extended far beyond his study. Finally we came to a stone stairway. We climbed this to leave behind the finery of the abbot's palace and entered the priory of the monks of Rocamadour.

This time, you will gather, I was able to make out where I was going. The priory itself was pretty impressive. Like the sanctuaries below it clung to the side of the cliff, but unlike them this was not a place for visitors. This was home to the many monks who supervised the tourist business. Despite the lateness of the hour there was the hum of activity. The brothers who prayed for the souls of the community were at prayer. Others were scrubbing long trestles ready for the preparation of vegetables and herbs for the next day's dishes. I saw some monks carrying piles of scrolls and documents, making for the scriptorium, where the illumination of parchment was a permanent work.

The abbot led us up another smaller flight of steps and we came to a long thin corridor. Here the sounds of activity diminished. The small windows set high in the stone walls gave little indication of the dizzying height we had reached.

At the end of this passage was a small lancet door. The sound of deep fitful coughing penetrated the carved wooden panels. To my surprise the abbot tapped gently on one of them before entering. It would have been a wonder if any sound was heard inside above the choking gasps and the racking spasms.

When the door opened, the small corridor was filled with the sounds of a fit of coughing worse than any we had yet heard. I said nothing but the abbot turned to Tommaso and explained, 'There are days when he can barely draw breath. Our doctors stay by his side nursing him day and night. They have diagnosed asthma and bronchial congestion.'

It struck me that whoever this poor wretch was, the last thing he needed was a visit from a stranger. Perhaps this thought also struck the abbot. 'We cannot stay long,' he said, 'our physicians have warned against tiring him. It is by God's grace he has survived the last attack. We await a gift of myrrh promised by his Holiness, Lord Boniface, to help with his recovery. Today, however, our physicians tell me he is doing better.'

The spasm of coughing continued. If this was Maimonides doing better, I didn't like to ponder on the worst days of his illness.

'I trust he will be able to talk to us,' said Tommaso. His words rang unfeeling in the passage where we waited. But he had a point seeing it was the purpose of our visit.

The coughing subsided and became a series of choking gasps. While we waited for the patient to find the breath to speak, the abbot explained further.

'Maimonides,' he said, 'is a great scholar. From an early age he showed a rare talent for languages and now he speaks four, Hebrew, Greek, Latin and Arabic. As well as French and English, of course,' he added.

I was relieved to hear that.

'For some years,' he went on, 'he was professor of philosophy and natural science at the studium of La Sorbonne in Paris, but now he has come to our monastery for a rest and convalescence. He found his lungs were made heavy by the damp air and the mists which rise from the Seine. The crowded streets around the studium and the drunkenness and brutish behaviour of the students, particularly the English and Germans, became too much for him to tolerate.'

I didn't know whether to apologise for my countrymen or not. Still that's students for you. Reginald had been sent home from the cathedral school at Exeter before his first examination for similar bad behaviour, though in his case it was probably a blessing.

The lay brother who had opened the door stood back and Maimonides' physician beckoned us to enter. The abbot went first followed closely by Tommaso. The guards either side of me pushed me forward.

The room I entered was little more than a cell. It was small and bare save for a narrow bed and a chest, on which were the instruments that had brought the patient his present relief. I noticed a bowl filled with the mucus of his wretched coughing.

To my surprise, Maimonides was not an old man. I would have guessed that barely two score years had passed since his birth. He had still the dark hair of his youth and his beard had no flecks of grey. Truly he must have been a prodigy. His skin however was dull with the pallor of illness. When he looked at me, I noticed, even in the pale light of the room, that there was a yellow shadow around his eyes. It seemed to me that it might take more than the arrival of the Pope's myrrh to cure him.

His breath still came uneasily to him and his throat gurgled with the effort, but he welcomed me kindly to his sickroom. He declared himself concerned for my wellbeing and wished me good heart in all my ventures.

My words of thanks in reply, I regret to say, were quite hurried. If I'd known then how much his good wishes would mean to me, I might have sounded more grateful. I understood, however, how the loutish behaviour of undergraduates was not for him. His calm speech and gentle manner suited the quiet of the library rather than the heady question and answer of the classroom.

On the wall of his cell I saw a triptych depicting the martyrdom of St Sebastian. A statue of the Blessed Mary stood by his bed. Maimonides noticed my quick look. 'I converted to Christianity while still a child,' he said. That explained a lot. Jews might be welcomed for their learning at some universities but to find a home with the monks of Rocamadour was another matter. In return for their hospitality, Maimonides worked in the monastery's library, writing, translating and recording items for the Book of Miracles, the monastery's precious record which kept the pilgrim business in such a healthy state. According to the abbot his wisdom was such that kings and bishops came to this small city set high on the cliffs to seek his advice. I reckoned the abbot knew he'd got the better of the bargain.

Tommaso, who was standing by the abbot, now spoke. His voice seemed low and harsh in this quiet room. 'Enough of these pleasantries,' he said. 'We have business to conduct. The manuscript

141

is lost and time is short.' He addressed Maimonides directly. 'Repeat, if you please, for this young Englishman what you confessed to the abbot when you asked for his absolution.'

I looked away. I wanted no part in threatening this sick man to reveal his final words when he believed death called, for threat I had detected in the voice of the officer of the church. He might be a servant of the holy seat but he was a mercenary for all that.

Maimonides, however, made nothing of Tommaso's words but beckoned me forward. I had to lean close to him to hear his words. He took my hand and pressed it. 'If God had willed otherwise,' he whispered, 'I would now be fulfilling a promise to your good king. We have known each other for a long time since the days he rescued me from the soldiers of Sultan Baibars and took me back to England. His voice broke and a deep cough came from his chest. The physician held the bowl while Maimonides cleared his throat of the brown phlegm.

While we waited for the fit to subside, the abbot told his story. 'In the days,' he said, 'when your King Edward was a prince fighting in the Holy Land, his soldiers came across a boy lying under the body of his dead mother. She had been killed by the forces of the Sultan of Egypt, who had taken the lands around Haifa, plundering and raping. He was brought before Edward who saw the character in the child. The prince ordered that he should be fed and his wounds dressed. With his home burnt and with no family to claim him, the crusaders took him back to England and placed him in a monastic school. There he adopted the faith of his rescuers and grew to be a gifted scholar.'

I listened to the life story of Maimonides with interest. It came as no surprise to me to hear of the chivalry of King Edward and his crusaders. That much I knew from my father. What Maimonides then explained, however, was of much more relevance to my current situation.

'Some weeks ago,' Maimonides said in his throaty voice, 'King Edward wrote to me. He sent a letter by a distinguished visitor to the priory. In this letter he told me of the sacred manuscript which had been taken from the library at Acre. He said that his spies informed him that the monk was seeking me at Rocamadour. He was kind enough to praise my learning and begged me to confirm the authenticity of the document. He told me, furthermore he was arranging for a young Englishman to come to Rocamadour. He asked me to seek out this young man and entrust the manuscript to him for its safe passage to England. This young man, he confided, would be unaware of the great task appointed to him, for ignorance was surely the greatest security against thieves. I resolved to do the King's bidding,' said Maimonides. 'I owed my life to him. But when I fell ill I feared that death was near. I asked the abbot to bless me and implored him to fulfil my promise.'

It made a good story, I grant, but most of it puzzled me. It was obvious they took me to be the young Englishman. On that score I could find no grounds for argument but as to the rest, I had come to Rocamadour simply as a tour guide for Bon Macip. I had taken this employment as a favour to Jacques Donadieu, Marguerita's father. He had come to my rescue on my arrival in France. But for that I would now be in the king's lands in Gascony. All else was my own choice. I said as much.

Maimonides made no reply. The silence in the room was almost overpowering. I looked from one to another. I tried again. 'I found myself in Cahors,' I protested, 'through the kindness of one Jacques Donadieu who rescued me from bandits in Libourne. I found employment with Penance Way simply to pay for my journey west.'

Despite the dignities of a sickroom I was now beginning to lose my temper. 'Now you tell me my lord king knew of this even before I did?'

Despite his sorry state, I hoped Maimonides would hear the sarcasm in my question, but all he did was to give a faint nod of the head.

'And pray what speculum did you use to discover this?' I demanded.

Maimonides breath rattled in his chest. He eased himself against the pillow behind his head. 'I had no need of a mirror,' he answered. 'Bon Macip informed me.'

'Bon Macip,' I repeated. 'What would Bon Macip know of this, and why would he inform you?'

'Bon Macip is my uncle,' Maimonides replied.

His answer shocked me. The devious diplomacy of King Edward was hard enough to take in. How Maimonides came to have

Bon Macip as his uncle was beyond understanding. Still I'd got Reginald. Not quite the same I admit but proof that all families have their problems.

'Why should Bon Macip know the thoughts of the king of England?' I demanded.

It was Tommaso who now spoke.

'Bon Macip's spies are everywhere,' he said. 'His tours travel all over Christendom. Doubtless he had heard of the journey of the monk and his precious parchment. We have long suspected that his organisation is involved in the movement of stolen artefacts. Illuminated manuscripts, psalters and breviaries are stolen from our churches every week. There is always a market for them. When Maimonides wrote to his uncle to bid him farewell in this life, Bon Macip realised that he had an opportunity to procure the manuscript.'

It seemed everyone knew of this monk and his journey except me. If I was expected to find his missing manuscript, I wanted to know what it was.

I asked the obvious question. I should have asked it sooner. 'This parchment,' I asked. 'What's so special about it?'

Not for the first time that night a profound silence seemed to overcome the abbot and Tommaso. The stillness in the room was broken only by the rattle of the sick man's chest. At a glance from the abbot, the physician and the lay brothers left the room.

Only then did Tommaso speak. 'The first part, we understand,' he said, 'recounts the deeds of St George.' I maintained a look of interest. I didn't completely lack manners. All England knew St George and his emblem, the great white banner with the red cross. The saint fought for the poor and defenceless. King Richard the Lion Heart had put his crusaders and his kingdom under the saint's protection. I said a quick prayer to the great warrior. I had need of him at this moment.

'For that alone,' Tommaso went on, 'the king would pay well, but it is the second part of the manuscript that Edward of England desires and raises the wrath of al-Ashraf.'

I said nothing. I looked from one man to another. All three were preoccupied with their thoughts.

Finally Tommaso said, 'It records the great journey of al-Khadir.'

I wasn't sure if I should have looked impressed. It was difficult as I had no idea who this al-Khadir was. I tried to look wise. In the end I had to admit my ignorance.

It was Maimonides who replied. 'al-Khadir,' he explained, 'is a great prophet guide. It is said he is a servant of God and has divine wisdom. In the traditions of the eastern lands he had many companions. Abraham and Moses walked with him for they sought his knowledge. The great Alexander, king of Macedonia, set out with him to reach the end of the world, the Land of Darkness, in search of the water of life.'

A fit of coughing overcame Maimonides. He struggled to breathe. I made to move towards him but a hand held me back. Tommaso gripped my arm. There was nothing to do save wait for the spasm to pass. I looked away. To me, Maimonides had need of this water, for he already walked in a land of darkness, towards the vale of death.

When he could breathe again, Maimonides continued his story. It was difficult to follow for the words rattled in his throat. Some were too faint to hear. 'The two companions,' said Maimonides, 'reached a parting of the ways. Each chose his path but it was only al-Khadir who reached the life-giving fountain and drank the waters. From that day he became immortal. He now lives forever and has great power. It is said that he can make all things grow, he can find water below the ground and he can talk the languages of all people. He walks the world from his earthly paradise and guides those who seek God.' The sick man struggled to breathe but no one else spoke. When his spluttering ended, Maimonides continued. 'He will give his divine secrets of eternal life to those worthy of his companionship,' he said. 'Anyone who walks with him will find energy beyond compare and will never tire of the task he faces.'

I was suitably impressed. I could see why my lord Edward desired the manuscript. The king was still a force in battle, but like my father he had lost the vigour of his youth. I wasn't sure about the immortality, but in his dealings with the troublesome Welsh and the turbulent Scots, not to mention the treacherous King of France, boundless energy was pretty helpful.

Before I could say anything Tommaso added with vigour, 'It is dangerous propaganda, of course, put about by the infidel. The Holy Father has instructed me to find the manuscript and take it to his seat in Rome.'

'King Edward wishes to have it,' I said. I well knew my duty to the Pope but it seemed to me my liege lord should have some say in this. I, too, for that matter. My father's ransom depended on it.

'Pope Boniface fears that if the manuscript falls into King Edward's hands he will be the envy of the rulers of Christendom, for he would surely use it to claim his superiority over all others.'

I understood it then. The pope held that position. The superior one I mean. The church didn't like rivals. My father told me often of the quarrels between our lord King and his priests.

'Can't we give it back,' I asked, 'if we find it?'

'That is what al-Ashraf fears,' replied the abbot who had remained silent while Tommaso answered my questions. 'If the Muslim world learns of its loss, his authority will fade.'

I still didn't understand. 'Isn't that what we want? I questioned. 'If al-Ashraf has no authority in the Holy Land, have we not won?

'Won what?' Tommaso asked. 'We have lost all in Outremer. Our success now is to build on al-Ashraf's fears. He will make no more moves against the Christians while he is uncertain of our plans. Give it back!' For once he let amusement show on his face. 'That's the last thing we want to do.'

His look told me what he thought I knew about high level diplomacy. Absolutely nothing.

A thought struck me. I agree it was a little late in the day. 'This manuscript,' I asked. 'If it's just a story about an unbeliever, why would all Christendom desire it?'

For all his shortness of breath, Maimonides rose from his pillow to answer that one.

'Al-Khadir,' he said, 'is the green man.'

CHAPTER 10

It was then I understood. You may consider I was slow to grasp the importance of this missing parchment. I would have to concede the point. Now, I knew what it meant, I turned over the significance in my mind.

In my corner of England we knew of the green man's coming. I had seen his face, growing like the trunk of a tree with his crown of leaves and the branches from his mouth. It was carved into the wall of our church. I had asked Father Thomas, the priest at our chapel, what it meant. 'He is life,' he had replied. 'He is the renewal of all things until the end of the world.'

We knew the green one came in all forms. I had heard many tales told of his gift of life. He never died but he gave all worthy men the chance to follow him and discover the truths of the world. It was said he had once challenged our own King Arthur and his knights. Sir Gawain smote his head from his body but the Green One lived on. He took his head and disappeared. Sir Gawain had to follow to keep his promise of the challenge.

As I have said, I heard these stories told in our small town. There were wise men and women who knew the nature of things unseen. Later they were written down for those with education to read but I had them fixed in my memory. Now I understood the prize which King Edward sought. A manuscript that told of the green man and his gift of everlasting life was indeed a treasure beyond price. I just could wish he hadn't chosen me to find it.

As the task I had in hand started to sink in, the physician returned. It was time for us to go. The monks came back to administer to their patient. We had tired Maimonides with our questioning and we were asked to leave. I was glad to escape the confines of the priory. The talk of life and death weighed heavily on my heart.

I was taken back to the chapel of St Michael. It was safer that way. Tommaso warned me to keep my eyes open and my wits alert. 'The agents of al-Ashraf are here,' he said, 'of that there is no doubt. Remember the Arab leader is determined to find the manuscript. If reports reach him that you have it, your life will be worth this much.' With that he had plucked a spider from its web in the rafters of the chapel and crushed it between his fingers.

He forgot to mention that he also had instructions from the pope to make sure he secured the same document. I could see I would have to watch my back at every turn.

I went to leave the chapel but Tommaso stopped me.

'The manuscript,' he said, 'I'll wager it is here in Rocamadour.' He pulled from the sleeve of his surcoat ten Florentine ducats. They shone in the first shafts of light that lay across the paving stones of the sanctuary. I did not take his wager. I coveted no prize but I realised the gesture had significance for Tommaso.

'I'm rarely wrong,' he went on, 'but where is it? Who has it? That is what I intend to find out. You say you do not know your pilgrims but you have talked with some. I have sat with them and studied from a distance. Now is the time for us to share what we know. Together we can make some sense of this.'

I hesitated. I had precious little to share, and furthermore I had no desire to hand this coveted document to an agent of the Pope. At the same time, without his help, I had little prospect of finding the manuscript. My duty was to my king, and it seemed that the fate of Outremer depended on it staying out of the hands of the Arab leader.

'I know almost nothing of my clients,' I said. Well, at least, it was almost the truth. 'All I do know is that there is one who was murdered.'

'You know this for certain?' Tommaso demanded.

I weighed up the situation. I had watched many a knight at the tourney do the same. For some the decision to charge with the lance won the day. For others a wrong assessment of the field meant defeat, even death.

I made my choice and showed Tommaso the knife which had killed the Templar. It was taking a big risk. I only had the abbot's word that this man I had known as a widowed merchant was an officer in Boniface VIII's army. If the servants of al-Ashraf were masters of disguise surely forging a papal pass to gain the abbot's ear would have offered no difficulty.

Tommaso took the knife carefully and studied it. He knew the strength of its pointed blade. Now he turned the handle in the palm of his hand. I had barely looked at the knife when I had taken it from the neck of the Templar. Now I saw for the first time the striations along the handle and the silver bolts that held the blade in place.

'What manner of dagger is this?' I asked. 'Who would wield such a weapon?' He was the soldier, surely he would know.

'I have only once seen a knife like this,' Tommaso replied, after some minutes had passed. 'In my youth when I fought for the king of Naples, I saw a similar horn forming the handle of a dagger. The knife was said to have the power of magic.' He shuddered slightly as he spoke.

'What magic is that? I asked. I, too, was feeling the curse of death even within the walls of this sanctuary.

'It is claimed,' said Tommaso, 'that a horn like this has the power to seek out its victim. Its aim is true. One blow will bring instant death.'

We both looked at the weapon. Certainly in the case of the Templar the claims made for the knife appeared to be true.

'It is nonsense of course,' said Tommaso. 'A dagger is as good as the man who wields it. I fear, however, the blade had poison at its tip.'

If that was meant to ease the moment it didn't work. A poisoned dagger would explain the lack of blood but it meant that we had an assassin amongst us who was obviously an expert.

'This horn,' I asked, 'what animal bore it in life?'

Tommaso studied me. Then he said, 'In truth I do not know but I have heard tell there is a strange animal across the sea in the lands south of Egypt. It is bigger than the largest ox, its skin is more wrinkled than an elephant and it bears not one but two of these great horns.'

I had heard enough. If any knife was the weapon of an infidel this surely was it.

Tommaso was still studying the dagger.

'I doubt a woman could hold this,' he surmised, 'but we must suspect all. There have been female assassins.'

I almost laughed. I hadn't even suspected the ladies on the pilgrimage. Who were they? Two nuns, Huguette with her useless arm, a married woman with her husband and Marguerita. It was ridiculous.

Tommaso was interested to learn that my young assistant was a woman but not surprised. I think he had long since worked that out. His words, however, reminded me that nothing here was what it seemed.

'That leaves us,' continued Tommaso, 'with three students, the husband Guy and his son Arnaud, a friar who follows St Francis and the Lord of Gourdon.'

'Lord of Gourdon,' I interrupted, 'you are mistaken I have no lord in my party.'

Tommaso looked at me with disdain. 'Heresy,' he said, 'is found everywhere, not just amongst the illiterate and uneducated.'

I knew what he said to be true. I had seldom heard of heresy in my home at Torre, but here in the Quercy it seemed it was everywhere. Bon Macip had warned me. 'We Jews,' he said, 'we make a profit while we may, before we are banished.' A slow sneer had spread over his thin face with its long curved nose, 'Until we are invited back wearing the red circle of our race. The coffers of many monarchs have need of our skills.'

'Heretics,' Bon Macip informed me, 'are another matter.' He should know. He made his money out of escorting the richest heretics on their journeys of penitence. The poor managed on their own, those who recanted that is. Stories of heretics who burnt for their beliefs were common around Cahors. That the heretic in my group was a local noble should not have surprised me.

I had no liking, however, for Tommaso's superior manner.

'And which of my pilgrims, in your long experience, might be the murderer?' I challenged. I said nothing about Guy and Jeanne and their visit to the hermit. Until the culprit was revealed, I felt as tour guide I should at least sound as if I cared about my group. Anyway I found I did. Care that is.

Tommaso was too clever to respond to my jibing. Rather he answered the question seriously. 'The students,' he said, 'are unlikely murderers. They had trouble managing their cart. When they walked they fell to the back. They talked only of their studies. If there is an assassin amongst them he would surely hesitate until he had applied the principles of Aristotle to the deed.'

I could but agree with him. I saw no threat in the two white-faced youths. I had concerns, as doubtless their mothers had too, that they would even find the energy to complete the pilgrimage. As for Bertrand, he hid some secret but it did not identify him as a murderer or a thief. I said nothing of this to Tommaso.

Tommaso was quiet for a time, reflecting no doubt on the suspects on his list. Me? I was quiet too but I added Tommaso to my own possible list. Not that it helped. My trouble was, I couldn't see any of the pilgrims having murdered one member of the party, let alone two.

I had a thought 'The man who rode the black horse,' I asked Tommaso, 'did you speak to him?' I didn't mention it was on that score I had fallen down on my duties as a tour leader.

'Very little,' said Tommaso, 'but I never mastered the language of Sicily. Neither Frenchman nor Italian can fathom the tongue of that strange island.'

I was amazed to hear this. It did explain why the stranger remained so silent, but I blamed Bon Macip for not informing me. Not that that should be any great surprise. He'd failed to explain almost everything about this venture. It was time, as Tommaso had warned, that I should believe nothing unless I had proven it to myself.

'Who was he?' I asked Tommaso. 'Was his death an accident or was he also murdered?'

'For the first,' replied Tommaso, 'I believe he was an agent of the King of Naples. There were some men from Sicily who remained loyal when Charles of Salerno was driven from that land. As for the second I have no answer. Not as yet.'

'King Charles,' I asked, 'why would he send an agent to join a tour with Penance Way?' The whole thing sounded bizarre. I knew something of this king they called the lame. For the state of his legs I have no accurate information, but for his reputation I have the opinion of my father who considered him a cold, secretive man. Before he followed his father to the throne of Naples, Charles had been the prisoner of the King of Aragon. It was my liege lord who had mediated to secure his release, for King Edward through his mother was his kinsman. The most beautiful ladies in Christendom they were called. Edward's mother, Eleanor of Provence and her sisters, Marguerite and Beatrice. The lady Marguerite was grandmother to Philip of France and Beatrice was the mother of Charles of Naples.

This you understand is what I heard from my father. I cannot vouch for the beauty of Queen Eleanor. I saw her but once when I was very young and she seemed very old. Many Provençal ladies came with her when she married King Henry. They sent for their kinsfolk. Edward's Queen, Eleanor of Castile did the same. She, good woman, was dead these past seven years but her retinue remained. It was often said that it was difficult to hear an English voice at court.

I kept these thoughts to myself, for I recalled that Tommaso's master Pope Boniface had been elected when the conclave was in Naples under the protection of King Charles. I remembered also that Tommaso had said that, when a young soldier, he had found employment at the king of Naples' court. The city of Montpellier was under the control of the King of Majorca. What agreements had been made between these kings that they should send a messenger to do the work of the Pope in Rocamadour. This was certainly a serious business.

You may think me surprisingly au fait with King Edward's family connections and with his foreign agreements. I have only the information given me by my father. As to his knowledge, I can but point out it came from the royal court. But then again, rumour is a cheap currency available to all.

Tommaso gave no answer to my question. I now began to think I had said too much. I tried a different tack.

'If the poor man carried anything of importance,' I said, 'it's a pity he had no time to present it. His pouch was empty when I found him.'

'You found him?' Tommaso questioned me. 'I had heard it was the monks on their nightly tour.'

I owned up. 'I had seen him first,' I said. 'He was already dead and his pouch had been searched and discarded.'

'Where is this pouch?' Tommaso's voice had grown harsh.

'I don't know,' I answered quietly. 'I left it there beside his body.'

'You are a fool!' shouted Tommaso. Then he corrected himself, years of training in interrogation had taught him to be calm.

'You did not think,' he said. I hadn't, that was true. Searching a dead man's possessions was new to me. I hadn't thought it would be a necessary skill for a budding spy, let alone a tour guide. Tommaso's next words did nothing to reassure me. 'Whatever the man carried,' he said, 'it may well have been hidden in the lining of his pouch. For all we know it was the manuscript for Maimonides to authenticate.'

I sank down on to the stone parapet around the steps at the entrance to the sanctuary. My heart was heavy. Had I lost the chance to find the precious manuscript so important to the king? If Edward desired it, I was determined to find it for I now understood that the ransom to secure my father's release depended on its safe arrival in England. I thought of Lord John waiting in some prison. For all I knew he had been injured during his capture. I had no time to waste, but my task was becoming more impossible by every turn.

Tommaso's voice broke through my despair. He spoke as if I were a new recruit in the papal army.

'Return to your party,' he ordered. 'Watch every one and find out what you can.' I needed no bidding from him to do that. From now on, I would be no one's fool.

'And you?' I asked. I wasn't having him doing all the ordering.

'I will go about my business,' he said. With that I had to be content.

I emerged from St Michael's chapel into the first rays of the morning sun. Rocamadour was already awake. The enticing odours of breakfast for the early risers rose to meet me as I descended the great stairway. Some eager pilgrims were seated at tables already set up along the main street, heartily enjoying large slices of freshly baked white bread and salted carp. The best inns offered their guests platters of roasted mutton and cakes of goat's cheese with bowls of red wine for sopping their bread.

Further along the main street, the souvenir trestles were already in place. They offered the tourist mementoes of their stay in this marvellous place: tiles painted with the cliffs of Rocamadour, small wooden statues of the saints, replicas of the bones of St Amadour, jars of holy water blessed by the Virgin. Rosaries made from pieces of amber for the richest pilgrims lay alongside pots of red fruits and coloured pebbles for the less well off. Small pieces of parchment with the name of the holy city written in a fair hand were available for those who had reached the end of their savings.

I was hungry but I didn't linger. I had much to consider. I could scarce believe all I had just heard. You will understand, I trust, my lack of skill in the procedures of international diplomacy, or espionage, as some would have it. I had heard things about my liege lord and his holiness the Pope which beggared belief. But that would wait for another day. My task now was to find King Edward's manuscript and take it to England.

First, however, I had to seek out Marguerita. I could no longer keep the news of Ridolfo's death from her. I needed, also, to ask her about the Sainte Coiffe. I had come to Rocamadour to find this relic for her great uncle, to save his embarrassment when its loss was discovered. I had done this in gratitude to her father for his aid when I was attacked in Libourne. Now I could not free myself from doubtful thoughts. If Bon Macip had learned of the king of England's interest in the manuscript, who had told him? Tommaso had said his spies were everywhere, but I knew of one man who had recently travelled in England. Jacques Donadieu had crossed to Gascony on the same ship as I. He had come straight from the court of Edward. I began to think it was not fortune which had led him to find me attacked on the path at Libourne. For all I knew it was his men who had put me in the ditch.

I feared I truly was the simpleton Tommaso had taken me for.

I hurried along the grand'rue to our inn. The tables were set up here and some of my party were already eating. The married couple were there although there was no sign of their son. They were treating themselves to coddled goose egg. Huguette was sitting with the nuns. Their breakfast was more in keeping with their calling. They ate slowly on rye bread and water.

The students, Hubert and Gaucelin were satisfying themselves with a flagon of wine. Free from the constraints of the seminary they were letting their hair down. Once again Bertrand was not with them, although he appeared a little later rubbing his eyes. Perhaps I wasn't the only one to have had a sleepless night. I looked around for Marguerita. There was no sign of her.

I bade my clients good morning and sat down on an empty bench. I waved away the boy who came to ask what I wanted to eat. Then I called him back. I needed time to think and would do so better with a full stomach. I made short shrift of a wedge of white bread spread with goat's cheese.

While I ate, I thought of my predicament. I had to speak to Marguerita but I also had a duty to my two dead clients. Tommaso was convinced their deaths were connected with agents determined to find the missing manuscript. I had accepted his word that these assassins were in the pay of the Arab leader but it was also possible they worked for him, Tommaso. The answer to that made no difference to me. I still worked for the king of England. If anyone was going to keep the manuscript, it was I.

My thoughts turned to the poor man who had died with his head bashed in. His pouch had been ransacked. Then I had taken it to be the work of thieves. There were plenty enough of those working their ill deeds among the crowds at Rocamadour. Now I had to consider the fact that he may have been carrying the manuscript. His killer needed both strength and guile. I tried to think back to the time of his death. It had been but yesterday evening I had found him dead, but so much had passed that night that I had to concentrate to remember where everyone had been.

I recalled sitting around our campfire. The heretic had gone to his bed or so I had learned. Huguette and the two sisters had also sought the dubious comfort of their cubicle. The married couple had gone into the sacred city while their son slept. The two students had sat for a while and then they too had left. Bertrand and Tommaso, or Guillaume as he was then, were missing. The Franciscan friar had stayed until the embers died.

I realised that this was hopeless, I couldn't account accurately for anyone's movements that evening. All the party had disappeared at some time or other. Any one of them could have ended the life of the silent pilgrim. Yet I still couldn't dismiss the possibility that he had fallen foul of one of the many criminals who infiltrated the crowds. Theft and violent death were common here. The monks who had disposed of the body had no doubt recorded the death as such in their official register.

I finished my bread and got up. Most of my pilgrims were still lingering at the table. Their duty to the good Lord done, this was the real holiday and they were intent on enjoying themselves. Some were counting the coins they had left for last minute souvenirs.

It was time to find Marguerita. I went inside the inn. A staircase rose to the side of a panelled chest where the innkeeper's wife was counting the coins already received that morning. I smiled at her as I climbed the narrow steep steps. She looked surprised that I was returning to my room but she said nothing. Tourists were obviously unpredictable.

Upstairs there was a dark narrow corridor. Most of the doors were closed but I came across the maid dragging a huge feather mattress towards the balcony. She remembered Marguerita. I was not surprised. Marguerita's questioning the previous day had been very forceful. The maid directed me to our room.

I tapped on the door and waited. Then I tapped again. I hesitated to enter. Much as I admire the form of a pretty maiden, I too recalled Marguerita's ability with words when she was moved to wrath. The minutes passed, however, and I heard no sound from within. The maid struggled past me with an armful of strewing grasses. I was aware of her gaze. She was no doubt pondering the difficulty of understanding a guest who needed directions to the room he had booked the day before.

When she had passed out of sight I opened the door and looked around the room. As inns go this was a good one. The bed was raised off the ground to escape the beetles that roamed the floor in the hours of darkness. The window had a cloth of damask edged with a fine pulled stitch. There was a chest and a chamber pot. Of Marguerita there was no sign. The bed gave no indication that a body had lain there, nor, indeed, the room that it had been occupied by any guest.

I went down to the small entrance room and looked for the innkeeper's wife. She too had disappeared. I emerged into the sun of the street. The brightness made me screw up my eyes. When I opened them, Huguette stood there.

'Young man,' she said. My heart sank as I had no time for complaints. She tapped me with her staff. 'I am going to the Place du Senhals to buy my sportelle.' she continued. 'I shall return at noon.'

I thanked her for the information, although in truth I had little use for it, or so I thought. As she turned to go the old woman said, 'I should take good care of that lad and not let him disappear into the night.'

I thought at first she meant the son of the married couple and then I realised she spoke of Marguerita.

I caught her arm. The good one. 'What lad?' I asked.

'Your assistant,' she replied. I remembered I had called Marguerita my assistant on the journey.

'What do you mean,' I asked, 'disappear into the night?'

'I need little sleep,' she replied. 'I saw your assistant leave the inn when the moon was high in the sky.'

'Where did he go?' I almost shouted but managed to keep my voice calm.

'That way,' she indicated with the arm I still held. She was pointing to the Sainte Voie that ascended from the city to the hill above Rocamadour.

'He was not alone,' Huguette then informed me.

My fears grew worse.

'Who was with him?' I asked.

'Two knights,' she replied. 'Two Knights of St John from the hospital on the hill.'

I stood there trying to take this in. What in Holy God's name was Marguerita doing with the knights. She had shown no sign of being unwell. Had she been taken ill in the night? What was going on? I turned to ask Huguette but she had gone. Her arm might be useless but her feet were in good shape.

As I stood there in disbelief at all that was happening, I felt a hand grasp my arm. I looked round sharply. I had been taken unawares.

'My friend,' a voice said, 'it is early in the day but you seem tired. The duties of a tour leader rest heavily, no doubt, on your shoulders.' It was the Franciscan friar.

I looked at him carefully. Did he know where I had been for the hours of night which had just passed. I saw nothing but concern in his open face. I decided I was worrying unnecessarily.

'I thank you for your care for my health,' I said, 'but I am well. I worry only for my clients. Our pilgrimage ends tomorrow and I want one and all to have a day that will always be remembered.' As a reply it was pretty pompous. That was another skill I had to hone.

The friar pressed my arm again. I was growing rather tired of his familiarity. I understood, however, that it was his calling. He had given up all. He asked nothing save the knowledge of helping those who listened to his words as he preached the salvation of souls. St Francis had taught his followers to go barefoot and offer Christian love to the poor and lonely, those who were cast out and set aside. They were to beg as they went and accept only charity in kind for their bare needs, never accepting payment.

I knew also of harsh voices which said no doors were closed to these travelling monks, especially when the good man of the house was far from home. I had heard rumours that no wench or wife was safe, for some friars, having offered their blessing, accepted charity of a different sort. Not that I had any misgivings on that score. I was sure the ladies in my group would give short shrift to any offer of comfort which went beyond the spiritual.

I don't recall requesting his assistance but perhaps my concerns showed on my face. He felt my tension and remarked kindly, 'If I can assist you with anything please ask me. I am used to the problems of the road.'

I was about to protest that I had no problems but I thought better of it. Instead I said, 'It prays on my thoughts that two members of our party have not enjoyed this pilgrimage. One died on the journey and one on arrival here. It is a great sadness to me.'

'I have prayed for the souls of both,' replied the friar. 'I hope their path to paradise will be smooth.'

'If they get there at all,' I said. I knew enough of the day of judgement to know that the path to paradise was a long one given to but a few. I had seen many pictures of the sins of this world and the punishments which followed many into the depths of purgatory.

'Have courage, my son,' the friar begged. 'The good Lord answers the prayers of the faithful.'

I thanked the friar again for his vigil in the sanctuary of the Madonna, for that is where I thought he had just been. I hoped Our Ldy's intercession would work its miracle.

'I fear our friend died a lonely death in the meadow below,' said the friar. It was true but I wondered who had told him.

When I asked, he said, 'I learned that from the knights who are arranging the burial. There are some brothers who help those who meet unexpected death. They make sure the body is interred with blessing of the church.'

I already knew that but I trust I had the look of someone who was listening carefully. The friar had a manner which commanded attention.

I took another chance. The stewards at the tourney would have brought me to the front of the lists.

'And missing people?' I asked. I tried to make the question sound casual. 'Do the same monks deal with those unfortunates?'

The friar's expression didn't change. 'You are thinking of your assistant?' he asked kindly. When I didn't reply, he added, 'I overheard our pilgrim friend with the withered arm. She seemed concerned for him.'

'It is true,' I said casually, as I wasn't sure how much he had heard.

'I must locate my assistant. I have errands for him.' I hated to think how Marguerita would have reacted to my words but if the friar could throw any light on her disappearance, I had to have his help. The Knights of St John were dedicated to their patients' care. I had had no success on my first visit to the hospital. There was more chance they would reveal news of Marguerita to one who had taken the church's vows.

The friar, however, said nothing about the knights who had accompanied Marguerita. Instead he clapped me on the back and strode off, promising to find out what he could. His stride was long and energetic. There were no problems of the road for him.

Not for the first time I thought of quitting this wretched employment and making my way home. What had I to show for my trouble. My mother, Reginald even, were awaiting my return but only if I had procured King Edward's help in finding the ransom for Lord John. I knew my hope now lay in finding the lost manuscript. Tommaso believed it was here. Whether he was my friend or my enemy made no difference. I had to find it, and quickly.

I determined to go back to the hospital. Some mystery lay there. The knights had taken charge of the body of the dead pilgrim. Ridolfo had been secretly buried there, and now Marguerita, from what I had heard, was last seen in their company. How willingly she had gone with them was anyone's guess. However kindly meant, I could not rely on the help of the friar. If there was any investigation to do, I was the one who should do it. With that resolve in my heart I set out. It was just as well lady fortune kept secret from me what lay ahead.

CHAPTER 11

It was still early for most pilgrims. The monks operated a queuing system at the great stairway. It was rigorously enforced. The first pilgrims that morning were the penitents. I looked to check if our heretic was amongst them but he was not to be seen. Today was his last opportunity to climb with the other pilgrims who were expiating a sin, but doubtless he had decided on making the painful climb much later in the day, possibly at the moment of dusk.

I didn't blame the penitents their choice of hour. I saw that they were stripped naked and laden with chains and anklets of iron. Some gloried in this display, but others crawled up the steps on their hands and knees in shame, the blood from their raw skin marking their path. I heard some pilgrims wailing and chanting their prayers and calling to the good Lord to give them the strength to reach the holy chapel of mother Mary and her son the Lord Jesus. Most looked as though they needed it. Some swooned with the effort of their travail. Penitent mothers were often separated from their children and they called in anguish for their return.

The monks did their best to oversee the crowds of people, but if the crowd grew too strong or too unmanageable, they closed the stairway and waited for the steps to clear. Most inns offered timetables indicating the most crowded tourist times. The best hotels organised a minute to minute account of the number of pilgrims making their way to the top. Small children were employed to run back and forth, keeping the proprietors up to date with the crush so that guests could be advised accordingly. Lunch time, as I had discovered myself, was a quiet moment, for most guests in the better quality inns were still at breakfast or on shopping trips.

I made my way out of the city and took the holy path that ascended to the hospital. First it led down into the meadows where we had stayed on our first night. At this time the tents were closed. The revelries of the previous evening kept most pilgrims here on their straw mats until well into the afternoon. Then they would rise hastily, buy a sportelle to prove their journey had been completed, and return to the festivities which started afresh each day at sunset.

The morning hour was fresh and the earth smelt sweet. If you averted your eyes from the litter around the tents, you could imagine yourself back in the lovely Devon countryside. At least that is what I told myself. A proper look, however, told me the truth. The towering limestone cliffs, the yellowing grass and the sluggish waters of the Alzou river were nothing like the rolling hills and the red soil of my home or the green meadows which bordered the fast flowing Dart on its way to the sea.

I put these thoughts away as I made my way up the hill on the other side of the stream. Thoughts of home reminded me of Reginald, and I recalled the trouble he had caused. The incident at the mill was only the most recent. There had been many similar scrapes before. Our villeins and cottagers served us well. I could only hope that was still the case on Lord John's return.

The thought of my father spurred me on. I strode out and climbed the last stages of the holy path to the hospital beyond. Here there was considerable activity. Wagons and carts laden with produce for the hospital had lined up outside the entrance gate. The first had bales of clean straw and bundles of strewing grass. Behind this was a cart filled with squawking chickens and fattened geese. At the back was a small cart holding baskets of vegetables. I recognised cabbage and spinach, beet and kale. There were bundles of greenish sticks tied with bind. This was new to me but it was popular with the gates man. I watched him take a bundle or two when no one was looking. The carter in charge of this wagon had disappeared for the moment. I noticed that he was sitting behind a rock swigging a jug of ale.

Suddenly the knight in charge completed his checks and the carts moved forward. I took the reins of the abandoned cart and followed them into the courtyard of the hospital. I made a hasty disappearance behind the largest wagon before I could be asked to unload my vegetables and looked around to get my bearings.

The stone wall of the hospital rose above me. To my left and adjacent to the hospital was the visitors' room where I had been seen on my first evening in Rocamdour. Relatives wishing to have information about the sick waited there. I would avoid that place on this occasion. I wanted to find out what exactly had happened to

Marguerita, but asking an ill-reasoned question might not produce a helpful answer.

To my right stood the chapel of the knights. A porch connected it to the main hall of the hospital. I had no knowledge of what else lay behind this entrance. Now was the time to find out. I nipped across to the porch when the coast was clear. It gave entrance, as I suspected, to the chapel but through another portal I found myself in the hospital kitchen. I saw the food being prepared for the patients. Nothing seemed to have been spared to suit different tastes. No wonder the penniless pilgrim begged for a night here. A lay brother busy at the kitchen fire looked at me with some interest, but I gave him a wink and nod and he turned back to his spit.

Through the door of the kitchen I passed into a hall filled with trestles. I took it to be the refectory of the knights. At this time it was empty, for the hour of lunch was still a long time away. I hurried through a door at the far end and found myself in a wide stone corridor with side cubicles. I peered inside the nearest and discovered it was a store for medical equipment. The instruments of the hospital were here, fine knives for cauterising and lancing abscesses, hammers for trepanning, needles and catgut for sewing wounds, bandages and splints, as well as tall jars which contained bran, no doubt for the leeches inside and pots of poultice for making hot plasters.

I had no further time to view the contents of any more shelves for I heard someone coming. Not wanting to enter the medicine store with its lethal weapons, I hid myself in the next cubicle. I shrank for cover against some sacks. In my haste I dislodged one. I quickly secured the top. I didn't want a storm of goose feathers escaping into the corridor.

I needn't have worried. The lay brother who passed was intent on carrying two huge buckets of water. The weight of the yoke across his shoulder pulled his head down. He was watching his footing and had no eyes for what was happening to the left or right. At the far end of the passage were two heavy-barred doors. From the noises emanating from them I realised I was near the wards of the hospital.

I stayed behind the brother until he reached the barred door. Then he carefully eased his hands from the yoke and pulled up the oak beam. It was obviously something he did regularly, for with little difficulty he edged around the half-open door and entered the hospital. He left the door slightly open presumably awaiting his return. I took the opportunity to peer inside.

What I saw amazed me. The hospital was one huge room divided into three by two lines of pillars. At the side of the aisles formed by the pillars were many beds. I thought of our own hospital at St Nicholas Priory in Exeter. It was always crowded. The beds were drawn close to each other often with two or three men or goodwives to a bed. Such was the crush that some patients died of their own malady and some of their neighbours.

Here each patient had his own mattress raised on a truckle bed, male patients to the right and women to the left. The room was clean, and, even as I watched, brothers laid dry strewing grasses between the beds. I saw with awe that the physicians cared for all without regard to their sex. The space between the beds permitted the priest to pass close to the dying to hear their last wishes.

I peered at the female patients being tended at the end nearest the door where I was peeking. As far as I was able, I scanned the faces of the women. It was not easy as some lay prone on their mattresses. Had I not seen the slight rise and fall of the linen sheets covering them I might have thought they had already succumbed to their ills. Others were wailing and praying. One poor wretch was being blessed by a priest. From her groans and gasps I doubted that she was finding much comfort in his presence. I could only hope he would smooth the path which lay ahead for her.

Two physicians made their way towards the end of the hospital where I was hiding. They were carrying the leeches. I shrank back behind the door and waited. I needed to find out if Marguerita was lying here in one of these beds. She had left the inn dressed in the clothes of a lad. I reckoned, however, that even the newest nurse would not have taken long to discover that her place was not among the male patients. I had no idea if she were alive or dead. The fact that she had been seen walking with the knights gave me some hope.

I waited for the brothers to pass through the door into the corridor behind. I glanced along it. With their backs to me, I could chance another study of the patients' faces. I had little time to spare. The other cubicles I had passed seemed to be storage rooms. Any time now lay brothers would be fetching more straw and dried meadow grass.

After a few minutes I knew that Marguerita was not there. All the female patients were either too old or afflicted with problems that could barely have arisen overnight. If I was to make any progress I would have to seek her elsewhere.

The coast was still clear, so I made my back to the door I had first entered and emerged from the hospital. To the side of the entrance was a cloister where the nursing brothers walked for respite from their labour. That suited me. I had need of time to reflect. Beyond the courtyard of the cloister, I saw the infirmarer's garden. The hortarius was nowhere in sight. I walked along its cobbled paths between parterres of flowers. The gardeners had tended them well. Tall irises and fritillaries guarded circles of mignonettes and pinks. Periwinkles and anemones hung over neat pebbled borders edged with violets and cowslips. Larger beds contained the tools of the infirmarer's trade: wormwood, chamomile and salvia grew there beside rows of balsam, comfrey and saxifrage. I passed a large pond full of fat red carp and reached a stone seat set beneath an arbour of damask roses and sweet briar. I sat there for some time. It was quiet and very peaceful.

I thought about Marguerita. The deaths of the first victims had upset me but I had barely known them. Marguerita was different. I already missed her pointed comments more than I cared to admit. I couldn't leave this place without knowledge of her safety. There were so many other unsolved mysteries here. The dead pilgrims, the missing Saint Coiffe, the precious manuscript desired by my king. All had an answer and I had failed to find any.

As I sat there locked in my miserable thoughts, I felt a hand on my arm. I turned immediately, raising that arm in the air and preparing to strike with the other. I'd been caught off my guard once before and I wasn't chancing an easy capture again.

My raised arm stayed in the air however, for on turning I heard a voice say, 'William, what in heaven's name are you doing here?'

It was Marguerita. I wasn't sure if I was more pleased to know she was alive or to hear her speak my given name.

I didn't show it, however. Instead I said, 'Holy Mary, Marguerita, it is you not I who should answer that question. I did

165

add, however, to prevent a diatribe from this feisty maiden, 'I was searching for you.' I lowered my arm and looked her in the face. I saw for the first time that her large brown eyes were fringed with long curved lashes that lay along her cheek when she lowered her gaze.

'It is for you to tell me what is happening,' I said. Although I had already decided to talk to her about Ridolfo's death, I needed to hear first what had brought her to this place.

She sat down beside me. I feared that our presence there would cause comment not to mention alarm, but she put my mind at rest by telling me that this pleasant space was where patients who had hope of recovery were permitted to walk.

'Are you one of them?' I asked.

'One of whom?' she sounded bewildered for the moment.

'A patient with hope of recovery?'

She laughed for the first time and replied, 'I am neither, not a patient nor in need of recovery.'

As I had come to expect, Marguerita's answer told me nothing, but I hoped these good tidings would help when I broke the news to her of Ridolfo's death.

Perhaps she read my thoughts. I have known strange magic like that happen before. The next moment she placed her head in her hands and said sadly, 'He is dead.' I said nothing. I knew who she meant but it was for her to tell me in her own way. I was relieved that I had been spared the task.

'Ridolfo has gone to a better place,' she said. She made it sound like an order. Knowing Marguerita as I now did, I was sure the good Lord would listen to her wishes.

'How can you be sure?' I asked. I needed no proof for I had seen him dead but I wondered who had convinced Marguerita.

'Two Knights of St John came for me yesterday evening,' she explained. 'I had asked too many questions about Ridolfo. He had been taken ill in the same inn where we are lodging. Sadly the physicians could not save him. The innkeeper feared that I had the same illness. He insisted I go with the knights to check that I was not infected. He didn't want an epidemic in his inn.'

I could imagine that. Talk of a contagion would do nothing for his tourist trade nor, for that matter, anyone else's business in

Rocamadour. I had come to care little for this city. For all its holy sanctuaries, it had grown rich on the sous of the faithful who flocked here from all the corners of Christendom.

'And would you have caught this illness?' I asked. 'Were you and Ridolfo that close?'

'Certainly not!' retorted Marguerita. 'We only met when I was with my father and he with his uncle. Do you think they, too, have caught this disease?' She tossed her head as she spoke. I had said enough. I breathed a sigh of relief. Her love for this Ridolfo seemed to have been based on his appearance. I had to concede that even as a corpse he had a handsome look. I kept this thought to myself and only asked her if the physicians at the hospital knew the name of the illness which had brought about Ridolfo's death.

'The doctors feared some strange eastern malady, even the plague,' said Marguerita. 'Ridolfo had just returned on a Venetian vessel from the Holy Land.'

The plague! I could see why that would worry the authorities here. Even a false rumour circulating amongst the crowds would be enough to cancel the tourist trade for that season. Many pilgrims came to Rocamadour to pray for a cure for an ailment which had resisted all treatment. They wouldn't relish catching another in the process.

I repeated my question. 'What then caused poor Ridolfo's death?' I asked. I added the 'poor', as, for all the brevity of their acquaintance, she was obviously very moved by thoughts of his death.

'It remains a mystery,' she replied. 'There are many strange ailments in the east. Some travellers can resist but Ridolfo... She did not complete the sentence for sobs choked her. I sat still. I made no move to comfort her for I knew this maiden by now. She would deal with her sorrow in her own way.

I said nothing. It was a relief to know it was not the plague but the knowledge that some unknown malady had disposed of Ridolfo was still worrying. For the time I kept those thoughts hidden.

Her weeping under control, Marguerita faced me squarely. 'We have a task, William,' she said. The use of my name for the second time was ominous. What plan had she in mind? Did it involve the Sainte Coiffe?

'William,' she said for the third time, 'I must tell you of some tragedy.' Before I could interrupt to tell her I had one of my own, she went on. 'The tall, quiet pilgrim who travelled with us here to Rocamadour. You remember, he rode a black horse.' I remembered only too well.

'That unfortunate man has also met his death,' she said. I knew that too. I was turning over in my mind how much to tell her when Marguerita continued. 'It is very sad, for he was travelling with something precious and now it is lost.'

For one startling moment I thought she was talking of the manuscript. Tommaso had considered this possibility and cursed me for not searching the man's pouch. Now I cursed myself as well.

'Do you know what this precious thing is?' I hoped my voice sounded casual.

Marguerita surveyed me with a mixture of annoyance and pity. It was not a welcome look. 'Of course,' she answered sharply, 'why do you think I am telling you this?'

Suitably chastised, I begged her to continue, and after a certain tossing of her head, she did as I requested.

'The pilgrim on the black horse,' said Marguerita, 'was in fact a doctor from the medical school at Montpellier.' I raised my eyes at that. Marguerita was pleased her information had had the desired effect. The fame of the medical training at Montpellier had spread throughout Christendom even to my corner of England.

Marguerita then explained, without my interruption, how this doctor was bringing to Rocamadour many precious stones, gems which could be ground into medicinal potions for the sick. 'I have learned they were a gift from the Pope,' she told me and added for further effect, 'their value is beyond price.'

I said nothing but I could have told Marguerita that I knew of one precious remedy the pilgrim carried, myrrh. Myrrh to help Maimonides was, without doubt, in that pouch.

'It is important that we investigate the disappearance of these stones,' said Marguerita passionately. 'I had seen enough suffering in the hospital. The doctors can do little but comfort the sick. We must do what we can to help. Please, William,' she implored, 'assist me with this task.'

I admired her concern but I had worries of my own. I looked at her eager face. I remembered the love in her eyes as she had welcomed home her father when I had first arrived in Cahors. She had annoyed me often on the journey here but it was for her determination to be treated as an equal. She had never caused me to question her support.

I turned it over in my mind. I had a holy relic and a priceless manuscript to find. Why not add a few precious stones to the list?

'Did you find out what jewels the doctor was carrying?' I asked.

Marguerita was ready. She listed them: lapis lazuli, myrrh, amber, garnet, frankincense, pearls, emeralds and gold. Some were being carried as prepared potions,' she added, 'others as jewels for preparation by the physicians for ministration to the sick.' Her face showed her concern. 'I trust the phials are not broken and the precious medicine lost. You will take care when you find them,' she ordered. I was touched by her confidence in me. I was beginning to understand also why Jacques Donadieu treated her as a son to take over his business.

'Whoever stole the precious stones,' I said, 'must have planned to sell them. It would need someone with medical knowledge to turn them into medicine. The sale would have to be done secretly on the black market.'

'They could not be sold openly here,' agreed Marguerita. 'The commander of the knights has ordered all the physicians at the hospital to watch for anyone trying to sell them.'

'So we have two possibilities,' I said, 'either the thief is a dealer in stones or he knows of one who handles stolen property. I thought back to Bertrand's disappearance. He had a contact in Rocamadour. A contact he wanted to keep secret. It was difficult to think that he was a thief or indeed a murderer. I had two reasons now, however, to find out. Did he have his sights on the precious stones or the manuscript of al-Khadir.

'We must return to Rocamadour,' I told Marguerita. 'There is something I should have done before.'

As usual Marguerita wanted to know everything. I told her enough to keep her with me but not enough to put her life in danger. From what the papal agent had said, I knew that the assassin was becoming desperate. The manuscript was still missing. It was dangerous to have any knowledge of it.

'Come with me,' I said. 'We will keep our suspicions to ourselves. We won't accuse anyone, but we will discover what happened to the man's pouch and the precious medicine.'

I made it sound an easy proposition. If I fared as well with this task as I had done with the others we would get precisely nowhere.

I faced her squarely. I hope I sounded more authoritative than I felt. 'Keep to yourself anything you learn. And do what I say without question.'

I added that last order for my benefit. I then said, 'It's for your safety.' That was for her benefit.

She was so delighted at my cooperation she agreed to everything. I was sure that wouldn't last long but for now it would do. We left the pretty tranquil courtyard and headed for Rocamadour.

'Will no one question your departure?' I asked her as we passed through the great stone portal which led to the Holy Way.

'This is a hospital,' she reminded me, 'not a prison. Now I have been declared free of any malady I may leave when I please.' She was walking fast to keep her steps in pace with mine. If she wanted to play the lad, now was the time to prove it.

'What shall we do when we get back to Rocamadour?' she asked, her voice rasping with the effort.

'Something I should have done earlier,' was all I told her. I was worried to hear the 'we'. I had no intention of involving Marguerita in my plan. That was some hope. I realised this as she continued to question me about our next move. Her agreement to follow without question had been very short lived.

When we arrived back in the rue de la Couronnerie, I tried to persuade Marguerita to wait by a stall offering an array of sweetmeats, but, this time, even the chance of trying some prune turnovers couldn't dissuade her from accompanying me.

'Why did you come to find me, if you are going to abandon me now?' she asked. There was no point in explaining that my keenness to discover her whereabouts had more to do with the problem of facing her father than the prospect of her assistance. I could see that I would have no success in overcoming the logic of her question. I submitted.

'All right,' I said, 'but this time we face possible danger. Do as I say without question. And this time I really mean it.'

Marguerita said nothing. I was glad. Her silence meant she realised what might lie ahead. Well that was my hope.

We retraced my steps of yesterday. Searching for Ridolfo that morning had improved my knowledge of the layout of Rocamadour. It seemed to take far less time than before to reach the cottage that Bertrand had entered so secretly. In that quarter of Rocamadour, as I have said, there were many alleyways. The steps rose steeply from the road. It was possible to find cover in the shadow of the great slabs of stone that acted as a stairway. We hung around watching the people who passed along the street. Many of them were new arrivals, coming in through the Porte Basse and making their way to the rooms they had reserved or to the tourist office for details of accommodation. Some were residents. You could pick them out easily enough. They hurried along looking neither to left or right. The charms of Rocamadour were well known to them. They had other thoughts on their mind.

'What are we looking for?' hissed Marguerita. 'If you told me I could help.'

That was what I was afraid of. 'A man,' I said.

'What man?' she asked.

'A man who seemed more than friendly with Bertrand, one of the students.' I replied. 'I followed them here yesterday. Now I am going to find out what it was all about. Another of our party has died and the precious stones he carried have been stolen. Bertrand must explain his actions.'

'Would you know the man again?' Marguerita asked. It was a question I had put to myself. The crowds were increasing. Rocamadour was rarely still, and, by this hour, the streets were becoming busy.

Suddenly Marguerita dashed into the middle of the street, almost colliding with an old washerwoman. Her basket of folded sheets tipped precariously sideways. I dodged around her and steadied the bundle. She gave me the frosty face she had prepared for Marguerita and hobbled into a nearby courtyard.

'What are you doing?' I asked Marguerita, catching her arm.

'This man you are looking for. He doesn't know me. I'm just taking a stroll in the sun,' she replied.

'For that matter,' I said, 'he doesn't know me either. We can walk together.' We walked past the house some six or seven times before our vigil was rewarded. I caught a glimpse of the man who had met with Bertrand and taken him to this cottage. He was approaching us on the other side of the road.

'Stay here,' I snapped at Marguerita. I let the man pass and then I caught him up. You may like to avoid learning what happened next. I'm a quiet fellow by nature but I've learnt a few good holds in my time. As long as my clumsy feet stay up I can keep a grip on any opponent. I won't give you the details but I soon had him fast. In his defence I have to say I caught him unawares. He wasn't much of a fighter for he capitulated immediately.

Well you wouldn't expect a lute maker to know much about arm holds, would you? For that's what he was, and by the appearance of his wares when we entered his cottage, a very good one. Lutes, reboes and voils were stacked around the walls on long low trestles. The smell of sweet wood dust and fish glue filled the room. When he had recovered from the shock of my attack, he had invited me in. Needless to say Marguerita came too.

Inside it was a cheerful place, a family home. The seven children playing there gave me the clue. I said that we had been asked to look out for Bertrand. It wasn't exactly the truth, although the responsibility of being a tour guide was beginning to weigh on me.

Bertrand, it turned out, was no thief or murderer. We learned instead that he had little intention of going to university. His parents' plans of a career in the church were not his. He had his sights set on a wandering life as a minstrel. He'd saved up the generous allowance his wealthy parents gave him for his studies at the seminary. He was going to inform them of his decision when he was far from home. It seemed he was planning to extend his gap year to the rest of his life. I could imagine why he had not informed his parents.

I don't speak with any authority you understand, never having been sent to a seat of learning. Reginald had once suggested he have a year off work. He had been rewarded with a good clout on the head. My mother was having none of that nonsense. She realised, no doubt, it was my brother's way of annoying her when she had asked him to mend his ways.

The instrument maker, a chap called Pierre, told us that Bertrand had insisted on the cloak and dagger stuff. He was scared that his friends would grass him up before he was far enough away from home. Having spoken to the two young men in question I would have had the same concerns. Not that I went along with Bertrand's plans. I had brought him to Rocamadour for a five-day visit. Already I had two clients who would not be returning to Cahors. I didn't need a third. Persuading the young man to abandon his plans, however, might prove as difficult as locating the Sainte Coiffe.

It was on that score Marguerita came in useful. Apparently she had later taken Bertrand on one side and talked him through his decision. Her position as my assistant, or so she assured him, gave her authority to speak on the subject. She covered life in general, the problems of feeling wretched and the prospects for the future, at considerable length. By the time she had finished even the most determined of dropouts would have reconsidered his position.

We stayed long enough with the lute maker to enjoy a moment's peace in his pleasant cottage. Then, having bid him good day and patted all the children on the head, we made our way back. We had solved one mystery, but it had got us nowhere in finding a culprit of any description.

When we reached the square near the Porte Hugon, Marguerita found a table by a stall and ordered two cups of honeyed water. The morning's adventure had given us quite a thirst. We drank slowly and in silence. I think both of us were going over the morning's events. Finally, Marguerita said, 'Bertrand is not our thief, we must think again.'

I thought it uncharitable to point out that's what I had been doing for the past two days. So far it had got me nowhere. Not that I had been thinking of the precious stones. The Sainte Coiffe had been more on my mind.

Now my thoughts turned again to dealers in stolen property. I knew one person who understood the market in relics. I doubted if his knowledge stopped at artefacts. Medical supplies also fetched a high price. That person was in Cahors.

'Bon Macip?' I asked Marguerita. 'What do you know of him?'

She showed no surprise at my sudden question but answered. 'Only that he organises tours. Of course he is a Jew and he has to watch his step. Any devious dealings and he would be banned from the city.'

'Not if his dealings were unknown to the town government,' I replied. 'Have you heard your father talk of him?' I knew full well that she had but I asked the question all the same.

Marguerita thought for a moment. 'He likes to dabble in money lending,' she said. 'My father says only fools would go to him for he charges a high interest on his loans. Nevertheless,' she went on, 'when the pledges are a bit suspect and the local businessmen won't take them, debtors are forced to go to him.'

'I'm not sure where this gets us,' I said. 'We know of nobody in debt to Bon Macip. The three students have wealthy parents, the friar has no need of money, the married couple seem well set up. The Lord of Gourdon, the heretic, he's very rich.'

'Lord of Gourdon?' Marguerita repeated. 'The heretic? I had no idea it was he.'

'Yes,' I replied, 'so I have learned. It was something Bon Macip failed to mention.'

'My father also,' Marguerita exclaimed, jumping to her feet in excitement. I pulled her back. I was anxious that we should not attract attention to ourselves.

'The Lord of Gourdon is our heretic?' she said again. The information had obviously startled her.

'Yes,' I replied. 'Apparently.'

'He's not rich,' she cried. 'The Lord of Gourdon is in serious debt.'

'How do you know this?' I asked.

'I don't for certain,' replied Marguerita, 'but I remember that my father said he had had an important visitor. He gave me no name for he had been sworn to secrecy but he told me the man was in need of a great deal of money. He had been convicted of giving shelter to heretics.'

She had no need to tell me any more. I remembered the huge donation to the repairs of Cahors Cathedral which had saved the heretic from a longer pilgrimage of penance. I had thought him a big tycoon. Now I was sorry for the fees I had charged him. Not too sorry, however, when I considered the style in which he travelled and the best suite he had reserved at the hotel.

'Where did he get the money?' I asked.

'I am not sure,' replied Marguerita, 'but my father said that he knew of no one who would take his pledge.'

'But if he had some treasure to sell his financial worries would be over.'

'Do you think it is he?' asked Marguerita. 'I cannot believe the Lord of Gourdon is a murderer.'

'Perhaps not, 'I said, 'but he's more than likely a thief.'

Marguerita was on her feet again. 'We must go immediately and find out,' she cried. I looked at her. I admired her eagerness and her concern.

'All right,' I agreed, 'we can make enquiries, but we can't just rush and accuse him. We'll go to the monastery,' I went on, 'you to keep watch and I to find the Lord of Gourdon. If he has the cures there are only two places he can go in Rocamadour to get payment commensurate with their value. The hospital of St John is one. The other is the physician's office in the monastery. You say the knights deplored the loss of valuable medicine. There is only one place left for him to visit.'

Marguerita said nothing. I had no idea what she had in mind. I just hoped it didn't involve interfering with my plan.

That was some hope.

I walked fast, thinking furiously as I went along. I barely noticed Marguerita but she matched my steps with her own, keeping close to my side.

Finally she called a halt. 'Slow down,' she shouted at me, 'At this pace we shall be exhausted before we get there.'

I stopped then and looked ahead. The doors of the monastery lay before us. I turned to Marguerita who was sitting by the side of the path. 'I must leave you here,' I said. 'I will have trouble entering the monastery. I have no invitation. A woman will never get past the entrance.'

With that Marguerita laughed and indicated her attire. She still wore the clothes of a lad. 'Wherever you are going, I am going too,' she said. 'It was our agreement.' I didn't exactly remember my words like that. Marguerita had conveniently forgotten the bit about, 'do as I tell you.'

I had no time to argue, however. At least that's what I told myself. If the truth's to be told, I knew I would lose.

We approached the door of the monastery. As I had thought the guard on duty refused us entry. I told him that I had an important message for the abbot concerning Maimonides but that did not work either.

'Who is this Maimonides,' whispered Marguerita. I explained who he was. I left out the bit about him being the nephew of Bon Macip. I did explain his illness and how the abbot awaited the myrrh being sent by the Pope.

'Leave this to me,' said Marguerita. She approached the guard. 'I am the representative of Master Jacques Donadieu,' she said, 'businessman and financier of Cahors. He is directed by his gracious majesty Philip of France to bring news from Paris to the Abbot of Tulle.' She approached closer to the guard and said something low under her voice which I didn't catch. Whatever it was, it worked. The gate swung open and we were ushered in.

'What did you say?' I asked Marguerita, as soon as we were out of earshot of the guard.

I told him the king's officers were at hand to make sure the message reached its destination,' she replied. She added blithely, 'It always works.'

Once inside the monastery we were led to the guest room where all visitors had to wait. The monks of Rocamadour were Benedictines not vowed to silence. Even so talk was rare and only the monks in charge of hospitality interviewed visitors. This was explained to me by Marguerita in hushed tones. I thought the word 'hospitality' was a bit rich seeing how difficult it had been to gain access. Then I remembered this was Rocamadour, and, like much else, the rules here were special to the place.

We had little time to talk for the almoner arrived. The mention of Maimonides now did the trick and we were taken to the chief physician. He was the same monk I had met but a few hours previously. I had obviously made little impression, for he showed no sign of recognition.

He welcomed me but with caution. Marguerita said nothing. She seemed bemused for once to be in the inner sanctum of a monastery. 'I come for news of the myrrh and other precious gifts from his holiness, the Pope,' I said. 'I understand they have been brought here.'

'The precious medicine has been found!' exclaimed the monk. 'This is indeed good news. Where is it? Maimonides grows weaker. We must make a tincture immediately.'

I explained that we had no actual knowledge of its whereabouts only a belief that someone would ask payment for it.

The monk wrung his hands in despair. 'We understand that,' he said. 'It was but a half-hour since that we received the same message, although it did not say anything about payment.'

That did surprise me. Marguerita, too. I think our faces showed our shock.

'May I ask who brought the message?' I enquired.

'That is the strange part,' replied the monk. The message was brought by a boy. He said a man had told him to come here and say that with God's help the medicine had been recovered. He paid him well to deliver the message.'

'Could he describe the man?' I asked.

'We asked that same question,' the physician said, 'but the boy gave us an even stranger answer. He said the man was hidden from view. He saw only his hand.'

We could learn no more. The heretic was not there. I had to find him. I was still convinced he could tell me something about the death of the silent pilgrim. We raced down the steep path that wound down into the city. Finally we paused to get our breath. 'Where are we going now?' gasped Marguerita.

'Back to the inn,' I said, with what breath I had. 'Come on, there is evil afoot here.'

CHAPTER 12

When we got back into the city, I left Marguerita sitting at a table in the place de la Carreta. It was still early in the morning but the taverns here provided snacks at any time of day. The plan was for her to wait for me there, while keeping a sharp lookout for members of our party. I would go back to the inn to find out what I could about the heretic's movements. Well that was the plan. I had calmed any protests from her by ordering a plate of almond and rose tartlets.

When I reached our inn, the rest of my group, as I suspected, had already disappeared. I hoped they were enjoying themselves. It was more than I could say for myself. The innkeeper's wife was at her usual place laying down the rules of the inn to some new arrivals. I enquired at what hour the heretic had risen and if she knew where he was spending the morning. I discovered that he was still in his bed.

'We have not disturbed him,' she said. For the benefit of some tourists hovering in the doorway, she added, 'We do not turn our guests out at the crack of dawn. Those tourists who wish to stay abed can do so. Of course,' she went on, in case I was an undercover inspector checking on the standards of hostelries, 'he has missed the airing of the mattresses.' With that, as if to reinforce her words, the maid appeared and indicated to her mistress the day's cleaning was done.

I climbed the stairs again and knocked at the door of the private suite, the innkeeper's wife having instructed me on the position of the best room in the hotel. It was not difficult to find. There was a sign outside the door advising other clients to refrain from any disturbance to the guest within.

I took no notice and hammered as loudly as I could on the panel. For good effect, I also shook the handle. To my surprise the door was not fastened securely. Under the force of my knocking it moved slowly inwards.

I went in and looked around. The notice on the door fell off and landed at my feet. There was no point in fixing it back to its panel. The occupant of the room, the Lord of Gourdon, convicted heretic and client of Penance Way, had no further need of it. He lay slumped over his desk, a knife with a tusk for a handle sticking out of his back.

I went further into the room and shut the door behind me. I had no desire to arouse the screams of a passing maid. I peered down at the dead man. There was no doubt the knife was the same one which had killed the Templar, the very same one I had given but an hour or so ago to Tommaso Cavelli, the so-called agent of the Pope securing the peace of Christendom.

I have promised you the truth. I confess a great hand of panic gripped me. I had thought my position was bad enough. How could I now explain being in the room of a murdered guest. Tommaso must have found the manuscript and killed to obtain it. If he had fooled the abbot, what chance did I have to explain my innocence. When had this terrible deed taken place? A gentle touch of the body had confirmed the heretic was not long dead.

As I leant across the body to feel for any pulse, the corner of something blue caught my eye. I recognised the heretic's pilgrim sack. He was the only member of the party who had brought such a smart item with him. His bag was dyed with indigo. All the other pilgrims had settled for the usual plain woven hemp.

I pulled the sack from under him. It was not a pleasant task. Drops of blood had fallen on it. I needed, however, to investigate its lining. I wasn't going to make that mistake twice.

As I looked for a corner I could grasp without being marked with blood, I noticed something gleaming on the floor. I studied it more closely. It was a circle of glass. It was small but I recognised it easily. The last time I had seen such a thing it had formed half of some spectacles. They had been on the nose of the Franciscan friar.

Now I was truly perplexed. I had told Marguerita that evil was taking place here. It had been just a saying. Now I really believed it. I searched every part of the room. I even raised the feather mattress to peer underneath. I looked for any secret place where something could be hidden. Eventually I had to admit defeat. I had found nothing, not a cloth, nor a document, not even any evidence that the dead man had stolen the medicine.

This was all too difficult to understand. The heretic had been murdered, of that there was no doubt. Was there another thief in my party? Had the assassin found a third victim? I still had no answers.

I left the room and hurried down the stairs. Guests were arriving and departing. The innkeeper's wife was preoccupied with the new arrivals, charging them at the highest price. I heard her tell them they were getting a good price, for the season was not yet in full swing. I slipped past them. No point in telling her that one of her guests would not be making a return visit.

I took but a few minutes to get back to the place de la Carreta. Marguerita was no longer seated at the table where I had left her. For now I was too shaken to worry about her.

I sat down on a low wall and thought about my options. I could go to the abbot. I soon dismissed that, he believed fully in Tommaso. He had accepted him as the agent of the Pope. My story was unbelievable even I realised that. The friar also. He was a man of God. Who was I to lay any crime at his door? As for me? I was nothing. At home I could rely to an extent on the name of my father. Reginald used that often enough. But what was I here? The dupe of an untrustworthy tour operator, the associate of criminals, and an Englishman at that. How could I accuse either an agent of the Pope or a brother of St Francis?

You will no doubt be pleased to learn that that was my lowest point. The mumblings of an idiot are no pleasure to hear. I pulled myself together. I tried to put myself in the place of a murderer and a thief. Even Reginald would have struggled with that one. I thought of the assassin sent by al-Ashraf. He was determined to recover the manuscript. For all I knew he had killed three times in his search. He must have believed all three of his victims had the document. If he had not yet found it what would he do next?

Tommaso and the friar were implicated in the death of the Lord of Gourdon. The only male pilgrims left to challenge them were Guy and his son. I decided to find them. If they had the manuscript their lives were in danger. I rose from my stony seat and made my way along the rue de la Coronnerie. I searched all the souvenir shops. Most of my clients would be stocking up on objects to impress the neighbours when they returned home. As I approached the great stairway, I caught a glimpse of the boy. Hurrying forward, I found him staring through the entrance of an emporium. It was a shop that sold everything. The boy was fingering the denier he held in the palm of his hand. It was difficult deciding on a suitable souvenir. I suspected that his parents had bought the obligatory sportelle and had left him to choose something more up to date to show off to his friends.

I approached him with a cheerful grin. At least, what I hoped passed for one in the circumstances. I saw his gaze was fixed on a gruesome looking corpse carved out of stone. First I admired his choice and then I spoke more casually.

'Shopping on your own?' I asked. As questions go it wasn't going to elicit much information. And it didn't. The boy simply nodded his head. I had to try a little harder.

'No one with you?' I enquired. This question produced no reaction at all. I decided to abandon subtlety and asked, 'Where are your parents?'

Even this produced no reply. The boy was now feeling in his pocket hoping to find some more coins. With his free hand, however, he pointed to the stairway and flapped his fingers in the air. I took this to mean they had gone back to the sanctuaries. That seemed a likely place to find them. I remembered how they had spoken of their first meeting by the chapel of Our Lady.

For the fourth time I pounded up the steps that led to the sacred city. It was becoming busy. The monks let me through with a large group of pilgrims. I dodged up around them, bumping a few as I went. I hoped the devout would think that my penance was to get to the top in the shortest possible time.

I reached the parvis in front of the church of the Blessed Virgin. Some penitents were moving slowly into the sacred chapel, others were studying the beautiful frescoes on the wall of St Michel. I scanned them quickly. I could see no sign of the married couple. I looked around the square. Then I spotted them. They were disappearing into the church of St Sauveur. I nipped round a poor cripple hobbling awkwardly towards the crypt of St Amadour. He stumbled over a stone slab in front of the steps. By the time I had steadied him, the married couple had disappeared from view.

I entered the church of St Sauveur quietly. I had no wish to disturb the faithful. Also I didn't know what I was going to say. Questions such as, 'Are you carrying a lost manuscript, some precious stones or perhaps a stolen relic?' didn't seem entirely appropriate. As I went in, a large group of pilgrims made their way

181

out. The nave cleared and I was able to see the couple moving towards the chancel screen. Their heads were bowed in reverence. I waited. I would let the good Lord deal with their prayers.

At the same moment, my eyes caught a glimpse of grey. The friar was standing by the wall in the shadow of the screen. He hadn't noticed me. He was looking at the couple who were moving towards him. I went forward and addressed them. 'It is time to meet in the tavern, 'The Happy Goose', where I have arranged our lunch,' I said. They thanked me and moved towards the door of the church. I hoped I wouldn't be there when they arrived to find no food waiting for them. The friar remained where he was. Then I saw that Tommaso was there also, leaning against a pillar.

The church was now empty. I stayed in the nave and called to both. 'The Lord of Gourdon is dead,' I said. 'But,' I continued, 'you both know that.'

Tommaso raised his head. 'William,' he said, 'beware this murderer.'

The friar moved forward a few steps. The light from the beautiful decorated window fell on his face. 'My boy,' he called, 'assist me with this culprit. He claims the protection of the Pope but he has ended the lives of three people.'

I looked from one to the other. No one moved.

Tommaso spoke again. 'Come on,' he demanded, 'help me with this arrest. This is the assassin.'

The friar smiled. 'Fine words,' he said, 'from a killer. I have taken the vows of St Francis. I do no harm to any living creature. Not even a murderer.'

I was fixed to the place where I stood. I feared to move forward. If I chose wrongly another death might follow. If Tommaso were in truth the culprit, then he would not permit me to live. If the friar had already murdered he wouldn't hesitate to do so for a fourth time. I could see my life depended on my choice.

In the seconds it took me to weigh up the problems of my situation, I heard footsteps behind me. I didn't turn but I braced myself. For all I knew it was an accomplice of the assassin.

I might have guessed, however, who it would be.

'William,' said Marguerita, 'what's going on?'

'Go away,' I hissed at her.

'Why?' she asked.

'Go away!' I shouted at her. 'There is a murderer here.'

With that she ran from the building.

I moved forward a foot. Both Tommaso and the friar tensed. The friar continued to smile. I saw that Tommaso had a more severe look. I tried to read their expressions, but decided it was another of my skills which was severely lacking. Tommaso started to move towards me. 'Wait,' called the friar. 'I beg you, do this boy no harm.'

'Do not listen to him,' said Tommaso, 'he cares nothing for your welfare.'

The friar called to me again. 'Three men have died,' he said, 'I could do nothing to save them. Now it is my duty to help you. With your assistance we will bring this murderer to justice.'

Tommaso leaned heavily against the pillar. 'If you approach him you will die,' he said. 'Trust me, and in the name of the Lord, I will arrest this scoundrel.'

It was time for me to make my move. The situation was changing. The murderer would soon wait no longer. He was ready to fight his way out.

'See here,' I said, to attract the attention of both men. 'I have no knowledge of the truth. I can only make my choice.' The die was cast. I had to put my faith in one of them. I went forward to assist Tommaso.

At that very moment there was the sound of a great bell. The ringing of the tolling echoed around the church. We were all startled. The tolling grew louder. Whoever was sounding the bell was pulling with all his strength.

For a split second the two men made no move. The noise grew even wilder. There was no time to consider more, for a group of armed guards rushed into the church, their weapons raised in attack. The monks on sentry duty could respond when the need arose.

The next seconds were all confusion. Tommaso staggered forward. I darted to his side. The friar ran for the door. Such was the speed of his escape he made it through the entrance and into the square outside the church. Extra guards were waiting there and he was manhandled to the ground. From my position I saw several pilgrims look in astonishment at the scene. It was a better souvenir of their visit than any thing they could buy on one of the stalls below.

I held Tommaso who was slipping to the floor. As he fell I saw the great wound on the back of his head. It was a miracle he had stood for so long. As he lay in my arms, he raised his head slightly. 'You left that a bit late in the day,' he said.

'He left it?' said Marguerita, who had appeared at our side. 'I'm probably condemned to eternal damnation for ringing the sacred bell.'

CHAPTER 13

Tommaso was taken into the abbot's palace. His wounds were severe but not life-threatening.

Two monks came to tend to his head. Marguerita and I stood by him. We watched as they cleaned the wound and dressed the bloody hole with a wax of clarified honey and rosin, into which they mixed a green salve of betony, borage and ribwort plantain. This was held to his head with a plaster of fine stretched linen.

I said a prayer for his recovery. For all his cantankerous nature, I had grown to like this man and appreciate his straightforward speech.

When the doctors had finished their work, he raised himself from the trestle where he had been placed.

'Did you doubt me in the church?' he asked.

'Only for a time,' I replied.

'I saw you come towards me. Was it to help or hinder?' He was determined to learn the truth.

'To assist you,' I replied, 'you were frowning at me. You looked ready to fight anyone. I liked that better than the friar's welcoming smile.'

'At least he is arrested now,' said Marguerita. We had both thanked her for her efforts.

'Did you really ring the miraculous bell?' I asked her. I had seen it had no tolling rope.

'I told the Virgin you were in dire trouble,' she replied, 'and Our Lady did the rest. She paused and I reflected on her answer. It would make a new entry in the Book of Miracles.

'I don't understand, though,' Marguerita went on. 'Why did the friar murder three people?'

'For the first he was no friar,' replied Tommaso. The wound on his head had not affected his speech. 'He claimed he was a Franciscan but he had no knowledge of the brotherhood, neither Spirituals nor Conventuals. I think that is why the Templar died. He had spent a lifetime in the service of the knights, both in the Holy Land and at the commanderie at Cahors. There was little he didn't know about those who committed their lives to the service of

185

God. If you recall,' he said, looking at me, 'the conversation that took place the first night when we camped at Couzou. I think it was then the Templar realised the friar was an imposter. After that his fate was sealed. The attack on you in Rocamadour,' he continued, 'was because the assassin could not be sure the Templar had not shared his concerns with you.'

'You witnessed the attack?' I protested. 'Why did you not share your own concerns with me?'

'As I told you,' Tommaso replied, 'I could not break my story. At least I was there,' he argued. 'If you had not been so clumsy, I would have gone to your aid.'

'Why did he kill the other two?' asked Marguerita? 'Had they also realised he was no friar?'

'The Lord of Gourdon certainly died at his hands,' replied Tommaso, 'but I believe that the doctor travelling with the medicine fell and hit his head. As far as I learned, the Lord of Gourdon had approached him to offer a good price for the precious stones. There was a scuffle and the doctor got the worst of it.'

'And the heretic took the medicine?' I asked.

'I found it in his room,' said Tommaso. I had gone to tackle him about the manuscript.' He looked at me. 'We had agreed there were only four men who could have killed the Templar. I wanted to eliminate him from my enquiries. When I got to the inn, I found the Lord of Gourdon seated by a desk studying a paper. Standing by him was the friar. He had his same smile, the smile of an assassin. He had convinced the heretic that he had come to offer him forgiveness. In reality he was seeking the manuscript, though doubtless the Lord of Gourdon feared that he knew about the theft of the medicine. When the friar saw me he welcomed me into the room. I approached the heretic to see what he was reading. I, too, wondered if it was the manuscript. For a moment, I dropped my guard,' he admitted sheepishly. 'It was then he hit me. When I woke from the blow on my head, I found myself lying in a room with a dead man. The assassin had left me for dead but he had found the knife and used it to kill the heretic.'

'This paper?' I asked, 'what was it?'

Despite the pain in his head, Tommaso laughed. 'You and I think alike,' he said. It was the highest compliment. 'It was the list of precious stones.'

'You found them,' I said.

'They were hidden in the seat of his chair, where he was sitting.' Tommaso replied.

No one spoke. We were thinking of the struggle he must have faced moving the dead man.

'I asked a boy to get a message to the priory,' Tommaso said. 'Did it get there?'

'The message did,' I answered, 'but not the medicine.'

'I wasn't going to trust the boy with the gems,' he replied.

'Where are they now?' Marguerita managed to ask the question before me.

'Don't worry,' replied Tommaso, 'I have them here.' With that he struggled to find a pocket inside his tunic. He pulled out a small brown bag. Inside were phials of powdered stones and boxes of precious gems. One contained small lumps of a yellowish brown colour.

'The myrrh?' I asked.

'Yes,' agreed Tommaso, 'Maimonides will have his cure.'

I was glad of that.

'The friar,' I said, 'at least, he will not kill again.'

Tommaso sighed at my ingenuousness. 'He may not,' he said 'but that is not the end of it. al-Ashraf has many spies. He will not rest until he has located the missing manuscript. There will be other assassins, but they will not all be dressed as Franciscan friars.'

'So we have achieved nothing,' I complained. 'The manuscript is still missing.' I looked directly at Tommaso. 'Will you continue the search?' I asked.

'I am paid by results,' said Tommaso. 'I will not return to Rome until I have the manuscript in my possession.'

I said nothing. I too was paid by results. By King Edward when I brought the manuscript back to England.

'This manuscript,' enquired Marguerita, 'Is it very important?'

'Very!' Both Tommaso and I spoke together.

'Ridolfo had a manuscript,' she said.

We both looked at her in amazement. Tommaso tried to lift himself from the trestle, but it was I who took her by the arm.

'Marguerita,' I said gently for the death of Ridolfo was still raw in her heart. 'What do you know of this manuscript?'

Marguerita looked at me. 'When Ridolfo lay dying,' she said, 'he told one of the lay brothers he had a precious document. He had found it on a sick monk who had begged him to take it secretly to Rocamadour and give it to a great man who lives here. I don't know what plans Ridolfo had,' she continued quietly for she now realised she was not the only reason for Ridolfo's journey to Rocamadour. 'but he still had the manuscript with him when he was taken to the hospital.'

'I am sure he wanted to follow the wishes of the monk,' I said. It was not exactly what I thought. Ridolfo was a businessman. He would have seen the opportunity of a quick sale. There was no need, however, to speak ill of the dead especially where Marguerita was concerned.

'What happened to the manuscript when he died?' asked Tommaso, always ready to get to the point.

'The brother took the manuscript,' reported Marguerita. 'I asked to have it as a keepsake of Ridolfo, but it was no longer in his possession.' Her eyes glistened as she explained. I said nothing. I did not want to distress her.

Tommaso, however, was a hardened interrogator. 'Speak, woman,' he demanded in his forthright manner, 'where is it now?' He met his match, however, in the daughter of Jacques Donadieu.

Marguerita sniffed loudly and tossed her head in the imperious way I had come to know so well. 'I've no idea.' she said.

I tried on the smile which usually worked well with pretty maidens, local country girls, that is. It just made Marguerita laugh but it broke the impasse. 'The brother sold it,' she said, 'for a good price, to a visiting monk.'

'This visiting monk,' I asked, 'where did he go?'

'Nowhere,' replied Marguerita, 'he is staying here in Rocamadour.'

Tommaso could barely contain himself. 'Do you know his name?' he asked in a more conciliatory tone.

'He was called Louis, I think.' she replied.

Despite his injury Tommaso would have gone immediately to the priory, but the physician refused to let him. Eventually, Tommaso gave in. I would go in his place. He made me promise to tell him if I obtained the document.

'I will tell you,' I agreed. I forgot to add that I had not promised to give it to him.

We left Tommaso in the care of the physician and went to find the abbot. Marguerita felt it her right to accompany me. She had told us who had the manuscript and she had played her part in unmasking the friar. But for once I was firm. The abbot would not welcome her presence even in the visitor's room and I needed his agreement if I were to persuade Louis to give up the treasure. I persuaded Marguerita to return to the inn and wait for me there.

I made my way once more to the abbot's study. He had been informed of the day's events for I was allowed entrance. Once more I was back in the room I had left but a few hours earlier. This time the abbot welcomed me as an invited guest.

I told him what I had learned from Marguerita. The abbot, for all his girth and extravagance, was a man of action. He quickly understood the situation and ordered that the brother called Louis should be brought immediately to his study.

I waited with great tension. The moment was near when I would see this precious document. The thought of King Edward's gratitude was pleasing. Tommaso's disappointment was not quite so pleasant to contemplate. As we waited, I went over the words I would use to inform him of my decision.

Eventually the sound of footsteps approached the door. The gentle knocking was followed by the appearance of the master of the novices. He was alone. No young monk accompanied him. He approached the abbot and spoke very quietly in his ear. I had no chance to hear what was said but I knew already it was bad news.

Finally the urgent conversation between the two ended and the abbot turned to me. 'Brother Louis is not here,' he said. 'The monastery has been searched and he is not to be found.'

Before I could protest that this was surely not the case, the master of novices continued, 'I have made the most serious enquiries. I have insisted that the truth is told. All I can learn is that the brother left the monastery unexpectedly two days ago. He was visiting us from his monastery at Sainte Marie d'Alet. It is believed that he returned there unexpectedly.'

'You could learn nothing else?' insisted the abbot.

'Nothing, Your Grace,' said the master, 'save that he rejoiced in the happiness he would bring the monks on his return.'

I felt sure I knew what that happiness would be. By the look on his face so did the abbot. 'I will write to my brother, the prior of Ste Marie,' he said, 'and request his assistance in this matter.'

I was certain that he would contact the abbey of Sainte Marie d'Alet wherever that was, but I doubted if he could rely on the abbot's assistance. When the value of the manuscript was discovered, it would remain hidden in the abbey library. It was always useful to have bargaining power where the Pope was concerned. I knew that from my father.

I thanked the abbot and begged permission to leave. There was no alternative, I decided, but to travel there and seek the manuscript myself. Even if the monks of Ste Marie offered the Lord of Rocamadour assistance, it would not include handing over the manuscript to me.

I did not make my way out of the palace when I left the abbot's study, rather I found the passages which I had been led through during the hours of night. Once again I climbed the narrow stairs and reached an arched door. I knocked and waited. This time there was no reply. I had need of Maimonides' help. Now I feared for his state of health. I felt sure, however, I would have learned if he had died. The abbot had spoken of him not an hour since.

I need not have worried. A monk hurrying by with his arms full of papers directed me to the scriptorium. There I found Maimonides sitting at a huge desk surrounded by piles of scrolls and bound books. He rose to greet me. In fact he did more than that. He enveloped me in his arms and kissed me soundly on both cheeks.

'Dear friend,' he said, 'thank you for coming to see me. I owe you a debt of gratitude. I understand you found the medicine sent by the Pope.'

I explained it had been the work of Tommaso.

'That is strange,' said Maimonides, 'he says I owe it all to you.'

'The medicine has already worked well,' I said, 'for you have made a miraculous recovery.'

Maimonides clapped me on the shoulder. It was the only action that linked him to his relative in Cahors. 'The medicine,' he laughed, 'who knows. I take what is given to me with gratitude but in the end it is the good Lord who disposes. There are days when I think the gates of heaven have opened for me and then,' he indicated the rows of manuscripts and tomes which surrounded us, 'he gives me the time to do my work here.'

'I have come to ask for your assistance,' I said.

'Sit here,' invited Maimonides, 'and tell me what you wish. As you know, I count Edward of England as my friend.'

'The precious manuscript of al-Khadir,' I said, 'I'm not sure if you have been told but it was here in Rocamadour.'

Maimonides bowed his head. 'I know,' he answered. 'I have learned many things, terrible things. I know of the deaths of three good men. It brings back memories of a time long ago.'

'The assassin travelled in my party of pilgrims,' I told him. 'He was dressed as a Franciscan. I was a fool. I took him to be a friar.'

Maimonides lifted his eyes to my face. 'Your King Edward,' he said, 'but for God's grace, he would have died in the Holy Land. I have told you that he took me with him to England but I did not say that our return was delayed for Edward lay at death's door for many months.'

I remembered my father talking of this. Now I recalled the reason. 'The poisoned dagger,' I said.

Maimonides searched my face. 'Do you know who wielded that dagger?' he asked. He did not wait for my reply for I had none. 'It was a Christian monk,' he replied. 'An assassin sent by Baibars of Egypt. Edward accepted him as a friend and almost paid with his life'.

There was a long silence. I tried to think of something more encouraging to say. I gave up. Nothing very helpful came to mind.

'This manuscript,' Maimonides asked. 'You will continue the search?'

'I have to,' I replied, 'my father's ransom depends on it.'

'I heard that the young monk called Louis was being sought. Was it he who had it?' Maimonides asked.

'Yes,' I replied, 'but he has left the monastery.'

'And you wish to follow him?'

'Yes,' I said again.

'He has travelled south?' queried Maimonides.

It was time to put my request. 'He has returned to the abbey of Sainte Marie d'Alet,' I said. 'I must go there but I have no knowledge of the road.' I hesitated and then blurted out the truth. 'In fact,' I admitted, 'I don't even know where it is.'

I thought Maimonides would simply tell me the way I should follow. Instead he frowned and looked straight into my eyes. 'Sainte Marie d'Alet,' he repeated. For a while he said no more. Then when he spoke it was to warn me that I was going to tread a dangerous path.

That was nothing new.

Maimonides expanded on his warning. 'Sainte Marie d'Alet,' he said, 'is indeed a sister monastery to our own here at Rocamadour. It is dedicated to the Virgin and the brothers there follow the rule of St Benedict as they do here. But that is all we have in common.'

'Where is it?' I asked. However far away or difficult the place might be, I was determined to get there.

'Sainte Marie lies close to Carcassonne,' Maimonides told me, 'There you enter the lands which still give their loyalty to the ancient house of Trencavel. The French king has claimed the territory but he finds it difficult to exercise his authority. He has a rival in the king of Majorca. Each town and village gives allegiance as it suits them.'

It didn't sound too different from the situation in Cahors. I was used to the quiet countryside around my home in Devonshire. I was glad we had one sovereign lord. In this strange land every man fought for his own authority.

'That is not all,' Maimonides continued. 'It is also the country of the Cathars. Take care you do not get embroiled in the heresies of the Bons Hommes, for the consequence is death.'

I thought of the Lord of Gourdon. He was only a faydit, who offered shelter to the non-believers of the church at Rome. He had recanted his ways. Not that it had done him much good. The costs of the pilgrimage had led to his death. A knife in the back or the fires of the Inquisition? It wasn't much of a choice.

'Whatever awaits me,' I said, 'I must go. My father's ransom depends on it.'

'Then go my friend,' replied Maimonides, 'take the road to Figeac, then south to the city of Albi and south again to Carcassonne. Take care when you reach that place. Stranger things happen there than you could begin to understand.'

As words of encouragement it left much to be desired. It did not deter me. Nothing much worse could happen than I had met here in Rocamadour.

I'd got that wrong again.

I thanked Maimonides for his assistance. Before I departed, he pressed something into my hand. It was a talisman in the shape of a six pointed cross.

'Take this, my friend,' he said. 'May the Lord watch over you but if you have need of assistance, show this to one, Mordecai ben David.'

I looked at him. His conversion to Christianity had taken place when he was still a child.

Maimonides appreciated the thoughts which passed through my head. 'I understand your puzzlement,' he said. 'My soul is in the hands of Jesus Christ but my family ties...' he looked away and said no more. For all I knew the memory of his long-dead mother filled his thoughts. I doubted if it was his uncle in Cahors.

I left him then, poring over his books. I hoped, fortune permitting, we would meet again.

The bells of Rocamadour were sounding noon as I reached the door of the inn where we had one more night to pass. As I entered I heard a familiar voice. Huguette was waiting in the small room which served as the inn's office. Marguerita was with her.

'Young man,' she said, when she saw me, 'great sadness has befallen us here. It is time we returned to Cahors. I have made enquiries and there is a house at Soulomès which can give us each a bed tonight. I suggest that we depart now. There are still many hours of day for the ease of travel. Tomorrow soon after the sun rises we shall reach our fair city. And this young lady,' she said indicating Marguerita, 'her father will be glad to welcome her home.' She turned to wag a good finger in Marguerita's face. 'You have come to no harm,' she went on, 'despite your tricks.'

With that, I swear the old woman winked at me. I looked at Huguette in a new light. 'What do you know of Marguerita's father?' I asked.

'Young man,' she replied, 'what do I know? I am employed by Master Donadieu to watch over his daughter and bring her back safely to her family.'

I remembered Bon Macip and his assurance that I would have assistance with my task. He hadn't mentioned it was to supervise Marguerita.

So it was decided. The pilgrims would cut short their visit to Rocamadour by one afternoon. No one was bothered especially when I told them they would be charged for only one night's stay. Actually that wasn't the case but I had not been exactly clear about how much they owed the innkeeper. Now I paid for the second night out of the profit I had made on the first. I owed them something for the disasters which had befallen the trip. Not that everybody felt the same. Arnaud told me it was his best holiday yet.

Huguette thanked me for my cooperation. I left it like that. I was touched by her decision. The house at Soulomès where she had reserved the rooms was doubtless the guest house of the Knights of the Temple. The returning pilgrims would give their sympathy for the death of one of their brothers. I now knew that the men who had taken the Templar were in the pay of the Franciscan. His body had not been returned for a fitting burial. I had learned this from Tommaso. I had been shocked by the information but it served to show me how very green I had been but a few days ago. I asked Huguette to add my own condolences to theirs.

As for me, I had no choice but to set off immediately for Sainte Marie d'Alet. The manuscript was already well ahead of me. I could delay no longer if I was to have any chance of finding it.

I said little to Marguerita. It was difficult to say goodbye. She had proved herself a worthy companion but I had to travel light with no thought of anyone except the task ahead. I hoped she would understand. I had one thing to confess however, before we parted.

'I had a commission,' I told her. 'It was to find the Sainte Coiffe. Your father asked for Bon Macip's assistance. I was available.' I didn't tell her of my suspicions about my first real meeting with her father. Of that encounter I was sure she was unaware. 'I have been unsuccessful,' I admitted. 'The day of Pentecost will arrive and your great uncle will have to explain why the sacred relic is missing. Tell your father I am sorry I have failed him.'

Marguerita made little of my apology but I later saw her deep in conversation with Huguette.

Soon the remaining pilgrims were ready for departure. They were now ten excluding me. When they were all assembled outside the Gate of the Fig, I stood on a stone and addressed them. Only four days had passed since I had done the same in the square at Cahors. Then I had been unsure of them, eager to impress them with my abilities as a tour guide. Now I spoke to them as friends.

'Good folks,' I said, 'I am your tour guide and I wish you a safe return. I have been proud to accompany you to Rocamadour but now duty calls me to another place. You have lodgings for the night kindly arranged by Huguette.' With that the boy gave a loud whistle of approval. He seemed to have perked up now he was on the way home. 'The abbot of Rocamadour,' I added, 'has provided a guard to watch over you on the road. I shall now ask my assistant to guide you back to Cahors.'

Marguerita gave me a look I couldn't read. 'If my assistant is willing,' I said.

'We have no need of you, William,' she retorted. 'I am sure we will find the road.'

The pilgrims made their way to their carriages. The students had agreed to take back the carriage of the heretic. I approached Bertrand. I saw he had a large box. 'Your lute?' I asked.

He looked rather sheepish but he confirmed my question.

Suddenly I felt quite old. 'Practise it at home,' I advised. 'You could have the best of two worlds.'

He knew what I meant.

'Thanks, I'll remember that,' he said.

One day he would make a good priest.

The married couple had piled their souvenirs into their cart and were ready to depart. Arnaud was talking to the students. I went to say goodbye. Jeanne took my hand. 'It's been a wonderful trip,' she said, as she pressed my fingers between hers. I was glad she had enjoyed herself. Satisfied customers were the best advertisement.

That was another of Bon Macip's first rules. For once I thought he'd got it right.

'I can't tell you what it means to me,' she said. Then promptly she did just that. Arnaud was now out of earshot. Nevertheless she drew me close to her. 'He is the same age as you,' she whispered. 'My first son...' She was overcome with emotion and it was Guy who finished her story.

'It is true,' he told me, 'we met in Rocamadour some eighteen years ago. It was my first pilgrimage. We pledged our troth here in the chapel of St Michael.' His wife leaned against him, her hands now covering her face. 'As you know,' he continued, 'we married and had our son Arnaud, a good boy.' He smiled with fatherly pride in the direction of his son who was now annoying the horses. I reserved judgment on the boy. 'We have made this pilgrimage,' said Guy, 'to find Jeanne's firstborn son. He was born here in Rocamadour.'

Rocamadour, it seemed, was not just for lovers' trysts. Her father had sent her here for the child's birth. It was where rich parents sent their wayward daughters.

My mother would not have agreed, about the word 'wayward' that is. She had given birth to two sons but how that had happened, she insisted, was a mystery she had yet to resolve. The boy Jeanne had borne, I learned, had been taken from her at his birth, by the knights at the hospital of St John.

'It has taken Jeanne all these years to tell me of this,' said her husband. 'Now she knows that her son lived.'

I realised what their visit to the ancient hermit had meant. He had once served in the hospital. Some information is not recorded on parchment.

'My son is a monk now,' Jeanne said. We saw him in the priory. He's just received his tonsure.' With that she clasped her husband around his neck. Guy gave me a smile. I think he realised his future had taken on a rosy glow.

Marguerita was handling our poor wagon. I went over to her as she returned from speaking to Huguette and climbed up to take the reins. 'You understand, Marguerita,' I said, 'I must hurry south to the abbey at Sainte Marie d'Alet. Explain to your father that urgent affairs take me there but I shall return to Cahors to settle our business. He will understand.'

'When will that be?' she asked.

'That is for lady fortune to decide,' I replied, 'but return I shall. I may have further need of a smart lad to assist me.'

She gave me one of her rare smiles and moved the cart forward to the front of the queue.

At the end of the line of carts the two nuns were sitting quietly in their transport. Huguette was with them. Some whispered conversation was taking place.

'Young man,' the old woman called. I went over to the cart. The nuns lowered their heads. Their wimples were dusty but still firmly in place.

'The sisters have a small confession,' said Huguette. 'They wish to make it to you.'

My heart sank. I was not prepared to receive the confidences of such ladies. One of the sisters rolled back her wide sleeve and removed a small box.

I wondered if it were some present, a souvenir perhaps of our visit. I prepared myself to thank them but to refuse it as graciously as I could. The other sister raised her head slightly. Her eyes were still lowered. I could see that this was not going to be easy.

Huguette took charge of the situation. 'The sisters wish to tell you they have this box.' I could see that clearly. I wondered if by some magic I was supposed to guess the contents. The pilgrims were waiting to leave. This was obviously going to take some time. I decided to take the initiative.

'Ladies! Good sisters!' I said, 'I thank you but I must refuse your gift.'

The sisters hid their faces behind their hands.

Huguette again spoke for them, 'They wish to say,' she explained, 'that they have found no moment to approach you. They are too modest to speak to you when you are alone and they could not talk to you when you had the sacristan's great niece by your side. They want you to know that they have the Sainte Coiffe.'

As they were sisters of the church, I could find no words to tell them just what I thought. I contented myself with ordering them to explain immediately why they had taken the sacred relic.

The sisters bowed their heads in submission but their silence continued. It was left to Huguette again to explain. It seemed the price of the Sainte Coiffe's return had lain with the sacristan himself. Apparently he was a difficult man. Knowing Marguerita's family, I could believe that. The sacristan had refused to allow the convent of the sisters to purchase some land they needed to extend their burial ground. In desperation the mother superior had thought up the plan to remove the Sainte Coiffe from the cathedral. The two sisters had taken the relic to Rocamadour for the Virgin's blessing and forgiveness for their actions. The convent felt sure that the holy lady would understand their plight and persuade the sacristan to agree to their request.

As Huguette explained their actions, the sisters held each other by the hand and kept their heads bowed. I thanked them for the information and told them to take the Sainte Coiffe to the sacristan immediately upon their return.

'Immediately,' I reiterated, 'after you have first spoken to your prioress.' The sisters said nothing but I am sure I heard them giggle.

I watched the party move off without me. I had no idea what Bon Macip would do next, but for now, he had had the last laugh. I made a vow to myself that I would have further dealings with him.

I thought about my mother. I thought about Lord John. I even managed a thought or two about Reginald. I missed them all. I wondered if they thought about me. Doubtless they waited for some news. I had none to give them. All I had was another mission.

I thought about my home and our village of Torre. I thought of the grassy slopes of my Dartmoor hills and the sweet west wind that moved the heather. Then sense took hold of me. I stopped this daydreaming. If I went on like this, I would achieve nothing. I waited for the carts to move out of sight and hurried back to the inn.

When I got there, I found a boy waiting. He had brought the horse I had ordered. I paid him for the mount with my remaining money. I would have to make my way south to Sainte Marie d'Alet using only my wits. I hoped they would prove good enough for the journey.

A clatter of hooves sounded in the road outside the inn. I looked up and saw Tommaso.

'Holy Mother of God!' I said, 'what's an invalid like you doing here?'

'I'll thank you to mind your words,' said Tommaso. 'I have senior rank over you.'

'Of that I am not sure,' I replied, 'but your head is tough, I'll give you that. Tell me where are you going?'

'Sainte Marie d'Alet,' said Tommaso. He obviously still had the ear of the abbot.

'You'll never keep up with me,' I said.

'And you'll never find the way,' Tommaso retorted.

'Then we had better travel together,' I replied.

'Exactly,' said Tommaso.

And so we did.

LATER
(BUT NOT THE END)

So I left Rocamadour. The country boy, I'd been, was gone. You may want to ask who had taken his place. For the answer to that question you will have to wait. I'm not keeping any information from you. The fact is I don't yet know myself.

We travelled slowly. For all his bravado, Tommaso was a sick man. I tended his head with the ointments the monks had placed in his pouch. There were many times he said very little. I think the effort to ride took all the energy he had.

I considered my position. I had come to this strange land in the company of one surly stranger. I was now moving on to some unknown destination as the companion of another.

Our path took us through the high Causse which we had crossed only five days before. We were making for Figeac. What lay ahead of us there and in the towns beyond only the Good Lord knew. I had given up working out how I would get the precious manuscript back to my liege lord in England. Locating it would be hard enough. If I managed that, my real troubles would only just begin. Getting hold of the document and keeping it from Tommaso were problems I didn't even want to contemplate.

The countryside here was similar to that we had passed through on the way to Rocamadour. The month of June was upon us. Sweet meadow flowers embroidered the slopes to both sides of our path. We were now on the highest part of the Causse. We felt the strength of the wind as it blew sharp over trees that bent to its force. Tommaso pulled his cloak around his shoulders. Despite the sun, his wound had lowered his body warmth. I resolved to watch him well. Worse than a miserable travelling companion was a dead one. I had had enough of worrying about corpses for the time being.

I turned my mind to more pleasant thoughts. I pictured my home. The trees in our orchard would now be in full flower. The catkins of the alder and willow would have given way to the heady blossom of the haw and quick thorns on the lower slopes of the moor. Higher up where the ponies ran free and our sheep grazed was Rippon Tor, its craggy granite nose rising above the clitter of stones which had rolled down its slopes, before memory began. Higher still were the old oaks of the Wishtwood. It is said that pixies live there. This, I should tell you, is the talk of our cottars. I have never verified it for myself.

The waters of our rivers the Dart, the Teign and the Bovey would be flowing fast. I thought of the meadows of purple grass, heather and gorse enclosed by the long stone walls of the high moor. There I had travelled with our packhorses on roads, newly made, linking the markets at Ashburton, Bovey Tracey and Moretonhampstead where some of our wool was sold for the trade in cloth.

I longed for the soft mewing cry of our buzzards and the sight of our goshawks and kites. There were many of these same birds here, you understand, but to me they seemed as foreign as the man who rode beside me.

I won't go on. Doubtless you will have had enough of these pangs of sickness for my home. I, too, for that matter. I pulled myself together. I had a mission to accomplish. I now knew the real task King Edward had set me. Not only my father's safe release hung in the balance, but his good name also. I was his son by adoption only, but if I were not the man to undertake the venture that lay ahead, then I had no right to use his name or accept the spurs promised by my king.

I looked at Tommaso. He was slumped on his mount but he was bearing the track well enough. He fought for money and for the patron who paid him. How could I judge him? I was about to do the same although my patron was a sovereign king rather than an anointed pope. Not that I planned to do much fighting. I would leave that to Tommaso if he were up to it.

As if he knew my thoughts, Tommaso lifted his injured head. 'The way ahead,' he said, 'is long and hard. You would do best to concentrate on the matters in hand.'

'And what would they be?' I asked.

'To get me off this sainted mare and give me something to drink.'

I could tell that our journey together would not be dull.

We made it eventually to Sainte Marie d'Alet but that, as they say, is another story.

TIPS FOR TRAVELLERS

IN ENGLAND

William Giffard was born in 1278 on the estate lands of the manor of Torre in the county of Devonshire in south-west England. Torre is now part of the town of Torquay, birthplace of Agatha Christie, which itself is part of the conurbation of Torbay. In the late thirteenth century, Torre was a thriving community subsisting for its market trade on the sheep reared on Dartmoor and the huge variety of fish which swam in the waters of the bay. The small quay was controlled by the abbot of Torre Abbey. Larger ships plied between Dartmouth, some eighteen miles south west of Torquay, and the French coast. Today, Brixham, part of Torbay, supports the largest fish market in England.

Lord John de Mohun, who lived at the manor of Torre, held vast estates in south-west England. This great landowner was a friend of King Edward I. He owed his position to his ancestor, William Brewer, a statesman held in high regard by four successive monarchs, Henry II, Richard I, John I and Edward's father Henry III. It was William who had given the lands at Torre for the building of Torre Abbey so the monks, who were also canons, could pray for the souls of Richard the Lionheart and his father Henry II.

On William's death, the estates had passed to his son William, who had died without issue. They then passed to his daughter Alicia, who had married Reginald de Mohun. At the time of this account Reginald's grandson, Lord John de Mohun, was lord of the manor at Torre where William Giffard was born.

Lord John's coat of arms, Or, a cross engrailed sable, can still be seen carved on the keystones under the vaulting of the gatehouse at Torre Abbey.

The Abbey of Torre, which overlooks the sea and the gardens bordering the promenade of Torquay, has just undergone the first stage of a major restoration. In its day it was the largest and richest Premonstratensian foundation in England. Founded in 1196 by the followers of St Norbert from Prémontré in France, by 1297 it was a major influence in local affairs. The monks at the abbey were largely responsible for the export of local produce from their harbour at Torre. The abbey owned vast tracts of land gifted to it by wealthy families for the saying of Mass for the dead.

The village of Blackawton, with its beautiful thirteenth century church, is in the South Hams of Devonshire in south-west England. In medieval times it was known as Avetone and was an important local centre. It had its own manorial court.

The harbour and town of Dartmouth on the south coast of Devonshire, now home to the Royal Britannia Naval College, was known in the thirteenth century as Dertemue. It was an important port then for passengers and goods alike. It is mentioned by Chaucer in 'The Canterbury Tales' as a major arrival centre for the import of wine from France, Spain and Portugal.

Dartmoor National Park is a granite plateau of 700 feet elevation in the centre of Devonshire. Hills, locally called tors, rise to 2000 feet while rivers dissect the upland in a series of deep valleys. It is bounded by the towns of Okehampton in the north, Tavistock to the west, Ivybridge in the south and eastwards by the ancient stannary town of Ashburton. In 1239 the forest of Dartmoor was granted to Richard, Earl of Cornwall, and from then the deforestation commenced, the high moor becoming a chase reserved for hunting.

IN FRANCE

The town of Libourne, on the river Dordogne just below its confluence with the Gironde, owes its origin to Edward I who, in 1269, had developed the small village he found there as a port friendly to the English. In 1286, in the face of the growing influence of King Philip IV of France, he fortified it as one of his walled bastide towns. Edward gave this task to Roger de Leyburn, one of his soldiers from Kent, as a reward for his services and the little Gascon settlement has taken his name.

The Romanesque church of Sainte Radegonde stands at the edge of the town of Talmont-sur-Gironde. The church was built in 1094 and was already old when William Giffard saw it, but the town itself was constructed in 1284 on the orders of Edward I, as a bastide to guard the entrance to the Gironde. Talmont lies 16 kilometres south of Royan and became well known as a staging post on the Via Turonensis to Santiago de Compostela. It is now considered one of the prettiest towns in France.

William's journey south can be followed today on modern roads. From Libourne, the last port approachable from the Gironde which splits just south of Blaye, take the D936 to Bergerac and then turn south towards Monbazillac. Follow the N21 until its junction with the D124. At this point turn towards Monsempron-Libos and continue to Fumel. From here follow the D911 though Duravel to Puy L'Evêque. Then continue on this road via Prayssac to Castelfranc. Here, cross the river Lot on the D45 until its junction with the D8. Turn left and follow the D8 through Albas, Luzech, Douelle and Pradines. Crossing the Lot again pick up the D911 into Cahors.

Duravel was well known in the Middle Ages as an important stopping place for pilgrims on the road between Cahors and Villeneuve-sur-Lot. In 1055 the barons of Pestilhac had built a priory there affiliated to the great abbey at Moissac. The bones of three eastern hermits, Agathon, Poemon and Hilarion were interred there and these relics drew huge crowds of penitents.

Puy L'Evêque, with its many medieval houses and towers, occupies a beautiful setting on the river Lot. Acquired from King Philip II of France by Bishop Guillaume de Cardaillac of Cahors in 1227 as a reward for assistance in the Albigensian crusade against the heretics of Toulouse, it once had a fortified palace used by successive bishops when dealing with the affairs of administration and justice in the eastern part of the diocese. It also acted as a safe haven offering respite from the stresses of governing the city of Cahors.

Cahors, the chief town and administrative centre of the modern department of the Lot, was once the capital of the Quercy, a semi-independent province roughly affiliated to the counts of Toulouse. In May 1297, the time of this story, Cahors was a largely independent city ruled nominally, by a Lord Bishop, and effectively, by a group of consuls mainly drawn from the rich banking merchants of the city.

Cahors lies in a loop of the river Lot, known in Occitan, the medieval language of the south, as the Olt. In the Middle Ages the merchants of Cahors developed a very successful network of commercial interests with England, Flanders, Norway and northern France. They maintained their standing at foreign courts through money lending. These bankers were so successful they brought upon themselves the wrath of the poet Dante. For the sin of usury he consigned them to Hell in the Divine Comedy, (Inferno, XI, 50).

The modern visitor will find nineteenth century name changes. La Place du Change is now known as La Place des Petites – Boucheries and La Rue Duras as La rue du Tapis-Vert. The gate which connected the citadel to the city of Cahors formerly known as the Porte del Miral is now La Place de la Citadelle, off the Rue Soubirous. La Place du Marché was known in William Giffard's time as either la Place de la Bladerie, (where wheat was stored) or La Place de la Conque, on account of the fountain supported by three nymphs blowing trumpets constructed by the Romans to receive some of the water flowing from the aqueduct which served the city.

The Sainte Coiffe, the sacred relic of Cahors Cathedral was brought back to the city from the Holy Land by Bishop Geraud III (Geraud de Cardaillac). Today, the Sainte Coiffe is housed in the crypt of Cahors Cathedral in the chapelle Saint Gausbert.

The Knights of the Temple or Templars had a large command centre at Cahors. At first they lived within the city walls on land, possibly now 93 Rue du Cheval Blanc, but in the early days of the thirteenth century they moved outside the city. The rules of their order required that they should provide assistance and shelter for pilgrims particularly the needy and the sick. The consuls of Cahors became worried at the presence of so many new arrivals bringing diseases into the city. The Templars were disbanded as a society in the early fourteenth century. In 1328 their property in Cahors was given by Pope John XXII to the order of La Chartreuse. The Cours and Rue de la Chartreuse can now be found in Cahors between the Rue Joachim Murat and Rue du President Wilson.

Pradines is a village to the north-west of Cahors on the banks of the Lot. It has a medieval shrine, dedicated to the Virgin Salve Regina. In the thirteenth century, this shrine was regularly visited by mothers wishing to protect their children from the ailments of childhood and particularly from the bites of mad dogs. Originally, the words *Salve Regina* were said by fishermen and sailors praying for deliverance from the perils of flooding and attacks by bandits.

To retrace the pilgrims' journey to Rocamadour, the modern traveller should leave Cahors keeping to the north bank of the Lot, and then take the D653 to Larroque-des-Arcs. From here turn northwards on the D7 until its junction with the D22. Continue on the D22 to Valroufié and then Francoulès. The D22 then cuts across country in a tortuous series of bends to Nadillac, but the wild Causse countryside is worth the effort. At Nadillac take the road to Cras and continue on to Le Moulin de Cras. Here you can cross the River Vers and join the D32 to St Martin de Vers. These roads are small country lanes. If you want easier driving, take the D49 from Francoulès until it joins the D166 just north of Cours. Continue on this road until it joins the D32 and turn north to St Martin-de-Vers. From here continue on the D32 to Labastide Murat, the modern name of the town known as Labastide Fortanière in the thirteenth century. Then, it was named after its founders, the Fortanière family of Gourdon. Now, the town is named after a more famous son, Joachim Murat, later King of Naples, born there in 1767. From Labastide take the D677 to Carlucet and continue until you reach a junction on your left, where you rejoin the D32. Continue on this road to Rocamadour via Couzou. The tourist in a hurry should take the D653 from Cahors to Larroque de Arcs and then continue along the river Lot on the D653 to Vers. Continue on the same road towards Labastide Murat via St Martin de Vers. Then follow the directions above to Rocamadour.

Soulomès is south-east of Labastide Murat. It was once a Templar commanderie of importance. The font in the Gothic church is covered in the unmistakable crosses carved by the Templars. The frescoes in the church might be thirteenth century or possibly slightly later addititons following the order's fall from grace. In 1307 the king of France had all the Templars in France arrested on charges of heretical practices. In one of the paintings Jesus is seen walking in a garden with Mary Magdalene. On the north wall is pictured the apostle St Thomas (Doubting Thomas). It is believed by some that the Templars may have thought that Jesus was married to Mary Magdalene and was the twin brother of Thomas.

Rocamadour lies 36 miles NNE of Cahors. This medieval village and its 'miraculous' holy sanctuaries still cling to every ledge of a sheer cliff rising above the right bank of the river Alzou. Rocamadour first attracted penitents in the early twelfth century. By the end of the thirteenth century, thanks to the entrepreneurial abilities of its abbots, it had become one of the main centres of pilgrimage in France. Many pilgrims to Rocamadour came down from Flanders. Often they were en route to Spain to visit the shrine of St James at Compostela. It was quite usual, however, for the pilgrims who came from Germany or the east of France to break their journey at Brioude, Aurillac or Cahors to make a quick excursion north before continuing their journey to Spain.

The medieval city owed its popularity as a pilgrim destination to Géraud d'Escorailles. Elected the superior of the monks at St Martin de Tulle, he commissioned the writing of the Book of Miracles. This beautifully illustrated book in its readable Latin describes in a clear style 126 miracles which, it was said, had taken place through the intercession of the Virgin Mary. People thronged to the site to have their ailments cured. The Virgin also protected those engaged in Holy War and particularly sailors who faced the perils of the sea.

The discovery of a perfectly preserved body at the entrance to the oratory in 1166, shortly after the publication of the Book of Miracles, seemed the final evidence that this indeed was a miraculous place. The bones were said to be those of St Amadour, a servant of the Virgin and the husband of St Veronica. Géraud d'Escorailles organised an excellent publicity campaign around these events and the rest, is history.

The centre of attraction for the pilgrims who flocked there during the twelfth and thirteenth centuries was the statue of the Virgin Mary. It was carved from the trunk of a tree in the twelfth century and was originally encased in a wooden shrine covered with gold leaf. The statue is seventy-six centimetres high and thirty centimetres wide at the base. Mary sits on a seat carved from the same wood in a hieratic pose with open hands and a slight smile on her lips. The infant Jesus sits on her left knee. In his left hand he holds the gospels.

The statue is black giving rise to the name, the Black Madonna. It was probably not this colour when it was carved. The wood has darkened over the centuries in the smoke of the candles and the incense burnt in her honour. The statue one sees today has been subject to restoration, not all good. The crowns, for example, which are now worn both by the Virgin and the infant Jesus are of recent fabrication.

Although Rocamadour was one of the main pilgrim destinations in the thirteenth century it was also a centre for trysts and social outings. The fashionable and well-to-do made the journey to enjoy the festivities not available in their own home towns and to meet lovers or people not acceptable in their own social circle.

Rocamadour is now the second most impressive site in modern France superseded only by Mont St Michel. Modern visitors are as amazed today by that first sight as the pilgrims were nine hundred years ago.

Bon Voyage